CUT-OUT

Other books by Bob Mayer

Eyes of the Hammer
Dragon SIM-13
SYNBAT

CUT-OUT

a novel by

BOB MAYER

LYFORD
Books

Copyright © 1995 by Bob Mayer

LYFORD Books
Published by Presidio Press
505 B San Marin Dr., Suite 300
Novato, CA 94945-1340

Library of Congress Cataloging-in-Publication Data

Mayer, Bob, 1959-
  Cut-out : a novel / by Bob Mayer.
    p.   cm.
  ISBN 0-89141-508-4
  1. Riley, Dave (Fictitious character)—Fiction. 2. Witnesses—
  Protection—United States—Fiction. 3. Soldiers—United States
  —Fiction.   I. Title.
  PS3563.A95227C88   1995
  813'.54—dc20   94-26197
                                                          CIP

Typography by ProImage
Printed in the United States of America

To Debbie I. for everything.

And thanks to my agent, Ethan Ellenberg; my editor, Joan Griffin; and the Out-To-Lunch Bunch.

CUT-OUT

CHAPTER 1

CHICAGO, ILLINOIS
27 SEPTEMBER, 3:15 P.M.

The two men in the beat-up Chevy had been sitting in the same position for more than two hours, their eyes hidden behind wraparound sunglasses, their minds tuned into the little earplug each wore in his left ear. On this busy street on the north side of Chicago, with active small businesses on the first floor of most of the apartment buildings, the men's presence had gone relatively undetected. Even if someone had noticed them, it was highly unlikely that anyone would approach to question their motives; like New Yorkers, most Chicagoans had long ago learned to ignore anything not thrust directly into their face as a threat.

"They been going at it for forty minutes, for chrissakes!" the shorter of the two men muttered, rubbing the spot where the cord ran behind his left earlobe.

A shrill, shuddering cry echoed tinnily in their ears, and the taller man turned to his partner and smiled. "She sure is a good actress."

"How do you know it's an act?" the other asked with a leer. "Could be real."

"Right. With that loser?"

A deeper series of grunts sounded for almost twenty seconds, then there was silence. A man's voice was heard, the first words in the third-floor apartment across the street in quite a while.

"I've got to go, Jill. I've got to get back to the office."

A woman's voice purred in reply. *"How about another twenty minutes, babe?"*

1

There was a pause, then the sound of a bed creaking. *"I'd love to, but I've really got to go. Tony's stopping by and I have to give him some paperwork."*

The taller of the watchers removed a revolver from a shoulder holster, snapped open the cylinder, and checked the rounds. "He's a stupid fuck, mentioning names like that."

His partner laughed, not a particularly pleasant sound, as he inspected his own weapon. "He's out of his league."

The tall man snapped the cylinder shut with a flick of his wrist, the noise of metal on metal loud in the close confines of the car. "He's about to get sent back to the minors."

They listened to the sounds of the couple dressing. Their eyes now focused on the front door of the building.

"Can I see you tomorrow?"

"Why wait until tomorrow? You can have me tonight—full time— if you really wanted, Phil."

"Oh, come on, babe. Don't start on that. I've explained it all to you a thousand times. It just isn't possible right now."

"Why? All you have to do is—"

"Please! Enough, all right? Just drop it for now."

There was a long pause, and the two men strained to hear the sound of the apartment door. They were disappointed when the woman's voice came back.

"All right. I'm sorry. It's just that I miss you so much and it gets so lonely here at night."

The short man started laughing again. "What a buncha bull. Does he really believe that crap?"

The taller man didn't bother to dignify the question with an answer.

"So. Can I see you tomorrow?" The man's voice was edged with pleading.

The voices faded slightly. They were moving out of the bedroom. *"Sure. Just give a call so I can be ready. All right? We'll do something a little different tomorrow."*

"What?"

"You'll just have to wait, hon."

At the sound of the apartment door closing, both men pulled out the earplugs and threw them under the seat alongside the receiver for the bug.

"Party time."

The short man stepped out of the car as the other started the engine. The short man was just outside the building's front door when Philip Cobb opened it, right hand fumbling in his pocket. Cobb was a tall man with a pudgy face and wore round spectacles. His hairline had moved back as the years had gone on, complementing the comfortable roll of fat around his waist, which defied his sporadic diets and exercise routines.

As the building door slammed shut behind him, Cobb saw the muzzle of a gun pointed at his face and froze in his tracks. A car pulled up to the curb with a screech, the door to the backseat swinging open.

"Get in the car, asshole."

"Who are you?" Cobb looked at the cold black eyes that were staring at him over the muzzle of the gun and realized the futility of the question.

"Get in the car."

Cobb stepped forward, feeling his body being pulled to the car by the command in the man's voice and the power of the weapon. He couldn't think; his brain refused to process information as a wave of cold fear swept over him. The man grabbed his suit jacket with his free hand and propelled him forward.

"Hey! You! What are you doing?"

The short man swung his gaze to the left; his gun quickly followed as he spotted the uniformed police officer walking toward them from the corner. While the officer was trying to pull his weapon out of his holster, the short man fired off three rounds in rapid succession. The cop dove behind a parked car. Cobb stood frozen, the sound of the gun echoing in his ears. The short man had let go of his jacket to shoot at the cop, and now he turned back toward Cobb, centering the muzzle of the gun on Cobb's forehead.

"Let's go!" the driver of the car screamed, gunning the engine. "Forget him!"

"I'm gonna finish him!" the short man yelled back as his finger tightened on the trigger. He flinched as the cop fired for the first time, the deep-throated blast of the pistol reverberating through the cool fall air.

Changing his mind, the short man turned and jumped into the open back door of the Chevy, and it was gone with a roar down the street. Cobb still hadn't moved.

The cop came running up, yelling into his portable radio. It was only then that Cobb realized he had soaked his pants. He staggered back against the welcome support of the building wall and resumed breathing.

"Are you all right?" the cop asked as he returned the radio to its slot on his belt. "I got backup coming and I sent out a description of the car. Did you know those guys?"

Cobb shook his head weakly. "I don't know who they were."

A crowd was starting to gather, and Cobb felt foolish with the large stain clearly visible on the front of his pants. The sound of sirens pierced the air.

"Are you all right, Phil?"

Cobb turned in surprise to see Jill standing in the doorway to the apartment building, clutching a robe around her.

"Get out of here," he hissed, glancing nervously at the police officer, who was trying to get the crowd back.

Jill bit her lip and nodded, backing reluctantly into the dark of the building foyer.

Two hours later, Cobb was still within twenty feet of the site of his almost death, sitting in the backseat of an unmarked police car, trying not to cough from the stench of the detective's cigar. Detective Guyton sat two feet away, staring at him with passionless eyes. He was a large man, his muscular bulk encased in a well-cut suit. His hair was gray, almost silver, and his face was flat and hard, with twenty-four years of street experience etched into it.

"So let's go over this one more time, Mr. Cobb. You're a real estate developer and you say you were here to see a client. A Miss Jill Fastone? Is that correct?"

"Yes."

Detective Guyton nodded. "Uh-huh. So why didn't you tell the officer who was first on the scene why you were here when he asked you two hours ago?"

"I was confused. I'd just been shot at, for Christ's sake."

"Couldn't be something funny going on between you and Miss Fastone, now could there, Mr. Cobb?" Guyton asked, glancing down at the wedding band on Cobb's left hand.

"No."

Guyton leaned forward. "Bullshit. Don't fuck with me. A cop almost got his head blown off saving your sorry ass. And you sit here and lie to me. I know who you are and I know who you work for.

Don't bullshit me anymore. The name Michael Torrentino mean any-thing to you?"

Cobb closed his eyes and sagged back against the worn upholstery. His already fragile world was crumbling.

"And don't you think I know who Jill Fastone is? She used to work for Torrentino—if you want to call what she does work. Maybe she still does. I know you do." Guyton shook his head. "You should have stayed in your little real estate office in the suburbs, Cobb. Did Fastone bring you into all this? Did you think you could start laundering money and being a middleman for the number one guy in 'The Outfit' here in Chicago and no one would notice? Wake up." Guyton tapped Cobb on the chest with a stubby finger. "You got any idea why those two guys tried to grab you?"

Cobb shook his head.

"You'd better talk to me," Guyton growled. "'Cause if you don't talk to me, you know what I'm gonna do?" He didn't bother to wait for an answer. "I'm not gonna take you downtown. I'm gonna let you get out of this car and go home. And I can guarantee you one thing: next time they try to whack you, they'll do it. You were lucky this time."

"But I don't know who they are or why they would try to kill me," Cobb whined, missing the look of satisfaction that settled on the detec-tive's face.

"You been juggling the numbers? Maybe skimming where you shouldn't have been?"

"No. I swear it."

Guyton regarded Cobb for a minute. "I think maybe you just ought to get out and go home, Cobb. You're starting to piss me off."

"But I didn't do anything wrong!" Cobb protested.

"I know. That's why you can go home. I've got all I need. Besides that, you're stinking up the back of my car."

Cobb's face showed his confusion and fear. "But what if they try again?" he asked.

Guyton shrugged. "It's your ass." He got out of the car, leaving Cobb alone to consider the reality of the situation.

The detective walked over to a man wearing a three-piece suit and carrying a clipboard. Jim O'Fallon, the assistant special agent in charge of the FBI's Organized Crime Task Force in Chicago, was a slim young man who appeared to be a recent college graduate. He looked at Guyton in the fading daylight. "Anything?"

"He's too scared to realize how fucked up his life is at the moment. It'll sink in. I'm letting him squirm for a while."

"Don't lose him," O'Fallon advised. "He could be a gold mine."

"Let's give him another hour or so and then you can make your pitch," Guyton said. "He'll be ready then."

"What about his family?" O'Fallon asked.

Guyton flipped open his notebook. "He's got a wife. They had one kid—died about a year and a half ago of a brain tumor. I got a car watching his house. She's home there."

"She know anything?"

Guyton shook his head. "Nope. She's in for a big surprise."

They both turned as Cobb got out of the car and walked over slowly. His face was twisted with conflicting emotions. "What can I do?"

O'Fallon and Guyton exchanged a brief smile.

CHAPTER 2

OPERATIONAL AREA BEAR (OA BEAR), UNCONVENTIONAL
WARFARE OPERATING AREA PINELAND (UWOA PINELAND)
23 OCTOBER, 11:15 P.M.

The three men crawled up to the edge of the airstrip and peered across at the old wooden hangar a hundred yards away. They were dressed in unmarked jungle fatigues and wore black watch caps. Their M16s lay next to them and their load-bearing equipment bristled with knives and ammunition pouches. The snout of night vision goggles poked out of the center of each man's face.

Through the green glow of the goggles, Dave Riley, the man on the left, could clearly see the three guards armed with AK-47s who were patrolling outside the hangar. The men with Riley had been watching the hangar for the past forty-eight hours, but there had been no movement other than the eight soldiers who were camped there, switching over their guard shifts every six hours.

Riley was the smallest of the three men, at only five feet seven inches and weighing 150 pounds. His dark skin was a legacy from his mother's side of the family—Puerto Rican; his name was his only obvious inheritance from his Irish father. His body was lean and hard, the result of working out several hours every day in the martial arts. His dark eyes were hidden behind the goggles and his short black hair was covered by the black watch cap.

"Still no sign of the prisoners," Captain Murphy whispered to Riley.

"We've only got two hours until exfil," Captain Potter muttered nervously from his position on the far end, glancing at his watch and pushing a little button to display the time.

Riley didn't say anything. They'd been on the ground now for two and a half days, ever since parachuting into an open field twelve miles to the northwest. The other ten members of the team were back at the operational rally point six hundred yards to the rear. Riley knew his place: he wasn't in charge here, and even though it rankled him not to be able to run things, he consoled himself with keeping his eyes and ears open and noting all that was happening.

"Look!" Murphy hissed.

In the goggles a bright light was coming from the south, along the edge of the airstrip.

"Headlights," Potter confirmed. "It must be them."

A twelve-passenger van pulled up in front of the hangar and parked, its headlights pointing at the large open doors. Two armed men leaped out and disappeared through the doors. From inside the van a voice could be heard yelling, "Get on your feet, pigs! Let's go."

A figure with his hands tied behind his back appeared in the door of the van and stumbled out, prevented from smashing his face into the ground only by the quick grab of a guard. A second figure appeared, this one a woman, her arms also tied, a guard with a loose grip on her shoulder pushing her out. She did fall, going to her knees and then slowly tumbling to her side in the dirt.

"Get up, bitch!" one of the guards screamed, kicking at the woman.

A large figure stepped out of the front passenger door of the van. "Get them inside."

"Colonel Juncker," Potter whispered. "I remember his picture from the intelligence briefing. He's the counterintelligence chief for the district."

Riley nodded. He had recognized the man as soon as he stepped out. There was no mistaking the large size or the outlandish camouflage fatigues festooned with ribbons and medals. According to the intelligence they had received, Juncker liked to stand out in a crowd. He also liked to kill, and needed only the slightest provocation.

A third figure appeared in the side door of the van.

"Who's that?" Potter whispered worriedly. "There were only supposed to be Davis and his wife." He turned to Murphy. "Did you get an ID on the first woman? Is she Davis's wife?"

Murphy was peering anxiously through the goggles. "I don't know. I couldn't tell."

"Well, who the hell could that be?" Potter asked again as the second bound woman was escorted into the dimly lit hangar and out of sight.

Riley remained silent, knowing that the unexpected presence of the second woman upset the carefully made plans of the team. Since he wasn't the team leader, though, it wasn't his place to intervene.

Murphy shifted nervously, his knee bumping into Riley's. "What do you think, Chief?"

Riley shrugged, the motion lost in the dark. "You know you've got Davis—he was the first one off. That's the key thing, isn't it?" he asked, throwing the problem back on the team leader.

Captain Murphy was silent for a few moments, then started moving back. "I'm going to the ORP. Potter, you keep surveillance on the target."

Riley followed Murphy, crawling on his belly until they were into the concealment of the woods, and then he got to his feet. They wound their way through the labyrinth of tree trunks and undergrowth until they arrived at the objective rally point (ORP). The other ten members of the team gathered round as Murphy passed on the information about the captives arriving and being taken into the hangar.

"How many extra guards?" one of the men asked.

"Two exited the van and went inside. Another came out with the second woman. And Colonel Juncker got out too."

"What about the driver of the van?"

"He didn't get out," Murphy replied.

"Is the van still there?"

"Yes."

There was a short silence. Then Murphy began to lay out the adjustments to the plan the team had worked out in isolation after being alerted for this mission. Riley listened, his mind considering the variations and what they would mean. When Murphy finished, he again pressed the button on the side of his watch and checked the time. "We move forward in twenty minutes."

Riley leaned back against his rucksack and tried to relax, slowing the flow of adrenaline that had begun to pump through his veins when the van appeared with the prisoners. No matter how many times he went out on an operation, or what type of mission it was, he still got wired. It didn't bother him though. Once, when his team was aboard a Combat Talon on the way to Panama, one of his teammates, wedged into the cargo webbing seat with his 50 pounds of parachute and 120 pounds of gear, had turned to Riley with a strange expression on his face.

"What's wrong?" Riley had asked.

"I'm not scared," the soldier replied. "And that really scares me."

Riley had known exactly what he meant: it was the flow of adrenaline that gave you the edge you needed for anything dangerous. Time seemed to slow down in a parachute jump. The four seconds from going out the door until the parachute finished deploying seemed like an eternity—an eternity in which, if something did go wrong, you felt you had time to take corrective action. Riley felt that way now as the seconds ticked by in the darkness.

"Let's move!" Murphy uttered quietly.

Riley slipped on the shoulder straps of his rucksack and stood up, taking his place right behind the team leader. They moved through the darkness, the night vision goggles illuminating the way. Sixty yards short of the tree line, they all shrugged off their rucks, leaving them in a pile, one man staying behind to guard the equipment. The rest moved up to where Potter was still watching the target. Riley peered out—the van was gone; Potter reported that it had taken Colonel Juncker and two guards with it. That was a loss, Riley knew. Juncker would have been a valuable secondary target.

They could hear muted yells from inside the hangar, and only one guard now stood outside. The others must have gone inside to watch the prisoners. Riley hoped that was all they were doing.

"It's time," Murphy whispered. The team broke up, melting away into the darkness to carry out their assigned tasks. Riley followed Murphy as the main assault element crept along the wood line, to a point just behind the hangar. The guard was on the other side, peering out at the runway, as if a threat could possibly come from that direction.

One of the team slipped forward and placed a charge on the battered door of the hangar. He crawled back and the team stood and waited, twenty feet away. With a bright flash and loud bang, the door blew open. A machine gun roared out of the trees to the team's far right; it was the support element firing across the front of the hangar, taking down the guard and creating a diversion.

The assault element sprinted forward, Riley in the trail, and burst through the door. There was a brief exchange of gunfire, and team members screamed for the prisoners to get down. Riley took in the scene as he stepped inside. Six guards lay on the floor, unmoving. The three prisoners also lay on the floor, a team member astride each of them, resecuring their wrists in front with plastic quick-cinches.

The male prisoner, Davis, began yelling and twisting on the floor, trying to free himself. "Who are you? What do you want?"

The team member straddling him leaned over. "We're U.S. Army. We're here to rescue you."

"No!" Davis screamed, still struggling. "You're here to kill us. Why else would you tie us up?"

"It's for your own safety." The team member continued to reassure Davis as the others searched the bodies of the guards and the rest of the hangar, looking for anything that might be of intelligence value. The two women were pulled to their feet. Davis finally stopped struggling long enough for two of the team members to help him up also.

"What about our children?" Mrs. Davis asked suddenly, her eyes darting fearfully from one dark figure to another in the dim light cast by Coleman lamps.

"They're safe, Mrs. Davis," Captain Murphy assured her. "We need to go now to meet our transport to get us out of here." He stepped past her and looked at the other woman—the unexpected third party. "Who are you?"

"She's Mary O'Bannion, our nanny," Davis answered. "She has to go with us."

Murphy shook his head. They'd already spent too much time on the target. The firing would have been heard. "My orders are to take only you and your wife, sir."

"If she doesn't go, then I don't go," Davis insisted, a flat expression coming over his lined face.

Murphy looked at Riley, who kept his face impassive. This was the captain's problem, not his. Riley made a show of looking at his watch.

The captain turned back. "All right. She goes with us. Let's move. Now!"

With one team member guiding each captive, they moved out of the hangar across the tall grass that bordered the landing field. Within a quarter mile they were on the edge of a dirt runway that extended off into the night in both directions. A guide from the marking party stood there, ushering them into an assembly area. The team knelt in a loose circle, and Murphy grabbed the handset attached to the radio on the commo man's back.

"Eagle, this is Bear Six. Over."

The only sound was the hiss of squelch as Murphy let up on the transmit button. All eyes were turned to the sky, watching for the plane that was to pick them up.

"Eagle, this is Bear Six. Over." Murphy waited only a few seconds this time, then repushed the send. "Eagle, this is Bear Six. I say again, this is Bear Six. If you can read me, break squelch twice. Over."

Silence.

"What frequency do you have that set on?" Murphy asked the commo man.

"Forty-six oh-six. Like we were briefed."

Riley was squatting in the dirt next to Murphy. He pulled back the cover on his watch and glanced at the luminous hands; the four-minute window for the exfiltration aircraft to pick them up had just begun.

"Eagle, this is Bear Six. Eagle, this is Bear Six. Break, any station this net, this is Bear Six. Over." Murphy let go of the transmit button. "Shit. Jackson, bring your radio over here." The other commo man obeyed, carrying his backpack, from which an FM radio antenna protruded. "What frequency are you set on?"

"Thirty-three forty."

"Shit," Murphy muttered. "Take it off."

Jackson removed the heavy rucksack, and Murphy tore open the flap, exposing the top of the radio. He pulled a minimag light off his load-bearing equipment and shined the light on the small dials. With clicks that sounded abnormally loud in the dark, he switched frequencies. "Eagle, this is Bear Six. Over."

Still no response. Riley checked his watch: 0200 exactly. Time for exfiltration. He tapped Murphy on the shoulder. "Is the LZ marked and lit?"

Murphy turned to the man who had met them here. "Are the bean-bags lit?"

"No, sir. We were waiting for you all to come."

Riley rolled his eyes, the gesture unseen in the dark. "Turn them on!"

The guide sprinted off into the dark to turn on the infrared (IR) lights that the marking party had laid out to designate the touchdown point for the incoming aircraft.

"Eagle, this is Bear Six. Over." Murphy's voice was tinged with panic. Riley looked up—he could faintly hear the distant mutter of an engine. Whether it was the airplane or a truck with enemy reinforcements he couldn't quite tell. He scanned the sky, knowing he would be very lucky to spot the blacked-out plane against the stars.

"Eagle, this is Bear Six. Over."

The entire team was leaning inward, straining to hear a reply on the radio. Murphy pulled the handset off the radio, then licked his finger and ran it around the inside of the connection, cleaning off any possible material that might be interfering with the transmission. He quickly reattached the handset. "Give me the long antenna," he ordered.

The commo man obediently reached into the carrying case on the side of his ruck and pulled out the long rigid antenna while Murphy unscrewed the short whip. Riley checked his watch: 0201. The exfil window would close in one minute. He glanced over at the rescued prisoners, who were sitting in the dirt. The man, Davis, had leaned over and was whispering in his wife's ear. The man who was supposed to be guarding them had his attention on the radio crisis.

"Eagle, this is Bear Six. Over."

Lights pierced the darkness a mile to the south, on the ground along the airfield. The commo man tapped Murphy on the shoulder and pointed in that direction. "Trouble coming!"

Murphy looked at the headlights, up at the empty night sky, over at the nominal safety of the tree line on the other side of the airstrip, and then at Riley, who could almost see the captain's mind working in those glances.

Another buzz caught their attention. With surprising speed a twin-engine Caribou swooped out of the sky, wheels touching down exactly where the marking party had laid out the rectangle of IR lights. A fierce wind of blown dirt and grass swept over the team, and the plane roared down the runway and jerked to a halt within a hundred yards. As the team stood up, the pilot spun the plane around and bounced back toward the rectangle, the back ramp lowering while the aircraft was still moving.

The pilot locked his brakes, the engines screaming and throwing out a strong backwash. The team grabbed the prisoners and ran, heads lowered, toward the ramp and into the darkened interior. Glancing over his shoulder as he went in, Riley could see the headlights turn toward the runway.

Riley counted heads as he moved up the interior of the aircraft. All the seats had been taken out, and the team members and rescued prisoners were sitting on the floor with their backs against the skin of the plane.

Riley reached the open cockpit, where the pilot sat, peering out his windshield through a set of PVS-7 night vision goggles. All the lights on the controls were muted to a dim level.

"Got 'em all?" the pilot yelled above the props and engines.

"All here. Go!" Riley replied.

The pilot didn't hesitate. Releasing the brakes, he pushed forward on the throttle and pulled back on the flaps. Riley was thrown backward onto the laps of those behind him. He scrambled up and peered out a window. The truck had halted, and he could see the twinkling of muzzle flashes from the back of the vehicle.

The plane lifted within fifty yards of the takeoff point and climbed at a very steep angle, everyone inside grabbing onto whatever they could to keep from sliding out the still-open back ramp. As they gained altitude—and the pilot found the time—the back ramp slowly slid up and closed.

Riley looked around the interior of the aircraft. The ambient light from the stars and the ground glow dimly lit up the cargo bay. He could sense, more than see, the relief each team member felt. They were smiling and talking excitedly to each other. Riley looked at Davis, who returned the glance blandly. His wife and the nanny sat on either side of him. Riley twisted around and got up on one knee to look out a window. The lights of several small towns sparkled a half mile below. Riley tried to orient himself along the flight path of the aircraft, which he remembered from the isolation brief. They were heading south-southwest. Sure that he knew where they were, Riley turned away from the window. No one else on the team had bothered to look out. They were all too busy clapping each other on the back, congratulating themselves for a job well done.

Seeing a gesture out of the corner of his eye, Riley made his way up to the pilot.

"I've got trouble with my left engine. Don't know what's wrong, but I'm going to have to shut it down."

Riley nodded. "You might have taken some rounds in it when we took off."

"Yeah, right." The pilot turned his attention back to the control panel. The roar of sound on the inside of the aircraft lessened slightly as the pilot began to turn off one of his two engines. Riley could see that a couple of the team members noted the change but had no idea what happened. Riley leaned over and yelled in Murphy's ear. "The pilot had to shut down one of his engines."

Murphy was startled and looked up at Riley with questioning eyes. He sat there for a few moments, then leaned to the man next to him to pass along the information. Riley turned his attention back to the pilot.

Five minutes later, the pilot shook his head. "I've got problems with the hydraulics. My primary is down and the secondary is sluggish. I'm going to have to set down. If I lose my backup hydraulics, we're history."

Riley looked over the pilot's shoulder, scanning the landscape ahead. "Any idea where you can put down?"

The pilot gestured with his chin, both hands on the controls. "There's a landing strip up ahead there to the left. See the control tower?"

"An airfield?" Riley said. "That means there will be people there."

The pilot shook his head. "It's blacked out. There's nobody there this time of night. It's all automated. If I was a friendly I could turn on the airfield landing lights by dialing up the correct frequency and just breaking squelch. But I ain't a friendly. Fortunately I don't need the landing lights to touch down there. We'll get down all right. After that, it's your show."

Riley immediately passed the news to Murphy. He then sat down and braced himself as the plane descended in abrupt jerks. The ride was so rough that the only way Riley knew they had touched down was when the back ramp started opening and the pilot applied the brakes. The plane came to a halt as the ramp touched the concrete of the runway.

"Everyone out!" Murphy yelled. The team ran down the ramp in a muddle of confusion, the rescued prisoners in their midst. Riley followed them off as the pilot shut down the aircraft.

The team was spread out behind the aircraft in an unorganized arc. One of the men took charge: "Assemble here! Two hundred meters back of the tail. Let's go! Let's go."

Riley joined the group. They were all gathered around, staring at Captain Murphy. The team leader took a few moments to collect himself, shifting from the exhilaration of an apparently successful mission and exfiltration to this emergency landing in enemy territory. He shook himself out of his stupor. "Let's get a perimeter here, off the runway in the grass." The team members turned and hastily set up a loose perimeter, then lay down and faced out in all directions.

Riley knelt next to Murphy, who turned and asked, "Do you know where we are, Chief?"

Riley nodded. "I do. Do you?"

Murphy shook his head.

Riley pointed to the west. "See that? What does it look like?"

"A control tower for an airfield."

"Good. What airstrips lie along the planned exfil route?"

Murphy's brow furrowed in concentration.

Riley didn't wait long. "Do you have your one to two-fifty map covering the exfil route?"

"No."

Riley took a deep breath and held it, then slowly let it out. He reached into his pocket and took out his own 1:250,000 scale map. He spread it on the ground, pulled a poncho liner out of his rucksack, and threw it over both Murphy and him. Shining his red-lens flashlight on the map, he pointed at the location where they had made the snatch.

"We took off from here. What direction was the initial leg of the exfil route?"

"South-southwest."

Riley drew a dirty finger along the map. "How long were we in flight?"

Murphy pushed the button on his watch and glanced at it. "Twenty minutes."

"What's a Caribou's cruising speed?"

"I don't know."

"A hundred and eighty knots," Riley said immediately. "How far is that in twenty minutes?" As he waited for the reply, Riley rolled his right shoulder in a circle, trying to work out the ache that had been bothering him for the last two hours.

"About sixty miles?" Murphy replied.

"About," Riley confirmed. "So where are we?"

Murphy looked at the map. His finger tentatively poked at an airstrip marked in black. "Here?"

"Right." Riley waited a second. "Well? What do we do now?"

"Call for emergency exfiltration." Murphy didn't wait for a confirmation. He threw aside the poncho and grabbed the handset for the radio. "Bear Base, this is Bear Six. Over."

The reply was instantaneous. "This is Bear Base. Over."

"Bear Base, this is Bear Six. We are down and request emergency pickup. Over."

"Roger, Bear Six. What is your location? Over."

Murphy turned to Riley and grabbed the map out of his hand. "Wait one." The team leader turned on his flashlight and checked the lines on the map. "Uh, Bear Base, our location is—wait one." Murphy looked around, then pulled out his compass and shot an azimuth to the control tower. He calculated for a few moments. "Bear Base, our location is grid Uniform Sierra one six eight three four seven. I say again, Uniform Sierra one six eight three four seven. Over."

"I read Uniform Sierra one six eight three four seven for emergency pickup. Is that correct? Over."

"Roger. Over."

"What is your status? Over."

Murphy frowned as he considered the question.

"Do you have any casualties?" the voice asked, more plainly. "Over."

"Negative. Over."

"Chopper on the way. Mark PZ with IR. Out."

Murphy gave the handset back to the commo man and stood. "Potter, mark out an LZ with IR chem lights."

"Who's got the chem lights?" Potter yelled. Riley winced as he glanced around the airfield. They were more than half a mile from the darkened control tower and the hangars at the base of it, but Riley was still very uncomfortable with the lack of noise discipline. They were inside enemy territory. He looked over at the Caribou. The pilot was working on his plane.

Riley was surprised to hear the distant chatter of a helicopter so quickly. The aircraft must have been on station, not far from the border. Potter was standing about fifty yards away, in the open field where he had laid out his chem lights. Riley grabbed Murphy's shoulder. "Tell the chopper not to approach from the south."

"What?"

The bird was close, no more than a half mile out. Riley pointed to Potter. "Tell the bird not to approach from the south. You see that tree there?" A lone thirty-foot pine tree reached up into the night sky less than forty yards from Potter's PZ. If the helicopter came in on a glide path from the south—which it most likely would—it would hit the tree.

Riley reached past Murphy and grabbed the handset. "Inbound helicopter, this is Bear One. Over." A relaxed voice came back, the sound of the blades close in the background. "This is Stalker Four Three. Over."

"PZ marked by IR chem lights. There's a tree—thirty feet high—on the south side of the PZ. Otherwise your approaches are all clear. Over."

"Roger. Tree on south side. We're coming in from the west and we'll stay on that. We're about thirty seconds out. Over."

Riley turned to face the west, and the MH-53 roared in just above the treetops on the other side of the runway. The double-bladed heli-copter settled onto the PZ with a massive blast of air. The back ramp was already down, and the team began running for the bird. In the confusion, the three rescued prisoners were practically being ignored. One man remembered his assignment and grabbed Davis's wife to lead her to the bird, but Davis and the nanny were on their own at the trail end of the pack. Riley grabbed the commo man, who had just begun to head for the bird. "Put your antenna down!" he yelled above the whine of the turbine engines. The radio operator sheepishly discon-nected the long antenna, which was poking up high enough to get caught in the rotors.

Riley brought up the rear and signalled thumbs-up to the crew chief waiting there. The MH-53 lifted and sprinted to the east for home. Riley walked along the center of the helicopter, past the team mem-bers who were seated on the web seats facing inward, until he reached Davis. Gesturing for the team member who sat next to the prisoner to move over, Riley sat down in between. He leaned over and yelled in Davis's right ear: "What do you think?"

Davis shook his head and lifted his hands. He had managed to break the plastic bindings the team members had put on him when they'd burst into the hangar.

"When did you do that?" Riley asked.

"On the way from the hangar to the airfield," Davis replied.

"No one checked you in all that time?"

"Nope."

Riley slumped back in the web seat and closed his eyes. It was early in the morning and all he wanted to do was get some sleep. But he had a feeling it was going to be a very long day.

NICHOLAS M. ROWE TRAINING FACILITY
CAMP MACKALL, NORTH CAROLINA
24 OCTOBER, 6:12 A.M.

The MH-53 landed at the helipad across the street from what genera-tions of Special Forces soldiers had called Camp Mackall, but in 1992 had been redesignated in honor of Colonel Rowe. The students quickly off-loaded the helicopter and moved out to the tin shacks that made up the forward operating base (FOB) for debriefing.

The sprawling compound was named after Col. Nick Rowe, a Special Forces (SF) officer who'd spent five years in captivity in Vietnam before escaping. He'd then led the way in the development of the Survival, Evasion, Resistance, and Escape (SERE) course in the Special Forces School before being assassinated in the Philippines in 1989 while on attaché duty.

The first Special Forces students in the fifties had lived at the compound under poncho hootches. As time went by, the facility had grown, with tar-paper shacks, then tin, being added. But despite the slow upgrade in facilities, the school still had the same aura about it— intense men working with all their guts to earn the right to wear the Green Beret.

Chief Riley had earned his beret in 1980. At that time, only SF-qualified men wore the beret with full flash—the small cloth shield pinned in front under the SF crest. Non-SF-qualified personnel assigned to a Special Forces unit for support purposes wore the green beret with a "candy stripe" across the flash to designate their different status. Even that was a sore point with many old veterans of Special Forces who felt that the beret should be reserved for those who had earned it. As the eighties dragged on, even that small distinctive piece of cloth was lost as the "Special Forces tab" was introduced. Sewn onto the left shoulder, just like a Ranger tab, this tab was designated to be the only way to tell if someone was Q-course qualified. That opened the door for the beret to be worn by anyone assigned to an SF unit, from cooks to truck drivers to clerks.

At the present moment Riley just didn't give a damn. He'd worn the beret with pride for well over a decade and had given his blood for his country on more than one occasion; in doing so, however, he had learned that his country was just as ready to crap on him as it was to reward him. His assignment to Fort Bragg as an instructor in A Company, 1st Battalion, 1st Special Warfare Training Group, was a prime example of that. It was the reward for his last mission.

Riley had done his job—he had stopped genetically engineered killing machines, the results of an experiment gone awry. But the army had not been happy with the technique he had used—flooding the tunnels under downtown Chicago. And others in very high places had not been happy with the fact that Riley now knew too much. The powers that be had started out with threats, but Riley had counterthreatened to expose the whole story about the government's secret project with synthetic battle forms. He'd won that round but lost the war: orders arrived the following week removing him from his team and assigning him to Fort Bragg as an instructor.

An assignment to the John F. Kennedy Special Warfare Center and School was not one sought by most Special Forces soldiers. Any man who truly wanted to be in SF wanted to be on a team, which meant being in a line SF group. The official reason given for Riley's assignment to the training group was "to allow him to recover fully from his wounds." Riley knew that the real reason was to get him away from the press, which was still wondering about unexplained deaths connected with the Chicago incident, and also to punish him—unofficially, of course.

Riley shook all those thoughts out of his head as he entered the shack where the team of student officers was gathered, the air loud with mutual congratulations and questions as the men relived the training mission they had just completed. Riley stood impassively in the back of the room, listening. He noted those who were talking and those who weren't. A few men were just looking at him. The official debriefer, a Department of the Army civilian with an intelligence background, would be here shortly to conduct an operational debrief just as if it had been a real mission.

The door opened and Davis walked in. He stood next to Riley. That quieted everyone down for a moment.

Riley stepped into the center of the room. "All right. Everybody grab a seat." He ran a hand through his dark hair, which was grimy from the past three days of living in the North Carolina pine forest. The hangar they had attacked was only four miles from their present location. The exfil flights had followed a roundabout route that ended back here.

Riley perched himself on the edge of the table that held the team's planning maps. "We covered infiltration and surveillance up until the arrival of the prisoners, yesterday afternoon out in the field. Right now, before the debriefer gets here, I want to do a quick immediate review of actions on the objective and exfiltration." Riley looked over at Davis. "This is Master Sergeant Frank Davis. He's a reservist who works with us every once in a while. Hammer," Riley said, using the man's nickname, "from your perspective as hostage, what did you think of the team's actions at the hangar?"

Davis was a short man, slightly taller than Riley, at five feet nine.

He was built like a fireplug, with thickly muscled arms bulging out of his shirtsleeves. Curly salt and pepper chest hair poked over the top button of his shirt, and his head was covered with gray. His face was ruddy and creased from exposure to the elements. His voice was loud, with a gravelly sound.

"Well, Chief, to sum it up in one sentence, I would say that if there had been real bullets in all those guns, I'd be dead right now."

The team rustled with irritation, but no one said anything.

Hammer continued. "I could hear you coming about four seconds before you hit the door of the hangar. Sounded like a bunch of orangutans stomping in the dirt as you ran up. And I know the guards could hear you. That's the first time I would have died—the guards would have gunned us down first and then hosed you all as you were charging in the door. But if that hadn't done in me and my ladies, you all would have done it for them as you came in. No one yelled 'Get down,' like you were told to, until *after* you had already 'killed' the guards. I was in the line of fire when a couple of you shot at the guards with your blanks.

"On the positive side, at least the guy who jumped on me checked the ties the 'guards' had put on me. I had them make the knots loose so I could get out of them if I had to. Whoever checked them found that out and replaced the ties with the plastic."

Hammer paused and held up the slim piece of plastic. "*But!* But I broke the tie you used on my hands on the way from the hangar to the landing zone. Those damn things don't work and—"

"We were told to use them by Major Burris," one of the students interrupted.

Hammer nodded. "Yeah. I know. But did Major Burris go on the mission with you?" He didn't wait for an answer. "When it's your ass on the line, you need to make damn sure that every piece of equipment you plan to use actually works. Duct tape works real good. Just carry a roll of hundred-mile-an-hour tape and put a few wraps of that around the wrists and even the hands. Make sure the person can't use his fingers."

Hammer was warming to his theme. "Remember one rule if you remember nothing else: in a hostage situation you have to assume everyone is a bad guy. There's nothing to say the bad guys won't switch clothes with the hostages, or won't tape toy guns into the hostages' hands and throw their real guns away and pretend like they're the victims the moment you start coming in the door. Treat everyone as bad guys until you can confirm they aren't.

"Another thing: you all lost track of me and my ladies when we made the emergency landing. Whoever was assigned to me took off and left me when it came time to get on the helicopter. Guys, the whole purpose of this mission was to bring me and my wife out alive. Yet you all threw that out the window when things got a little hairy. I could have wandered off and not gotten on that bird and no one would have been the wiser."

Riley could see that some of the students were listening and absorbing Hammer's comments, but he also noticed that the man's lack of formality was irritating some of the officers. It was a problem Riley had encountered often in the past four months of teaching personnel who outranked him. In the effort to impart information, he was sometimes lax in observing military custom. It usually wasn't a problem once the students knew the instructor and had gained respect for him, but in this case, they knew nothing about Hammer other than his role of hostage in this direct action mission.

Riley stepped up and pointed at Captain Murphy. "Sir, did it ever occur to you to ask the pilot of the Caribou where we were once we did the 'emergency' landing?" Riley let a few moments of silence go by, then gestured around the room. "Did it ever occur to any of you?" He didn't wait for an answer this time. "You have to use your sources. You also left the pilot there without even checking to see what his status was. You don't leave someone behind. Never. Also, you left the plane sitting there intact. I know this was a training exercise, but in real life you would have to blow that plane and not let it fall into enemy hands."

Riley sighed. "And what's with all these digital watches? When people were checking the time, I saw more little mechanical fireflies than real ones out there in the woods." Riley peeled the Velcro cover off his battered army-issue watch. "Doesn't anyone wear a regular watch with a luminous face?"

There was much more Riley needed to go into, but at that moment the door opened and the debriefer stepped in with his tape recorder. Riley nodded at the man and then gestured for Hammer to leave with him. He could listen to the tape later. Right now he'd had about all he could take.

Riley and Hammer walked over to the FOB operations shed without a word, each lost in his own thoughts and unwinding mentally. Inside the shack, the company sergeant major presided over a pot of hot coffee. He smiled as the men walked in. "Welcome back. Have fun?"

Riley took off his combat vest, threw it near his locker, and sank into a metal folding chair, gratefully accepting the steaming coffee. "As always, Sergeant Major. My fun meter is all pegged out."

"Maybe this will help." The sergeant major held out an envelope. "Arrived this morning with the mail."

Riley's face broke out in his first smile of the day as he saw the return address—Chicago—and the handwriting. Hammer and the sergeant major smiled in turn. "Someone you want to hear from, I can see," said the sergeant major. "I need to make sure the chow hall has breakfast ready for all the teams coming in this morning." He slid out the door. Hammer made himself scarce by going over to a cot and throwing himself on it. He was snoring within three minutes.

Alone with his letter, Riley slit open the envelope. Three sheets of white paper fell out. Folded inside was a cartoon showing a man facing two doors labeled: Damned if you do, and Damned if you don't. He scanned the letter quickly before going back and reading it more carefully.

Hey Dave,

Thought of you when I saw this cartoon. Same shit going on here and I imagine same shit going on with you. Last week when we talked you sounded pretty bummed. So I thought I'd cheer up your day with my chicken scrawl. I'm writing this sitting at my desk trying to ignore the twelve cases I got stacked up and need to close out. I'll be damn glad when winter gets here—it gets most of the assholes off the street.

Things are crazy as always. Not only do we have the usual street killings going on, but now we got the wise guys acting up and taking potshots at each other. The feds sent in a new task force to fight organized crime, and all they've managed to do is fuck everything up while making a few headlines in their fancy suits. I'm glad I can stay away from most of the crap—not that I have much choice.

They still have me working all the junk cases. I'm on the Chief's

shit list so I'm keeping my head down and not making any waves.
Some of these people have long memories. If everyone who knows
what really happened wasn't so scared about the truth getting
out—well, enough about that. I guess the world's not gonna end.

Riley read the rest of the letter, then slid it into his breast pocket
and headed for the mess hall. Donna Giannini had been assigned by
the Chicago Police Department to help him during his last mission in
Chicago. They'd uncovered a highly classified Pentagon "black project,"
and afterward a security lid had been clamped down on the whole affair.
She was put on administrative leave with pay while the higher-ups
tried to figure out what to do about her. Eventually the feds did nothing, but her superiors in the police department resented the fact that
she knew more than they did. So she was moved off active homicide
cases and given one shit detail after another. Now the job was closing down the paperwork on old cases. She initially joked about it, but
the joke got old as she was given jobs well below her rank of police
lieutenant. Still, Riley admitted to himself as he pushed open the door
to the chow hall, she'd kept a better attitude about her fate than he
had about his.

Donna had visited him in the hospital when he was recovering from
wounds received in Chicago, and since then they'd managed to get
together three times. But lately she'd been vague any time he'd brought
up plans. The letter was a nice surprise and lifted his spirits after the
disappointment of the military exercise.

CHAPTER 3

Lisa Cobb listened to the judge with a mixture of relief and resignation. It wasn't over yet, but at least this step was coming to a close and the future could start to take some new shape. The agony of the last month and a half faded with each sentence the magistrate intoned.

"Michael Torrentino, having been found guilty of violating the Racketeer Influenced and Corrupt Organization Act, you are hereby sentenced to twenty years' confinement in the federal penitentiary.

"Anthony Lorenzo, having been found guilty of violating the Racketeer Influenced and Corrupt Organization Act, you are hereby sentenced to twenty years' confinement in the federal penitentiary.

"Louis Torrentino, having been found guilty of violating the Racketeer Influenced and Corrupt Organization Act, you are hereby sentenced to twenty years' confinement in the federal penitentiary.

"Court is dismissed. All are asked to remain seated until the prisoners are escorted from the room."

A flock of U.S. marshals gathered around the three and parted them from their well-heeled lawyers. As they walked by the Cobbs, Michael Torrentino turned and looked directly at Lisa's husband, sitting next to her. Torrentino lifted his manacled hands, pointed a finger at Philip Cobb, and mimicked firing a pistol.

"You're history, Cobb. We'll get you. No matter where—" His next words were lost as a marshal pushed him past. The other two defendants didn't even look, as if their disdain spoke what they felt. They passed out the double doors in the rear. Then the courtroom was abuzz

25

with reporters either heading out to call in the news or dashing to lawyers on both sides to get reactions to the sentences.

Detective Guyton and Special Agent O'Fallon ignored the reporters and leaned over the railing that separated spectators from participants. Bending down toward the Cobbs, Guyton tapped Philip on the shoulder. "Don't let it get to you and don't worry about what Torrentino said. You did the right thing."

Philip Cobb had the look of a defeated man, his formerly round face drawn and lined. "I didn't have much choice."

"If you hadn't gotten involved with them in the first place, we wouldn't be sitting here with our entire lives destroyed." The hopelessness in Lisa Cobb's voice was obvious to all three men. She was short, only three inches over five feet, and her previously slender build had grown almost anorexic from the stress of the past month. Her short blond hair was combed straight and pulled back severely, highlighting her heart-shaped face. She wore no makeup, nor did she need to; her pale skin was almost translucent. Her despair had been growing for weeks now, and as quickly as she let it show, she pulled it back in. "I'm sorry, Phil. I just can't—"

"It's all right," her husband said, gathering her in his arms and looking over her shoulder into the unsympathetic eyes of Guyton. Cobb shifted his gaze uneasily to O'Fallon. "When do we get out of here?"

The agent pointed at a tall, dark-haired woman standing in the back of the courtroom. The woman was well dressed and appeared to be in her midthirties. She had the cold look of sexless efficiency that many career women feel forced to adopt, particularly those in male-dominated fields. "That's your contact from the Witness Protection Program. She takes you from here." O'Fallon reached into his jacket, pulled out a card, and handed it to Lisa. "If you have any problems or need anything, give me a call." He crooked a finger at the woman, who came forward.

"Captain Chris Donnelly, this is Philip Cobb and his wife, Lisa."

The U.S. marshal didn't bother extending a hand. She just nodded at the two of them. "We're getting your stuff transferred to our car." She looked at the crowd of people. "Let's get out of this circus."

Lisa turned to O'Fallon before following her husband. "I don't like what happened, but I do appreciate your handling of things."

O'Fallon shrugged. "We made the best of a bad situation. I'm sorry you got dragged into it."

Lisa ignored Guyton and followed her husband and Donnelly. As they entered the hallway outside the courtroom, two men wearing three-piece suits and sunglasses took up flank positions, pushing away the horde of reporters who were screaming questions.

"Mr. Cobb, how do you feel having turned on the most powerful organized crime figure in Chicago?"

"What are you going to do now, Mr. Cobb?"

"How do you feel being called the 'real estate agent who put away Michael Torrentino'?"

"Do you feel the comparison between you and Al Capone's book-keeper is appropriate?"

"How does it feel to see them sent to jail and walk away a free man when you were guilty too under the RICO Act?"

Lisa tried to shut out the yelling as she followed Donnelly into a small anteroom. She held onto her husband's arm, more to prevent herself from collapsing than as a sign of closeness.

"From here on out you two are my responsibility," Donnelly explained. "As part of that, you have to do what I say." She pointed at a small table. "Place all your personal belongings on the tabletop."

Philip put his wallet there while Lisa emptied the contents of her purse. Donnelly went through it all expertly, pulling out driver's licenses, credit cards—anything that had their name on it. "You're going sterile. You'll get your new IDs when you get picked up." She found the card O'Fallon had given Lisa, looked at it, then tossed it in the discard pile. "You can't have anything like that," she said. She handed back the considerably thinner wallet and lighter purse.

"Where are we going now?" Philip asked.

"We're getting you out of the city right away. The farther you are from Chicago, the better."

"You still didn't say where," Philip repeated.

"We're going to North Carolina. Charlotte, to be exact."

"Are we flying?" Philip asked.

Donnelly shook her head. "No. The airports may be watched, and even if we use false names, you still might be spotted. Once you get on a plane, they'll know your destination and have time to set something up. We're driving all the way down there, so you'd better get comfortable. It's standard procedure in a case like this."

"Doesn't the government have its own planes?" Philip asked. "That way we wouldn't be tracked on a commercial flight."

"Yes, we have our own planes," Donnelly replied. "But that's involving a few too many people for our operation. We want the minimum number to have even the slightest idea where you're going."

Philip wiped his brow with a damp handkerchief. "Can I go to the bathroom before we leave?"

Donnelly pointed. "Go through that way and use the private one off the judge's chamber."

Philip left and Lisa stood alone, the impersonal gaze of Donnelly and her two men flickering over her. Philip was back in five minutes, and Donnelly led the way out the door and through the back of the courthouse, bypassing the reporters gathered out front on the courthouse steps. The two guards hustled the Cobbs into the backseat of a waiting sedan with darkened windows. Donnelly slid into the passenger seat up front.

"What if they follow this car?" Philip asked nervously, glancing over his shoulder out the back window as the driver pulled the car into the heavy traffic outside the federal courthouse.

Donnelly's face was unemotional. "Don't worry. Even if they are now, we'll lose them before we're out of the state. Trust us." She turned to Philip. "You turned state's evidence to get this deal. Torrentino's people have good reason not to be very happy with you. You made the choices that put you in this position. My recommendation is not to make it any harder."

"What happens when we get to Charlotte?" Philip asked.

"That's where we do what's called a dead drop," Donnelly said. Seeing the confused expressions on both their faces, she explained further. "I know who you are, as do the people in my field office. We're taking you to Charlotte and we're going to put you in a motel just outside of town. Another field office will pick you up. I don't know which one and I won't ever know. That way my people and I will have no idea where you are. The people picking you up at the motel will have your new identities but they won't know who you were. The motel is a 'cut-out' between the sections of the Witness Protection Program. We're a very compartmentalized organization because we have to be. Each compartment has no idea of what's happening in the other compartments. It makes everything more secure."

"Who will know who we really are and where we are?" Lisa asked.

"The main office in D.C. will have that information, but I can assure you that it will never get out. There are only four people on the access roster to that information and all have the highest clearances. The biggest threat you have of being discovered," she added, "is if you do something yourself to give away your former identity. There's little doubt that Torrentino's people will be looking for you, and they have connections with organized crime all over the country."

"Great, just great," Philip muttered nervously.

A look of disgust flickered across Donnelly's face. Lisa Cobb saw it, even though her husband hadn't. It was the same look she'd caught on almost everyone's face since the day the police had shown up at her door to tell her an attempt had been made on her husband's life. Her initial concern had changed to shock as the circumstances of the attack became clear to her. Philip's involvement with organized crime, followed by the information that he had been in that building visiting a mistress, had hit like a double blast from a shotgun, shattering the illusion in which Lisa had wrapped her life.

Lisa Cobb had grown up on the south side of Chicago, and that experience had convinced her that somehow she was smarter than those who'd had a more sheltered upbringing. She garnered a scholarship to the University of Chicago, where she found herself in a new environment—one where street smarts paid little dividend. She received her degree in graphic art and threw herself into a job with a small local newspaper outside of Chicago.

She met Philip after her second year there when he came to town to teach a seminar on real estate investment. He represented a different world to her—the world into which she was now trying to fit. It had just seemed the right thing when after three months he asked her to marry him. A year later their daughter, Melissa, was born. Lisa left her job and threw herself full time into being a mother. For four years life had gone well; Philip's business boomed and they moved out of the city into an exclusive suburb.

Their lives fell apart three years ago when Melissa, then four, began having trouble walking. She would fall over unexpectedly and complain of dizziness. Lisa took her to a doctor; the verdict surpassed her worst fears—a malignant growth in the child's brain.

For two years Melissa battled the cancer, and Lisa devoted herself to supporting her daughter. The toll on Philip was something Lisa had ignored, to a certain extent not even allowing him to participate in the effort to save their daughter. Not only had she ignored the emotional cost of the illness, but in her preoccupation with Melissa, Lisa had failed to notice the signs that Philip's business was failing miserably. As the real estate boom came to an end, he was left holding numerous downtown office properties that he couldn't unload. That burden, combined with the high cost of Melissa's medical treatments, rapidly ate up whatever savings they had and put them deep into debt.

Lisa shivered in the backseat, her head resting uncomfortably against the cold glass of the darkened side window. Lately she'd come to realize that she had tuned out Philip to the point where she had no idea what he was doing.

That realization forced her to confront another, darker, one: how much had her lack of interest and attention led her husband to do what he did? Lisa closed her eyes and forced her mind off that path. She didn't want to think about it. She surrendered herself to the wave of exhaustion that she'd been keeping at bay and was asleep within minutes, the mutter of the engine and the noise of the tires soothing her mind as the miles from Chicago and their lost life accumulated.

CHARLOTTE, NORTH CAROLINA
28 OCTOBER, 11:47 P.M.

Lisa opened her eyes and looked blearily around the rear of the car, trying to determine what was different. It took a few seconds but then she realized that they were no longer moving. The dome light went on as Donnelly opened the front passenger door and beckoned. "Time to go," she said, getting out.

"What?" Philip mumbled, peering out the window at the dimly lit parking lot. A one-story motel—The Continental—was spread out in front of them. The office was to the far left, along with a flashing light that beckoned to the road weary on the interstate. Underneath the light was a sign indicating that the Firefly Lounge was open until two in the morning. A scattering of cars was gathered around the entrance to the lounge, but the motel's business seemed to be slow, with only two cars parked in front of rooms. The rumble of the interstate was close by, and a string of fast-food restaurants and an all-night truck stop marked the two-lane road on which the motel was located.

"Are we there?" Philip asked as they exited the back of the car.

In response, Donnelly pointed at the door directly in front of them. "Room one-oh-seven. Here's the key."

Philip didn't move. "Aren't you going to stay with us?"

Donnelly shook her head. "My job was to get you here. I've done that."

"But who's going to protect us?" Philip protested.

"No one knows you're here except us and the people picking you up," Donnelly explained wearily.

"Well, where are the people picking us up?" Philip demanded.

"They'll be here in the morning. We need time to clear out, and we weren't sure exactly what time we'd get here. We made better time than I expected."

"But why can't you stay until they arrive?" he asked.

Donnelly's patience was wearing thin. "I don't know the people who are meeting you. They don't know me or my people, and I don't want them to. That helps ensure your safety and the safety of all the other people in the system. I've already explained this to you several times." She jerked her head toward the door of the room, where the driver had unceremoniously dumped their suitcases. "Now, it's time for you to go in there, and it's time for me to head for home."

"What if we were followed?" Philip pressed.

Donnelly's patience snapped. She leaned forward, putting her face less than a foot from his. "I've listened to you whine for ten hours. I don't want to hear any more and I don't have to. I've done my job. We weren't followed, I can assure you of that. You'll be picked up in the morning; meanwhile you'll be safe." She pulled two cards out of her pocket and handed one to Philip and one to Lisa. The card had a phone number printed in the center and a four-digit code on the bottom right. "This is the number to call if you ever have any problems. Use that personal code to identify yourself and pass the security check." She glanced over her shoulder as she settled back into the car. "Good-bye."

29 OCTOBER, 12:03 A.M.

Lisa threw herself onto the bed and stared up blankly at the ceiling. Her husband had gone directly into the shower, and she could hear the roar of the water through the thin wall. The weeks between the day her world had fallen apart and the end of the trial seemed like a blur. She didn't even feel as though she was really here in North Carolina. A part of her kept expecting to wake up from the nightmare.

Philip came out of the bathroom and threw on his clothes.

"Where are you going?" she asked as he headed for the outside door.

"I'm going to get some sodas from the machine. You want one?"

Lisa shook her head and sank back on the bed. Five minutes later, Philip was back, two Pepsis in hand. He popped one, pouring it into the plastic glass from the bathroom, and set the other on top of the TV. He was nervous, flitting about the room, glancing out the curtains every so often, checking his watch constantly.

"She said it would be morning before the other people showed," Lisa noted from the bed.

"Yeah, I know." Philip lit a cigarette and sank down into one of the chairs.

"I can't believe they'd just leave us like this," Lisa said.

"They don't care. They got what they wanted from me and now I'm just a pain to them."

Philip sat in the chair, his eyes unfocused. Lisa lay on the bed in her misery, still not quite sure how to resolve all that had happened in the past months and shelve it away in her mind. She realized some time ago that her big mistake had been marrying Philip in the first place, but it was a realization too late in coming. She was twenty-nine now and she'd given seven years of her life to a man who'd effectively trashed hers in one day. Lisa knew a little about the mob from her youth, and she very much doubted that they would be sympathetic if she tried explaining how she no longer loved the man who had turned state's evidence. They would most likely not even give her a chance to explain. Divorce had not been an option in the whirlwind of events following the attempt on Philip's life.

Philip suddenly stood, startling her. "I'm going down to the lounge. You try and get some sleep."

Lisa frowned. "Why don't you stay in the room?"

"I'm going nuts in here," he snapped and then he was gone.

Lisa felt the emptiness close in—the same emptiness she'd felt eight years ago in her drafty studio in suburban Chicago. She rolled off the bed and pulled on her jacket. Anything would be better than staying here alone. She left the room and walked along the covered sidewalk toward the lounge. She pushed open the door and stepped in, pausing for a moment to allow her eyes to adjust to the dim light inside. Philip was nowhere to be seen. There were about a dozen people lined up at the bar and a scattering of couples at the tables between the bar and the booths that lined the far wall.

Lisa felt slightly foolish. Perhaps Philip had gone to the men's room. She moved toward the bar, keeping an eye on the rest room doors at the far end of the lounge. She took a stool at the end of the bar, with a comfortable separation of one empty chair between her and the next person. After ordering a ginger ale from the bartender, she turned in her seat and checked the room again.

Her heart froze as she spotted Philip seated in a booth, a woman at his side. Thoughts tumbled in her brain. Who was the woman? A part of her wanted to believe it was someone Philip had just picked up in the bar, but the way the two sat close together made it clear that they were familiar with each other. The answer strained to be heard, but Lisa didn't want to accept it. She had never met the woman who had been so instrumental in the destruction of her life, but somehow she knew that the woman seated with Philip was Jill Fastone. How could the woman have known where they were?

Philip must have called her! Lisa was so shocked that her anger stayed at bay for a half minute. Tripping on the heels of the anger, though, came nausea. She staggered off the bar stool toward the ladies' room, not caring if Philip saw her. She shoved the door open and knelt by the toilet, heaving up the scant contents of her stomach.

12:17 A.M.

In the bar Philip turned to Jill, at a loss. Nothing was making much sense anymore. "Let's get out of here," he said.

Jill had a vaguely smug look on her face. "Where to?"

Philip was already on his feet. "The room. We're going to have to straighten all this out. I have to tell her. I can give up my old life but I can't give up you."

Jill laughed, shaking her head, as she followed him out.

12:18 A.M.

"This is Surveillance. They're back. I've got two entering one-oh-seven."

The team leader—code name Master—acknowledged the transmission from the back of the panel van parked in the darkness on the far side of the motel, out of sight of the Cobbs' room. "This is Master. Roger. Description? Over."

"One male. One female. Description for both fits, but the lighting's lousy and I can't confirm it. Over."

"What about the escort? Over."

"Gone. No sign of anyone covering them. They're all alone. Over."

"Roger. Hold. Out." Master leaned back in his chair and ran a hand through his hair. He was a large man, his arms corded with muscles, his hair prematurely gray. His face was permanently set in a scowl. What people noticed about him on first meeting were his eyes. They were such a pale shade of blue that they immediately drew people's attention. On missions where he could be spotted, he normally wore colored contact lenses.

He pressed both hands together and cracked his knuckles. The waiting was the worst part. It was too early. Too many people about. Later would be better. But the window of opportunity was narrow. He made his decision and checked his watch. "All elements, this is Master. It's now twelve eighteen mark twenty seconds. We go at twelve twenty-one. All elements report in with a confirmation on that. Over."

"Door. Roger. Over."

"Support. Roger. All clear. Over."

"Surveillance. Roger. All clear from up here. Over."

Master glanced at the man sitting in front of the communications console. "Anything?"

The man pulled one of the cups off his left ear and pointed at the glowing computer screen. "Nearest patrol car is four miles away." The use of computers in police vehicles—while of great benefit to the officers—made the location of those cars available to anyone who had the right equipment to lock into the police band and decrypt the continuous transmission those computers send back to patrol headquarters.

12:19 A.M.

"You need to tell her when she comes in," Jill insisted.

Philip wrung his hands. "Listen—I couldn't just let it go and never talk to you again but this—this was wrong of me. I shouldn't have done it."

Jill drove home her attack. "But you did! And you know why you did? Because you love me. What has she done for you in the past year? Huh?"

Philip pressed his palms against his temples and closed his eyes. He wished everything and everybody would disappear.

Jill Fastone smiled, the game done. "Oh, don't take it all so seriously, Philip. It doesn't matter anyway." Her right hand dropped into her purse. "You don't think I came down here because I love you, do you? You're such a fool."

Philip looked up in confusion. "What?"

She pulled the silenced pistol out of her purse and aimed it squarely at his chest. "You first and then your wife when she gets back."

"But why?" Philip protested in surprise.

Fastone ignored the question. "First, there's something you need to tell me, isn't there?"

Philip stared. "What are you talking about?"

"You know what I'm talking about," she answered. "Where's the money?"

12:21 A.M.

The unmarked panel van slid in front of room 107. Three men smoothly exited the sliding side door, leaving it open. They wore black ski masks, and small boom mikes hung in front of their lips. The middle man was the one in charge, and he was whispering their progress in his mike as they approached the door.

The lead man slid the passkey into the lock while the second man stood by with a sledgehammer in case the chain had been put on. There was no need, because the knob turned and the door swung open. The leader took aim and fired the weapon in his hand. A small metal dart shot out, reeling out a thin line behind it, and struck Philip Cobb in the chest, attaching to his shirt. The first man released the doorknob and fired his own electric stunner, hitting the woman, who was swinging around toward them, a pistol in her hand.

Both men pressed switches on the handles of the weapons. The couple's look of surprise changed to one of rigid pain as the volts coursed through their bodies, locking up their muscles and freezing them. The third man swung the door shut behind them. The second man ran forward and pulled the pistol out of Jill Fastone's hands. The entry had taken all of three seconds.

The leader strode up to Philip Cobb and peered at his face. "Master, I've got a confirmed ID on the primary target. Over." He pulled out a white plastic drop cloth that had been tucked under his belt, threw it on the ground, and kicked Cobb's legs out from under him. Philip landed on the drop cloth with a thud, the scream he was trying to let loose stuck in his throat by the electric current. His eyes, already opened wide, watched the man pull out a pistol with his free hand and point it at him, right between the eyes.

"Primary ready for termination. Over." The bulky silencer on the end of the barrel was rock steady.

"This is Master. Terminate. Over."

The man pulled the trigger, and a soft-nosed bullet tore through the center of Philip Cobb's forehead. The mercury inside the metal jacket expanded, sending shards of metal through his brain. The bullet disintegrated and spent its force inside the skull, killing Cobb but making a minimal mess. His head thumped back on the plastic, with only a slight dribble of blood oozing from the black hole in the center of his forehead.

"Shit, it ain't her!" the first man exclaimed.

The leader shifted his gaze from the body. The woman was lying on a similar plastic sheet; the first man had his gun centered on her, but he was looking at the leader. "It ain't her," he repeated. He held up her silenced pistol. "And she had this on her aimed at him"—he jerked a thumb at Philip's body—"when we came in."

"Master, this is Door. We've got a negative confirmation on secondary target. Over."

In the van, Master leaned forward in his seat and grabbed the boom mike, as if by holding it the message would come out clearer. "What do you mean it isn't her? Maybe they did a make-over. Over."

"Negative. I'm telling you it isn't her. Over."

"Who the hell is it then? Over."

The cell leader gestured for the lead man to turn off the stunner. He pressed his pistol in the middle of the woman's forehead. "Check the bag," he ordered.

The lead man grabbed the woman's purse and pulled out her wallet. He flipped it open and saw her Illinois driver's license. "Jill Fastone," he informed the cell leader, who promptly relayed the information over the radio. "She was in here with the primary and she was holding a weapon on him. Over."

Master recognized the name from the mission briefing. He quickly calculated his next move, feeling precious seconds ticking away. "This is Master. Terminate. Over. Break. Surveillance, we're missing the secondary target. Find her. Over."

The door to the ladies' room swung open and the waitress peered around. "Are you all right, miss?"

Lisa raised her head from the sink and met the other woman's eyes. "I'm all right. Something I ate."

"I was just checking on you—the way you ran in here and all," the waitress explained.

Lisa blinked and tried to sort out her thoughts. She couldn't confront Philip here in the bar, and not with that woman next to him. She decided to go to the room and wait for him. "I think I'll just go back to my room and lie down."

Lisa walked out on unsteady legs, her eyes seeking the booth where she had seen Philip and the woman. They were gone. Lisa continued toward the door to the lounge, fearing the coming stormy confrontation.

"Please," Jill Fastone whispered, her eyes riveted on the large black bore pointed at her. "Please don't."

"What are you doing here?" the cell leader asked.

She shook her head. "Please. Just let me go. I won't say anything."

He held up her pistol. "What were you going to do with this? Who sent you?"

"I can help you!" she pleaded. "I can give you information about—"

"Let's go!" The third man hissed, not interested in what she had to say. "Master said terminate. We've been in here for seventy-five seconds."

The cell leader pulled the trigger, and Jill Fastone's body settled onto the plastic with a thump and a twitch. "Let's wrap 'em and go," the cell leader ordered. They rolled the bodies in the white plastic. The third man, who'd been watching out the window all this time, cracked open the door and took a quick look. "All clear."

The cell leader and the first man picked up Philip Cobb's body and headed out the door.

"This is Surveillance. I've got what looks like the secondary leaving the lounge. Over."

"Door, did you get that? Over."

The cell leader looked up from his end of the body they were carrying and spotted the woman on the sidewalk fifty feet away. "Fuck!"

Lisa Cobb stared at the two men with the bundle between them, and she realized they were staring back at her. They dropped the bundle, and she gasped as Philip's body rolled out of the plastic. The men were pulling guns from their jackets. She turned and ran.

The door cell leader hissed into his microphone, "Where's she going? Over."

"Into the lounge. Over."

"This is Master. Clean up and let's get the fuck out of here. Over."

"What about the secondary? Over." The door cell leader watched the woman disappear into the lounge; he was torn between taking care of the dead body at his feet and the live one running away.

"You want to follow her in there?" Master's voice snapped at him over the air. "Do as I goddamn tell you. Clean up and clear out. Surveillance, you maintain. Over."

The men dumped Philip Cobb's body unceremoniously into the back of the van. Jill Fastone's followed. The three men swept the room, removing all signs of occupancy and relocking the door on the way out.

The van pulled away from the motel and was on the interstate heading north within two minutes.

"Do you have a phone?" Lisa demanded of the bartender.

He looked at the desperate woman and jerked his head toward the rest rooms. "There's a pay phone back there."

Lisa glanced at the front door, expecting at any minute to see the two men come hurtling through, guns ablaze. She reached across the bar and grabbed the man's arm. "I need to call the police! Right away."

The bartender extracted his arm from her grip and peered at her, his mind struggling with the conflict between the woman's obvious panic and the house rules. He grudgingly reached under the bar and pulled out a phone.

Lisa grabbed the receiver and punched in 911. The other end was picked up on the second ring.

"I've got a call!" the commo man yelled out. "A unit to respond to this location. Possible two-five-one."

Master twisted in his chair. "Who's responding?"

The commo man glanced at his screen as he listened. "One-four." He tapped the glass. "This one. About five minutes out."

"This is Master. Everyone pull back to alternate assembly point. Over."

"This is Surveillance. What about the woman? We'll lose her! Over."

Master leaned forward and spoke slowly into his mike. "This is Master. We won't lose her." His voice became ice cold. "The next person who questions my orders is dead. Out."

CHAPTER 4

The cop looked around the empty motel room and then back at Lisa Cobb. "Doesn't look to me like anybody was in here, never mind someone getting killed." He scanned a page of his notebook. "The desk says this room is reserved for a Mr. and Mrs. Lockhart, but they never checked in."

Lisa sank down in the cheap chair and stared around her. Philip was dead. Everything was gone. All she had was the few dollars in her purse. She didn't exist as a real person anymore.

"And," the cop added, "since you can't show me any ID, I think we might have a problem here. I talked to the bartender and he told me that one of the waitresses says you were sick in the bathroom just before you called nine-one-one." He considered Lisa. "I don't smell any alcohol on you, miss, but there isn't anything to back up what you're saying. I'd take you in and run you for drugs, but I get off shift in thirty minutes."

He stuffed his notebook back in his breast pocket. "I don't know what your story is, lady, but don't waste our time. If your boyfriend dumped you here and is gone down the interstate now, then call someone who can come get you." He gestured for the door. "Get out of here and I'll forget all about this."

"But I'm in the Federal Witness Protection Program and my husband was too, and they killed him!" she explained for the fourth time.

The cop nodded. "Right. And you were just sitting here in a motel and the mob found you and killed him and left you alive and made everything disappear. Uh-huh." He pointed at the door again. "I've heard better stories than that to get out of a speeding ticket. Get going."

Lisa stepped out of the room, feeling the early morning chill sink into her bones. The cop opened the door to his car and paused, watching Lisa. She turned and walked down the sidewalk, not sure where she was going but knowing she had to get away from the motel. Her body was working on automatic, her mind no longer able to function after too many shocks.

"The cop called in clear."

Master leaned forward. "She's not with him?"

"Negative."

"Nothing from the room?"

An irritated look flashed over the commo man's face, but his back was to the other man. "The cop's going off shift. He called in nothing on the woman or the room," he repeated.

Master's foot pushed the transmit button. "Surveillance, this is Master."

In the van parked next to his at the rest stop, the man sitting in the passenger seat pressed his own transmit. "This is Surveillance. Over."

"It's clear. Move in and reacquire the secondary target. Over."

With a squeal of tires, the van roared out of the parking lot, heading back to exit 12.

The radio crackled in the van. "Master, this is Door. I know what to do with the remains of the primary, but what should I do with the other one? Over."

Master thought about that for a few moments, then a nasty smile crossed his face. He pressed the transmit button with the answer.

The lights of the all-night truck stop beckoned just before the on-ramp to the interstate. Lisa walked along the side of the road, her shoes crunching in the gravel. The patrol car drove by slowly, the officer swiveling his head to look at her pointedly. She saw his brake lights come on; he was waiting to see what she did. She walked across the oil-spattered asphalt and into the diner. A couple of truck drivers eyed her briefly over their steaming cups of coffee as she settled onto a stool. She looked out the window and the cop car was gone.

"Coffee," she said as the waitress came up. She had to think. She opened her purse to grab a dollar bill and spotted the card that Donnelly had given her. She grabbed it the way a drowning person would a life preserver.

"Can I have some change, please?" Lisa said quietly, giving several dollar bills to the waitress.

She took the change and went outside to the pay phone on the wall. A set of headlights shining from the off-ramp caught her eye. A van with dark windows rolled by slowly. Lisa caught her breath—the van looked exactly like the one Philip's body had been thrown into. She dropped the phone and quickly walked back into the illusive safety of the diner, then watched from the window as the van disappeared into the darker shadows of a closed gas station on the far side of the road.

"Got trouble, little lady?"

Lisa tore her eyes away and stared at a man in grease-stained overalls. A big wad of chaw poked his cheek out to the left, and the broken veins in his nose spoke of large quantities of alcohol imbibed over the years. The skin around his eyes crinkled as he smiled. "That's my rig there," he said, pointing at a run-down tractor truck with a livestock trailer attached. "You need to get out of here?" he persisted.

Lisa glanced across the street one more time and then nodded. "Yes. Where are you going?"

He grinned and stuck out his hand. "Carrying a load to slaughter up at Greensboro. Name's Ted, but back home in Texas they call me Bubba."

"Lisa."

"Let's roll, Lisa."

"Secondary is getting into a tractor trailer. Georgia license AFT-649. Too many people to do anything here. Over."

"Shit," Master swore to himself. He keyed his mike. "Maintain contact." He opened a drawer and pulled out a bottle of aspirin.

"You just get in a fight with your husband or something?" Bubba asked.

"What?" Lisa said, her red-rimmed eyes momentarily looking away from the rearview mirror.

"Well, you got a wedding band on your finger there, and you been crying, and some asshole's following us," Bubba reported succinctly.

Lisa thought quickly. The van had been behind them now for the last ten miles, ever since they'd pulled onto the interstate. "It's him. He's been beating me."

"What?" Bubba glanced over with his forehead furrowed.

"My husband. He's been beating me. I've got to get away from him."

Bubba sat in silence for a few moments. "Son of a bitch," he said, pounding the steering wheel. "Son of a bitch. I *hate* assholes who hit women." He looked over. "You got any kids?"

Lisa felt her heart lurch. "I had a daughter."

"Had?"

"She died two years ago."

"Shit, ma'am, I'm sorry." Bubba's face tightened. "He didn't kill her, did he?"

Lisa couldn't do it anymore. She slumped forward, head in hands, and the tears came out in great heaving sobs.

"Oh, shit," Bubba groaned. "I'm sorry, ma'am. I'm real sorry." He looked in the rearview mirror and spit a gob of chaw out the partially open side window. The van was about two hundred feet back. You fucking asshole, he said to himself. He eased up on the gas pedal, and the van crept to within a hundred feet before the driver started to compensate. Bubba slammed his foot on the brakes and, with a startling screech, the rig slid, wheels locked.

The driver of the surveillance van cursed as the rear of the tractor trailer loomed in front of them, closing at a dangerous rate. He slammed on his brakes and threw the wheel to the left. The van hit the shoulder of the road at twenty miles an hour. A tree suddenly appeared in front of the van, and the driver threw up his hands in front of his face as the front end crumpled inward.

"Yea-hah!" Bubba screamed. "Did you see . . ." He paused as he looked at Lisa. His voice dropped to the closest he could manage to a concerned whisper. "You all right?"

Lisa nodded, wiping her sleeve across her face.

"Well, you won't have to worry about your husband for a while, ma'am."

Lisa nodded, unable to speak.

"Hey, listen," Bubba continued uncertainly, the excitement of the moment wearing off. "Where you heading? You got some folks to stay with?"

Lisa sucked in her breath and tried to get control.

"You can drop me off wherever you're going."

Bubba looked at her and opened his mouth to speak but then shut it. He drove on.

"This is Surveillance. We've lost the target and we need maintenance help. I-85, mile marker forty-two. Over."

The commo man twisted in his seat to look at Master, then quickly turned back to his computers as his boss's face contorted in anger. "This is Master. Say again. Over."

"We've lost the target and are broken down at mile marker forty-two. Over."

Master's hands gripped the edge of the console in front of him until the white showed clearly on his knuckles. Somehow he managed to control his voice. "We'll clear you out. Over."

He kicked the panel separating him and the commo man from the driver. "Get moving!" he yelled.

"What about the target?" the commo man dared ask.

"We'll get her," Master muttered, picking up the secure portable phone. "We'll get the bitch."

"I need to make a call," Lisa said as she spotted the sign for a rest area.

"Sure thing, miss." Bubba had been getting nervous during the past thirty minutes, half-expecting a state trooper to pull him over for running that van off the road. The guy must have reported it by now. All this time the woman had simply been sitting there, not responding to his attempts at conversation, staring blankly out the windshield. He pulled into the rest area and rolled up to the bank of phones.

"I'll wait here," he said. Lisa hopped out without a word.

She made her way to a phone and pulled out the change she'd gotten at the diner. On the card Donnelly had given her she noted that the number had an 800 prefix—someone had been thinking. She punched in the number and it was picked up on the third ring. A recorded voice talked to her: "Enter your code, please."

With a shaking hand she punched in the four-digit code written on the corner of the card. There was a buzz and then an extremely long pause. Lisa was beginning to think she needed to redial when a sleepy voice came on the line. "Yes?"

It all poured out in a torrent. "This is Mrs. Cobb. I was given this

number by Agent Donnelly. She said to call if there were any problems and . . . and my husband, he's been killed. I saw his body. They
were carrying it out of the motel room. And they're after me. They
were following—"

The voice was fully alert now. A distinct New England accent. "Hold
on. Wait a second, Mrs. Cobb." There was the sound of movement.
"You say your husband is dead? When? Where?"

The story came out in a rush, the voice on the other end occasionally asking questions to clarify. When Lisa ground to a halt, she finally realized she didn't even know to whom she was talking. "What's
your name?" she asked.

"You can call me Simon." The voice continued. "All right, Mrs.
Cobb. Where exactly are you right now?"

"The rest area on I-85 just before Greensboro."

"North- or southbound?"

"Northbound."

"All right. From what you told me, you're not in danger right now.
Stay where you are and I'll get people there as quickly as possible."

Lisa looked around the rest area. A dozen or so trucks with their
parking lights on were in the truck parking area. Two cars with misted
windows sat in front of the building housing the rest rooms.

"How long before someone will get here?" she asked.

"I'll have people there within an hour," Simon replied.

"How will I know who they are?" she asked.

"They'll know who you are. Just wait there."

"All right."

The phone went dead in her hand and she stared at it for thirty seconds.
She put it back slowly on the hook and walked wearily over to Bubba's
rig.

"Get through?" he asked as she stepped up and opened the passenger door.

"Yes. My friend will be here within the hour to pick me up. I really appreciate your help."

Bubba nodded, his eyes meeting her red-rimmed ones and then scanning
the dark parking lot. "Well, I don't have to deliver this load until six.
I can wait."

"Oh, no," Lisa protested. "I'll be fine waiting in the building. You've
been a big help and I don't want you to get in trouble."

Bubba shook his head. "It ain't right for a lady to be waiting in one of these places all alone. There's strange people come through here at night."

"I'll be fine, and I've already inconvenienced you enough."

Bubba frowned and spit into his plastic coffee cup. "Ain't no inconvenience to help a lady."

"Please," Lisa pleaded. "I'll be fine."

Bubba sat back in his seat and sighed. "Well, all right, ma'am. But you take care, you hear?"

"I will," Lisa said. She leaned across the large stick shift and kissed Bubba gently on his right cheek. "Thanks for everything." Tears welled up in her eyes again.

Bubba's already red face went a shade darker, and he mumbled something inarticulate as Lisa climbed down from the cab.

She walked under the lights to the back entrance of the small rest stop building, entered the brightly lit interior, and sank down wearily on a hard wooden bench facing the front where the cars were parked. She glanced at the large clock hanging on the wall—ten minutes since she'd gotten off the phone with Simon. She leaned back against the wood and her head immediately started to droop, her eyes feeling the urge to close, her body no longer capable of producing any more adrenaline to keep it going. She snapped her head up and peered about, struggling to keep awake. For the next forty-two minutes she alternately slipped into a sleep more like exhausted unconsciousness, then woke to a fretful but disoriented awareness.

At precisely 2:23 A.M. a car pulled to the front of the rest area building, its lights reflecting off the glass. Lisa awoke with a start and blinked, blinded by the high beams. Two men got out of the car and headed toward the building. Lisa stood—it had to be the people Simon had sent. She reached the door just before they did and stepped outside. "Mrs. Cobb?" one of the men called out, holding up a hand in greeting, his form silhouetted by the lights of the car.

The last bit of energy drained out of Lisa and she leaned back against the door, glad the nightmare was finally over. "Yes."

The man's other hand raised and there was something in it. Lisa's mind tried to react, but it was slowed by a quagmire of exhaustion and shock. There was a sharp snap, and something flashed across the six feet of space separating them and snagged the front of her windbreaker. Lisa's eyes turned downward in confusion and then she tried futilely to scream as the electric current tore through her body.

The two men hustled her into the back of the car and slammed the doors. "Let's go!" the man with the electric stunner yelled at the driver. The car pulled away from the rest area building and headed for the interstate.

The man looked down at Lisa lying on the floor in the back and allowed a small, satisfied smile to play over his face. He picked up the headset that was plugged into the radio.

"Master, this is Julian. We have the secondary target under control. I confirm the target. Over."

"This is Master. Terminate. Out."

Julian pulled out his pistol and centered the muzzle on Lisa's forehead. The car swayed as the driver pulled onto the ramp connecting the rest area with the highway. "Turn off the power," he ordered the other man, who promptly released the trigger on the stunner.

"Good-bye, bitch." As his finger tightened on the trigger, the right side of the car burst inward, throwing Julian against the left door, his shot tearing through the floor. The car was being pushed across the white lines on the highway and into the grassy median.

In his cab, Bubba let out a rebel yell. He grabbed the Colt Python he kept stashed next to the seat as protection. The car had rolled over on its left side in the grass; the wheels were still turning as Bubba hopped down from his cab.

The passenger door flew open and a head appeared.

"Hands where I can see 'em, asshole!" Bubba yelled, leveling his pistol at the man climbing out. Bubba moved closer and yelled again: "You all right, miss?" His eyes widened as an automatic weapon appeared in the man's right hand. Bubba fired two wild shots and dove for safety underneath his trailer. A return burst of fire tore into the livestock in the trailer, and the cattle screamed wildly in pain. Blood splattered against the side panels and the trailer rocked as the animals panicked.

The rear door of the car sprang open and Julian and the other man crawled out.

"Watch out!" the driver yelled from his perch in the open passenger door. "It's some fucking cowboy with a gun—"

The man's words were cut off as a large red spot blossomed in the center of his forehead. His head snapped back as the rear of his skull was torn off by the trajectory of the .357 magnum slug. The body slumped back into the vehicle.

Julian and the other man immediately hit the ground, peering up at the road. "See him?" Julian hissed.

"Negative. He must be behind the trailer."

Julian nodded. He flicked the selector lever of his FA-MAS Commando rifle from single shot through the three-round burst to fully automatic, then settled the butt of the weapon firmly into his shoulder. He rolled to his knee and sighted down the laser sight built into the top handle of the short weapon. The red dot slid along the asphalt in front of the trailer from right to left, the arc of bullets following it, hitting the hard surface and ricocheting off—a line parallel to and eight inches above the road surface.

One of the twenty-five rounds ripped into Bubba's left calf, the high velocity of the 5.56mm NATO round splintering the bone and tearing off a huge chunk of muscle as it tumbled through and continued on. Bubba fell to the ground, shock already setting in—as much from the surprise of being hit as from the bullet.

Julian smoothly pressed back the release, dropping the magazine that rested between the trigger and the rear of the stock—the innovation that allowed the French-made weapon to be only sixteen inches long—and slammed a new magazine home in less than two seconds.

Bubba was trying to get up on his one good leg and crawl behind the wheel of the trailer when Julian centered the red dot on his chest. A long, savage burst tore into the prone man. The first two rounds killed him, but Julian continued firing, bullets punching into the body and rolling it a good ten feet away from the truck.

Julian stood slowly and walked forward, surveying the mess. The left front of the tractor truck was dented where the driver had slammed into the car. Julian had no idea who this crazy person was, but it didn't matter now. Cleanup was the number one priority. Luckily no traffic had come along during the brief firefight, but they couldn't count on that much longer.

"Get on the radio," he snapped at the other man. "We need all the help we can get right away to clean this up."

The other man turned and ran back to the car. His shout startled Julian. "She's gone!"

"What?" Julian asked, sensing an already screwed-up mission going farther down the tubes.

"She's not here."

Julian spun and scanned the immediate area. A set of lights roared down the interstate toward him. He drew up the MAS to firing position, then relaxed as he recognized the van. It slid to a halt and Master stepped out, surveying the scene with his lips set in a tight slash. Julian ran up to him.

"We've got one body there. Cobb's gone."

"Where to?" Master demanded.

Julian shrugged and looked about helplessly. "She must have run while I was terminating the interference."

Master looked around, taking in the car on its side, the body of Bubba, the dented tractor trailer rig with animals in back, some still screaming in pain. "Kill those animals and drive the rig back into the rest area. I'll take care of the car."

"What about the woman?" Julian asked.

"Our first priority is to clean up this pile of shit before we get state troopers all over the place!" Master yelled over his shoulder as he started toward the van.

On the far side of the interstate, huddled in the thick shrubbery planted there, Lisa Cobb shivered with fear, her body incapable of running any farther. She'd scrambled out the back door of the car right behind the two men and sprinted away into the darkness, without looking back.

Now as she watched the truck being backed into the rest area, she knew what had happened: Bubba must have stayed in the truck rest area and spotted her being abducted. Tears filled her eyes as she watched the body of her brief friend and protector thrown into the van that had pulled up.

She blinked as the car from which she had escaped went up in flames. The men all jumped into the van and it sped off into the darkness. Lisa remained hidden, refusing to come out, even ten minutes later when the lights of state police cars and fire trucks appeared in the darkness and lit up the night.

Chapter 5

The change of guard occurred gradually as the caretakers of the night slowly closed down and passed the duty to those who made their way in with the rising sun—all well before the required time of eight. It was habit and tradition in the Chicago Police Department—you always came on duty at least fifteen minutes, more like a half hour, before your shift was supposed to start, so the person you were replacing could leave a little earlier.

Lieutenant Donna Giannini made her way through her old domain, Homicide, on the way to the little cubicle where she'd been exiled. She wasn't replacing anyone—her job was done only during the day. She was a short, slender woman with black hair, slightly tinged with gray, cut tight against her skull. She wore black slacks, flat shoes, and a thick sweater. Her Mediterranean ancestry showed up clearly in her olive skin.

Giannini paused at the table holding the large coffeepot, retrieved her mug, and poured herself a generous dose of the strong brew. As she turned to leave, Vince Lorenzo spotted her and gave a yell. "Hey, Lieutenant!"

"Yeah?" Giannini didn't like Lorenzo, and she knew he didn't particularly care for her either. She waited, her right hand curled around the warmth of the mug. It was a game—it always was—Lorenzo had his feet on his desk, expecting her to come over. She held her ground, knowing, by virtue of her rank of lieutenant and his of sergeant, that

51

he should come to her. The only problem was that she was a lieutenant without a following, which made everyone question her position.

Lorenzo gave it ten seconds, then swung his legs off the desk and lumbered to his feet. He shifted through the mess of papers on his desk and extracted a message slip. Beer belly leading the way, he shuffled over to Giannini. "Got a strange message for you." He scratched his head. "This guy—he's called about six times. I told him you wouldn't be in until about seven thirty, but he sounded kind of upset." A smirk played around his mouth. Giannini could almost read his mind as he speculated about her personal life.

"Can I have the message, please?" Giannini asked patiently.

"Oh, yeah." He proferred the piece of paper. "He wouldn't leave his name," he added.

She looked at the scrawled message. "Remember ices at Antonio's? Stickball at the school?"

"Kind of weird, eh?" Lorenzo asked, his curiosity now clearly in the open. "He said he'd call back."

"Did he say what he was calling about?" Giannini asked, half her mind already in a long-ago place.

"Nope."

"He calls again, you put him through right away."

"I go off shift," Lorenzo said smugly.

"Then make sure you brief Carter and the rest of the guys on the day shift," she snapped. Without another word, Giannini left Homicide and walked down the hallway to the former supply closet that now served as her office. She spun the dial on the padlock and swung open the door. Once inside, it was impossible to close the door, because the chair, when pulled out from the desk, was in the way. She sat down and looked at the message, her thoughts shifting backward through the years.

Antonio's had been the corner grocery store in the neighborhood where Giannini grew up. It was a treat to buy one of the nickle Italian ices there. And then, after getting an ice, she'd walk down to the playground at the public school and play stickball—using a broom handle and a Spaulding rubber ball in the inner-city version of baseball. The strike zone was marked on the side of the school with chalk. It was pitcher against batter—scores made by blasting the ball over the chain-link fence.

Several people from Giannini's childhood could have left that message, but she knew instinctively who it was—Tom Volpe. That name brought a rush of conflicting feelings—memories of hot, lazy summer days spent talking, lost in the innocence of youth, flanked by the harsher memories of entering adulthood and divergent paths. The last time the two had talked was more than four years ago, Giannini remembered.

The phone startled her out of her memories, and she grabbed the receiver in the middle of the second ring. "Giannini."

"Donna, do you know who this is?"

Giannini recognized the voice, but she didn't understand why her old friend wouldn't identify himself. "Yeah, I know who it is. Listen, To—"

"Shh!" Tom hissed, cutting off Giannini. "Don't use my name."

"What's going on?"

"My sister's in big trouble and she needs help."

"Your sister?"

"Yeah—you remember her, don't you?"

"Yeah, I remember her. What kind of help does she need?"

"She says people are trying to kill her. She says someone already killed her husband and they're still after her."

Giannini frowned. "Why are you calling me? Why don't you call nine-one-one?"

"She's not here in Chicago."

This was getting crazier, Giannini thought. "Well, where is she?"

"North Carolina."

Giannini took a deep breath. "Let's go back to the original question—why are you calling me?"

"She says she can't trust anyone. She called me, and the only person I could think of who might be able to help is you."

"All right," Giannini said, playing along. "What can I do?"

There was a long pause, and Giannini recognized it for what it was: her friend had not thought this through.

"She needs protection. She says there have been two attempts on her life in the past twenty-four hours."

Giannini leaned forward in her chair and grabbed a notepad and pencil. "Take it slow and tell me what happened."

"I can't. Not on the phone."

"It isn't bugged," Giannini assured her friend. People watch too many crime shows on TV, she thought.

"I can't count on that. The last call my sister made almost got her killed, and she told me not to let out her identity over the phone." The voice hurried on. "Listen, she's in North Carolina. Can you get down there?"

Giannini tried once more to get some facts. "Who tried to kill her?"

There was a pause. "The Outfit."

Giannini frowned. "Why? Listen, you've got to tell me something about what's going on."

A long sigh. "Okay. I'll trust that this line is clear. Remember the big trial we just had this summer involving The Outfit?"

"Torrentino?"

"Yeah."

"So?"

"My sister's married name is Cobb."

All of Giannini's senses went on alert. She'd followed the trial—everyone in Chicago had. And she knew who Philip Cobb was, but she hadn't heard anything about a wife being involved. She wondered why the feds weren't taking care of this.

"Can you make it down there, Donna?"

Giannini thought furiously. "It would take me a while."

"She may not have a while."

"How about if I contact the feds? They can get someone to her much faster."

"No! She said definitely not. She already tried that once." The voice on the other end sounded desperate.

Giannini's thoughts settled on a possible solution. "I've got an idea."

"What?"

"I've got a friend who might be able to help your sister. Can you get hold of her?"

"She's calling me back in thirty minutes."

FORT BRAGG, NORTH CAROLINA
29 OCTOBER, 9:04 A.M.

The new Special Forces academic facility, or ACFAC, as it was called by those who worked there, was one of the most strangely constructed buildings Riley had ever seen. His office was on the fourth floor on the east end of the building, the only stairs that went from the first to the fourth floor on the east end began in the back of a classroom that was usually in use, thereby making the stairs effectively worthless. His other options were to take stairs in the center of the building or the lone elevator on the east end.

That was only the beginning of what disgusted Riley with his modern Fort Bragg workplace. Another problem with the design of the building became immediately noticeable as Riley pushed through the heavy fire doors that opened onto the offices for 1st Battalion, 1st Special Warfare Group. The work area was a large open room, more than a hundred yards wide and deep. To designate company and individual work areas, the powers that be had simply installed six-foot-high blue partitions, to form numerous cubicles each with space for two desks back to back. It was easy to get lost in this maze; in addition, everyone was too close together, with the chain of command all sitting within spitting distance. It made a free spirit like Riley uncomfortable.

Despite the advantages of being in a modern building, Riley and all the other worker bees missed the old World War II barracks that SF had used at Fort Bragg. In those aging, unattractive buildings, they'd had the latitude to design and modify the interiors any way they pleased.

Riley threw his small backpack onto the crowded desk and slumped down into his chair as he eyed the training schedule hanging on the cubicle wall. His team—Team 3, direct action—was on the light part of its teaching cycle, having just finished the mission planning and field training exercise at Camp Mackall. One of his noncommissioned officers (NCOs) had to teach a target analysis class later in the week, but other than that, there was nothing formally scheduled. Riley planned to give the five NCOs assigned to him some days off, and he would use the time to update lesson plans and outlines—a chore no one enjoyed.

A Company was broken down into four teams—direct action, strategic reconnaissance, foreign internal defense, and unconventional warfare. When a student officer reported to Fort Bragg for the Q-course, he'd already passed the biggest hurdle to becoming Special Forces qualified—the three-week Selection and Assessment (S & A) course at Camp Mackall. S & A was modeled after the selection course used for Delta Force, which in turn had been modeled after the course the British used for their Special Air Service (SAS). It was a land navigation course that involved marching many miles through the North Carolina wilderness with a heavy rucksack on the back. The participants were not told what the time limits were from point to point, or how many points they would have to complete, which increased the physical and mental stress as the days and nights went by.

Passing S & A allowed a student to become slotted into the Q-course, and that was where Riley and his team took over. A Company handled the incoming officers; B through E Companies took over the enlisted specialties from weapons man through commo man. Several months were spent learning the individual specialties, then the surviving students were assigned training teams and sent to Camp Mackall for a final training exercise called Robin Sage. For the students the course was a one-time grind. For the instructors it was a never-ending rotation, as the long-range training calendar on the wall of Riley's cubicle constantly reminded him.

Riley stared with consummate distrust at the laptop computer he'd been issued when assigned to A Company. Every officer who came in as a student to A Company was issued one of the computers for use during the course. Riley imagined that somehow it helped training, but he would have preferred to see each student issued a 9mm pistol and spend the sixteen hours learning to operate that weapon instead of a computer. Riley often joked with the commander of A Company, Major Welch, that he was going to put his computer in his rucksack on the next jump and see how it fared.

The phone rang and Riley ignored it. He made it a rule never to answer the phone in the company area. Usually the company training NCO up front handled all calls, and Riley didn't see "secretary" listed anywhere in his job description. Besides, phone calls usually meant something was screwed up; in the army nobody ever called to say things were going well or as planned.

The phone kept up its insistent braying, past the normal three or four rings. Riley gave it eight, then reluctantly picked up the receiver. "A Company, 1st Battalion, Chief Riley."

"Dave, it's Donna."

Riley's feet swung off his desk in surprise. Giannini had never called him at work. "What's up?"

"I've got a friend who's in trouble and she needs help and she's down in your neck of the woods."

Riley digested the run-on sentence without a blink. "What kind of trouble?"

"I don't know. She says someone killed her husband and now they're trying to kill her."

"Sounds like pretty big trouble," Riley commented warily. "Sounds like police-type trouble."

"I'm not sure exactly what's going on, Dave, but I think she *is* in big trouble and needs help. She may have professional killers after her, and there may be a reason why she can't go to the police."

"Where's she at?"

"Gordontown. It's about five miles from I-85 just below Greensboro."

Riley twisted in his seat and glanced at the map tacked on the wall. Many of the exercises in which he was involved were run off the Fort Bragg Military Reservation, particularly one called Troy Trek, which covered almost a hundred miles in and around the Uwharrie National Forest, in central North Carolina. He spotted Gordontown on the northwest side of the national forest.

"Yeah, I see it. How do I contact her?"

"You don't. She contacts you. I passed on to her what you and your truck look like. You go to the center of town and park outside the courthouse, across from the police station, and she'll link up with you."

"What's going on?" Riley asked. "Why all the secrecy? If someone killed her husband and is trying to kill her, why doesn't she go to the cops?"

"She says she doesn't trust the cops. I don't know too much about what's going on. When you meet her, ask *her* what the story is and straighten all this out."

Riley leaned back in his seat and closed his eyes, considering the situation. Giannini didn't give him much time for reflection. "Hey, listen, Dave. I'm asking this as a personal favor."

She didn't bother to add that he owed her one—indeed Riley owed her his life—but he had already added it into his mental calculations. "All right. I'm on my way."

"Thanks, Dave. Get in contact with me once you talk to her and tell *me* what's going on."

"Okay." Riley hung up the phone and headed out. He stuck his head inside the company commander's door before exiting the fourth floor. "Hey, sir, I've got to take care of some stuff. I'll be out the rest of the day."

"Roger." Major Welch didn't even bother to look up from the mountain of paperwork. His men spent more than half their time out of the building, mostly at Camp Mackall, so Riley's absence would be nothing unusual.

Trust was something that good commanders in Special Forces granted their men as a normal part of everyday activities.

Instead of immediately heading west, Riley took a detour off post to his town house. It was a two-story, two-bedroom place off Yadkin Road, one of the main drags onto Fort Bragg. He ran inside and hauled a footlocker out of the back of his closet. After surveying the contents and considering the situation, he pulled out a 9mm Beretta pistol in a shoulder holster and strapped it on inside his camouflage fatigue shirt. Then he grabbed a High Standard silenced .22-caliber automatic pistol and wrapped it in a towel. He carried it out to his black Bronco II and put it between the front seats, handle up for ready access.

Reversing direction, he drove back on post, past the 7th and 3d Special Forces Group areas to Chicken Road. From there it was a straight shot due west, along the south side of Fort Bragg, out to Camp Mackall. Then Riley would take back roads up to Gordontown.

CHAPTER 6

The town square in the center of Gordontown featured a courthouse with police headquarters directly across the street. Lisa Cobb sat in the small restaurant two doors down from the police station and sipped on her eighth cup of coffee. Her time had been split between watching, drinking, and going to the bathroom.

Calling her brother had been an act of desperation, but Tommy had bailed her out of more than one scrape in her life. When both their parents died in a car wreck when she was fourteen, it had been Tommy, seven years older, who had taken care of her and helped put her through college. Lisa was grateful for his help, but sometimes she wished he had been as generous with his advice as he had been with his money. It was only *after* her husband had been picked up by the police that Tommy had expressed his disapproval of Philip and of her marriage— a disapproval that dated from the time she had first gone out with the man. From anyone else, Lisa might have made a charge of hindsight, but she believed Tommy—he had never lied to her. He had not spoken his mind back then, he said, because he thought it was futile: people in love will never believe they're making a mistake. While awaiting the trial, he'd urged her to divorce Philip, but to Lisa that was not an option. She felt she couldn't abandon her husband at this worst possible time; it seemed as immoral as what he had done to her. Tommy tried to convince her, telling her it wouldn't get any better. But the thought of starting a new life alone on the shattered remains of her

59

old one had seemed overwhelming. More than anything, what she had wanted was time—time removed from crisis to sort things out, and the Program had seemed to offer her that. How ironic that the "solution" had unraveled the remaining strands of her life. Now she had nothing left.

Lisa spotted the black Ford Bronco II on its first loop around the square. The vehicle and driver fit the description her brother had forwarded to her on the second phone call. She gave it three loops and watched as the Bronco pulled into a spot facing the courthouse steps. Then she forced herself to wait another ten minutes—the memory of the incident at the rest stop all too fresh in her mind.

She finally stepped out into the sun-drenched street and came up on the vehicle from behind. She was surprised when the passenger door swung open without the driver even turning his head. She hopped in, and he had the truck started and out into the traffic before he even looked at her.

"I'm Dave Riley." He wore camouflage fatigues, and a faded green beret lay between the seats on top of a crumpled towel.

"Lisa Cobb."

He nodded, his eyes flicking from the rearview mirror to the streets and buildings and finally to her, then immediately back to a scan of the surroundings.

"Have you spotted anyone here in town who might be one of the people who have been after you?"

"No."

"We're heading to Fayetteville, which is about two hours away. I'm going to put you up in my apartment, where you'll be safe. I need to know what's going on, so why don't you start from the very beginning and tell me all that's happened."

The last thing Lisa felt like doing was tracing the events of the past twenty-four hours. She wanted to sit back in the cushions of the seat, close her eyes, and escape from the world. The cross-country walk toward the lights of the town, then the hours spent shivering on the outskirts before entering at daylight, had drained what little energy she had left. She knew she looked ragged, although she had done the best she could to clean up in the rest room of the coffee shop.

"Please," Riley said, this time really looking at her as he halted briefly at a stop sign. "I know you're probably beat, but to help you I've got to know what's going on. Your brother got in contact with a friend of mine on the Chicago police force, and she also needs to know so she can help. As soon as we get to Fayetteville, I'll give her a call and fill her in. So if you can hang in there for another couple of hours, I promise you a hot shower and some good rack time."

Lisa nodded and began her tale.

CHICAGO
29 OCTOBER, 12:38 P.M.

The police file on the Torrentino case filled four cardboard boxes. Giannini shuddered to think what the court file looked like; it would probably fill her office and flow out into the corridor. At least who-ever had put it together had labeled the folders. She began her search, thumbing through the volumes of paperwork, looking for anything that might help her understand what was going on. Within five min-utes, she knew there was something wrong with the file—pages were missing and certain names had been blacked out on all copies.

Forty minutes later, a large shadow filled her doorway. She glanced up to see Mike Guyton leaning against the doorframe, cleaning his teeth with a toothpick.

"A little bird told me someone had pulled the Torrentino case."

Giannini didn't say anything, waiting for Guyton to get to the point.

"It's closed, Giannini."

"Yeah, I can read."

Irritation flashed across Guyton's face. "So why are you looking at it?"

"That's my job, in case you haven't heard. To go through these old cases and then put them away downstairs."

Guyton shook his head. "Not the Torrentino case. The captain didn't give that to you to close out. *I* closed it out two weeks ago. You drew it out of the basement."

Shit, Giannini thought to herself. Caught in one lie already. Why was Guyton so uptight about this? He must have told the clerk downstairs to call him if anyone asked for the Torrentino file. Guyton had been in the papers big time throughout the trial, sharing the fame and credit for breaking the case with the FBI task force—a most unusual scene of cooperation between local and federal authorities. Most likely, Giannini figured, he was worried about anybody messing with his prize baby.

Unless he was worried about the pages that weren't in the file. Giannini felt a small worm of fear begin to crawl about in her gut.

"All right, Mike, you caught me. I'm just curious is all. I wanted to check it out."

"Get curious somewhere else, doll." He pointed at the boxes. "Those go back downstairs right now."

Giannini bristled but held herself in check as the big man turned and swaggered down the hall. She knew he'd be waiting to get a phone call from the clerk confirming that the file had been replaced, so she quickly packed up the boxes and returned them to the holding area.

CHARLOTTE
29 OCTOBER 1:16 P.M.

The phone was picked up on the first buzz and Master began speaking immediately. "Master here. Primary was terminated. Secondary is still free. Everything's been swept clean."

"You've had two tries now." The voice on the other end was blunt. "We can't afford any more screwups."

A muscle twitched on the side of Master's face. "She was lucky." The other members of his team were silent, sitting amidst debris from several fast-food restaurants scattered about the motel room.

"Luck is a variable that shouldn't stand up in the face of superior firepower."

The muscle flicked several times, but Master continued. "We lost contact on the secondary. We need help in locating her."

There was a long pause. "I'll get back to you." The phone went dead.

FAYETTEVILLE, NORTH CAROLINA
29 OCTOBER, 1:42 P.M.

"You're sure it was the same people at the rest area and at the motel?"

Lisa frowned. "No, I'm not sure. I didn't get a good look at the two men at the motel, and I really didn't have much chance to check out the men at the rest area. But it had to be the same people."

Riley nodded. "I suppose." It had taken Lisa almost an hour to tell her story from the Chicago courtroom to Gordontown. Riley had remained silent until just now, letting the words pour out. "So, you think they—whoever they are—found you because your husband called this Fastone woman?"

Lisa had spent the time in Gordontown running through the events of the past twenty-four hours, trying to make some sense of the madness. "I think it's the only way they could have found us. He must have told her about Charlotte when he went to the bathroom just before we left the courthouse. He probably used the judge's own phone—he was gone long enough."

"So you figure Fastone flew into Charlotte, and then your husband called her again when he went out to get those sodas and told her exactly where you were?"

"He must have coordinated with her to stay at a certain place and called her there," Lisa said. "And the mob must have followed her down and then followed her to the motel."

"Unless she was working with them," Riley noted. "You only recognized your husband's body, right?"

Lisa blinked and tried to concentrate. "Yes."

"For all you know, she set him up."

Lisa closed her eyes and leaned back against the headrest. "Maybe. But does it matter now? He's dead."

"We *assume* he's dead," Riley corrected. "So why didn't you call the number this lady in Chicago gave you again?"

"I tried that once," Lisa snapped. "The bad guys got there before the good ones. They must have that number bugged or something."

"The bad guys probably followed you to the rest area."

Lisa shook her head. "I told you Bubba ran the van following us off the road. They could have found me only by tracing the phone call, or whatever it is they do to find out where you're calling from."

Riley had already considered that. "If they were professional, they had more than one vehicle following you. Bubba probably just took out their lead chase vehicle. There was most likely another one farther back. Running that van off the road just forced them to take some extra time to get coordinated for the second attack. Since you called from a pay phone, there's no way your end of the conversation could have been bugged or traced. And I very much doubt that the Witness Protection Program's end was tapped."

"Are you saying I should call that number again?"

"We're going to have to eventually, but not right away. And when we do, we'll take some precautions." Riley glanced over at her. "Why'd you call your brother for help?"

"He's the only one I could trust."

"Why'd he call Giannini?"

"I guess because he trusts her. They went out together a long time ago. Even got engaged."

Riley raised an eyebrow. "What happened?"

"He went into the navy. He wanted her to move to San Diego. She wanted to keep working as a cop. They called it off rather amicably. I think they were both scared of committing." She didn't add that Tom had been laid off at his construction job and had gone into the navy to ensure a steady income to help support her schooling.

"So, he's back in Chicago?" Riley asked, wondering at the twinge of emotion that provoked the question.

"Yes." Lisa looked at him, ignoring for a moment her own misery. "How do you know Donna?"

"Long story," Riley muttered, his mind flashing back to a rapidly flooding tunnel beneath the streets of Chicago and Giannini pulling him along to safety.

Lisa gestured at his uniform. "What do you do in the army?"

That was a question civilians often asked and was actually hard to answer. "I'm in the Special Forces." At her blank look, Riley amplified his answer. "The Green Berets."

"Oh." She waited a second and then repeated her question. "But what do you do?"

"Right now I teach at the school where we train new soldiers for the Special Forces."

Her next question was more to the point. "Why does Donna think you can protect me?"

Riley's face was a blank. "I've had some training and experience that might be applicable."

"Applicable?" Lisa persisted.

"You're safe," Riley assured her. "We're not being followed, and no one knows you're here with me except for Giannini—and she surely isn't going to tell anyone." Riley pulled up in front of his town house. "End of the road."

He let her in and pointed out the shower and the bedroom. "I've got to check on some things. You get cleaned up and get some sleep.

There's a sweat suit that should fit you in the second drawer of the dresser. Everything's going to be all right."

Riley sat at the kitchen bar downstairs and considered everything he'd been told, then he picked up the phone and dialed Giannini's work number. She answered right away.

"Donna, it's Dave."

"Did you get her?"

"Yeah. She's safe and sound. Taking a shower as we speak."

"What's going on, Dave?"

As succinctly as possible, Dave related Lisa's story.

Giannini concurred with Lisa's assumptions. "They must have tracked Jill Fastone down there, or she gave them the information. I checked the file on the Torrentino case, Dave. Fastone was involved with Michael Torrentino for several years. I find it very hard to believe that she just happened to dump the biggest mobster in Chicago for some married real estate developer. They used her to draw Philip Cobb into the organization. They needed someone clean and from the outside to launder money for them, and they must have used his affair to keep him on a leash."

"Then Fastone set him up," Riley said.

"Must have." Giannini paused. "There was something funny about the case files, though."

"What do you mean?"

"Some pages were missing and some names were blacked out."

"Any way you can find out what's missing?"

Giannini explained about Guyton. "I don't think that's an avenue I want to pursue," she concluded.

"If they got Lisa's husband, why do they still want to kill her?" Riley pressed.

"To send a message," Giannini said.

"How are they sending a message when no one knows about the hit?"

"Oh, you can be sure the word will get out on the street. It's the new wave—something the mob learned from the Colombians: families are no longer safe. They'll keep after Lisa until she's either dead or out of their reach somehow."

Riley pulled the 9mm out of the shoulder holster and laid it on the countertop. "We need to get her back under the protection of the feds."

"I can't believe those idiots left them alone and unguarded in that motel," Giannini said.

"I can understand it," Riley said. Lisa had repeated to him what Donnelly had told them just before departing. "They have to have some sort of cut-out at the local level to prevent compromise inside their own organization. If Lisa's husband hadn't gotten in contact with his girlfriend, they'd have been all right. The screwup wasn't on the feds' end—it was Philip Cobb's."

"Are you going to call the number she was given?" Giannini asked.

Riley ran a finger along the blackened metal of the gun barrel. "Not right away. Let the assholes sweat a little first. If their people showed up at the rest area, they must have come across the result of the fight. I'll call them first thing tomorrow." He frowned. "Funny thing, though. There was nothing on the news this morning or in the local paper. You'd think two dead people on the interstate would make the news."

"Maybe the feds clamped down on it when they were notified," Giannini said. "Another pile of shit swept under the rug. You should know about that."

"Yeah," Riley agreed. "Or it simply might have happened too late to make the morning paper."

"I'll get in contact with Lisa's brother and let him know she's all right."

"Okay."

"And Dave—"

"Yeah?"

"Thanks."

Riley put down the phone, then punched in the number for Moon Hall—the guest quarters for military personnel on Fort Bragg—and rang through to Hammer's room.

The voice that answered sounded quite happy. "Tony's funeral home. You stab 'em, we slab 'em."

"Hammer?"

"Yo!"

"This is Dave Riley."

"What's up, Chief?"

"What have they got you doing tomorrow?"

"Shooting ice cream and eating marbles." There was a pause, then Hammer's voice turned serious. "Not much, Chief. Why? You have something for me?"

"Yeah, but it's not exactly official work. I can cover for you at the company. I've got a woman here at my place who needs someone to guard her for a little while. I can do it tonight, but I need to show up at work tomorrow and I was hoping you might be able to come out here and watch over her while I'm at PT."

"Sure thing, Chief. She good-looking?"

"Her husband just got killed the other night and I think the mob is after her to finish the job."

All the humor was gone from Hammer's voice. "What time do you want me at your place?"

"Zero-five-thirty."

"Roger. I'll be there. Run a few miles for me, eh, laddie?" Hammer asked no more questions, simply accepting what Riley told him at face value.

Riley hung up the phone and settled down on his couch to think.

Upstairs the tears finally flowed, soaking the sheets. It was all gone— Melissa, her old life, and now Philip. Everything was over. Lisa grabbed the pillow and pulled it tight to her chest, wrapping her arms around it, as sobs racked her body.

CHAPTER 7

CHICAGO
30 OCTOBER, 7:45 A.M.

"So what's up?" Giannini asked as she made her way through Homicide, grabbing her daily morning cup of coffee.

"It ain't what's up, it's what's down. Permanently down," Lorenzo cracked. "That's what we deal with."

Giannini rolled her eyes. "You stay awake all night thinking that one up?"

Lorenzo was a dud—everyone knew it—and that's why he was anchored to his desk in Homicide instead of being out on the streets doing a real job. She glanced around. Lorenzo was all alone, which had prompted her first question. "Where is everyone?"

"Out at the filtration plant."

"What do they have?"

"A body."

Giannini reeled in her temper. She didn't need this shit. "Everyone's gone for one body?"

"A wise-guy hit."

Giannini could just picture Lorenzo sitting up late at night, practicing impressions of various TV detectives. "Who got killed?"

Lorenzo glanced down at his desk. "Some dame named Fastone."

Giannini slowly put down her coffee mug. "The filtration plant?"

Lorenzo looked puzzled. "Yeah, but why . . ." His next words were lost as Giannini headed out the door.

FAYETTEVILLE
30 OCTOBER, 8:50 A.M.

Hammer was sitting on the couch, his attention divided between the
sliding glass doors leading onto the small patio, and the front door.
He heard Lisa Cobb upstairs long before he ever saw her. He listened
to the progression from the bedroom to the shower, back to the bedroom, and now down the carpeted stairs.

Seeing him in the living room, Lisa stopped in alarm. "Who are you?"

"Frank Davis, but most people call me Hammer—and no, I don't
do rap. I had this name a long time before that guy showed up. I'm a
friend of Dave's. He asked me to look after you while he went to work.
He said he'd be back later this morning to make the phone call he
talked to you about. He said there were some things he had to work
on before you could make that call."

"Am I just going to get passed from person to person?" she asked,
her body tense. She was wearing a loose set of gray sweats, and she
knew she looked only slightly better than she had yesterday. She moved
slowly, trying not to aggravate a long bruise up her right side, a result of the car getting rolled.

Hammer gave his most charming smile. "You have to look at the
quality of the people who are doing the passing."

She observed his camouflage fatigues. "You work with Riley?"

"Part-time. I'm a reservist here at Bragg for six weeks of active duty
training. As such, I am expendable—which means that no one will
miss me at the company this morning. But if Chief Riley isn't there,
he gets missed."

Lisa poured herself a cup of coffee and seemed to be relaxing a bit.
"If you don't mind me asking, why does everyone call you Hammer?"

"Everyone doesn't call me Hammer," Davis replied. "Just those who
know me and those I let." He sighed. "Well, I guess it ain't no big
deal. I was assigned to CCN-North when I was in Fifth Group in Vietnam.
That's Combat Control North—a sort of special outfit that did a bunch
of dirty jobs no one else was capable of. We were under MACV-SOG."
He saw her confused look and continued to explain. "That's Military
Assistance Command Vietnam, Studies and Observation Group, which
was a fancy way of saying a bunch of guys who did what our government said we didn't do. Anyway, I ran a few missions with them. Everyone
had a nickname. They called me Hammer because I carried a Stoner

machine gun that I had 'borrowed' from some navy SEALs, and when I fired that thing my teammates said it was like bringing the hammer down on the enemy."

It didn't make much sense to Lisa, but she was grateful to talk about anything but her predicament. "Why'd you get out of active duty?"

Hammer enjoyed talking, and the fact that Lisa was good-looking only added to his verbosity. "I left active duty after I got back to the States, but I stayed in the reserves. Then in eighty-nine I went back on active duty for Operation Just Cause—you know, the invasion of Panama. The general running Special Ops down there was one of my old commanders from CCN. So he got me in on some of the door busting when they were tracking people down. I was on the teams that took down Noriega's number three and five men." He stated it so calmly and matter-of-factly that Lisa didn't quite believe him. She wondered what "took down" meant.

"What do you do in your civilian life?" Lisa asked.

Hammer shrugged. "A little of this, a little of that."

"What do we do now?"

"We wait."

FORT BRAGG
30 OCTOBER, 8:50 A.M.

A four-mile run on the sand paths of the "Mata mile." Thirty minutes of stomach and arm work. Thirty minutes of katas. Riley felt good, his muscles stretched out and tingling with that slight edge of fatigue brought about by a good workout. He felt good mentally too; he'd finally mastered the final kata, or ritualized form, required of the third-degree black belt in Tae Kwon Do. He would be taking the test in two weeks and felt ready.

He pulled the band around the top of his jungle boot and slipped the bottom of his fatigue pants underneath, securing it. Standing, he checked himself in the mirror—good to go. He left the shower room and looked in on his company in 1st Battalion's offices. The commander and sergeant major were out at Mackall, listening to briefbacks from the student class as they prepared for a strategic reconnaissance mission—Team 2's area. Riley left a few instructions with the senior sergeant on his team and then headed downstairs to 2d Battalion's area.

The third floor was a replica of the fourth—a large open room criss-crossed with blue partitions. His first stop was F Company, which ran the counterterrorist training. Riley spent several minutes talking with a sergeant he knew there and received a few pieces of specialized equipment. After thanking the man, he asked where the Operations and Intelligence (O & I) committee was located in the labyrinth of cubicles. The sergeant gestured vaguely toward the rear of the room. "Somewhere back there, Chief. And take care of that equipment—it's my ass if they find out I lent it to you."

Riley had to ask twice more for the O & I committee, surprised that people who worked every day within fifty feet of each other had no idea where the others were. Finally finding the right place, he had to ask again to track down the correct person. "Sergeant Major Alexander around?"

"Two cubicles over, Chief."

Riley poked his head into the indicated square and spotted the familiar figure. "Sergeant Major."

Alexander looked up from his desk and frowned for a brief second, then his face cleared as he recognized his visitor. "Chief Riley. How the hell are you? Haven't seen you in what, two years?"

Alexander had been assigned to Riley's team during the EYES missions in Colombia. Riley had found his name on the large organizational chart that hung in his company sergeant major's office when he'd looked up the O & I committee. Special Forces, despite the recent increase in numbers, was still a relatively small, close-knit community, especially among those who had spent more than ten years in it. Alexander's name had leaped out at him as he scanned the chart, looking for someone who could do him a favor. Alexander was the senior NCO; his name was second, right below the major who commanded the teaching cadre.

Never one for small talk, Riley nevertheless tried for a few minutes, inquiring about Alexander's family and the committee. Finally, he wound his way around to the purpose of his visit.

"Sergeant Major, do you have any exercises scheduled this afternoon or evening?"

"What kind of exercises?" Alexander didn't wait for an answer. "We've got two classes in session and both are running ops." He didn't need to consult a training schedule. "Class six is running a surveillance exercise and class seven is doing photography."

Riley nodded. "Can I borrow some of the people you have on the surveillance op?"

"Borrow?" Alexander peered closely at Riley. "What exactly do you mean by borrow? To do what?"

"I'm running an operation with the officers—an E & E exercise—and I'd like to put some of your guys on surveillance to cover a personal meeting. See if the officers spot the surveillance—you know what I'm talking about."

Alexander leaned back in his swivel chair and regarded Riley for a few seconds. "You know that the training schedule is next to the Bible around here. You don't change it, especially not on the day of the training."

"I'm not asking you to change the training schedule," Riley explained. "They'll still be doing surveillance—just in a different location and with a different objective."

Riley could see that the sergeant major wasn't buying his story. There was a long silence, then Alexander stood up and gave a yell: "Martin!"

A worn-looking master sergeant appeared a few seconds later. "Yes, Sergeant Major?"

"A change in plans." Alexander poked a thumb at Riley. "The chief here will brief you on what your students will be doing later today on their practical exercise in surveillance. We have a slight change of training locale."

Master Sergeant Martin looked none too thrilled, but as a veteran of the ACFAC, he was used to changes. "Right, Sergeant Major."

CHARLOTTE
30 OCTOBER, 10:30 A.M.

Master grabbed the portable phone on the first ring. "Anything?"

"We're still searching. We'll find her. You've got to be ready to move quickly. The longer she's free, the more dangerous she becomes."

"What if she's no longer around here?"

"We'll get her no matter where she is. You just worry about your area." The connection went dead.

Master put down the phone and went back to hand-loading shells for his Glock pistol. He hated waiting.

CHICAGO
30 OCTOBER, 11:15 A.M.

The Central District Filtration Plant jutted out into Lake Michigan just
above the spot where the Chicago River entered the lake. Private First
Class Milton Lee Olive III Park took up the land where the plant connected
with the main shoreline. Giannini drove around the police barrier that
had been placed at the end of the parking lot for the recreation area.
A uniformed cop waved her to a parking spot.

Before leaving the car, she opened the trunk and pulled on a set of
worn coveralls. She'd learned that trick on her first case in Homicide
when she got a small spot of the victim's blood on the clothes she
wore to the crime scene. That automatically made her clothes part of
the evidence, and she had to turn them in. This morning she also pulled
off her flats and put on an old pair of cheap tennis shoes. Properly
dressed to enter the area, she slipped under the yellow tape.

She made her way to the first response team, which was quarter-
ing the scene, gradually working their way in. Unlike crime dramas
on TV, it sometimes took four to eight hours to make it back to the
body's location. Ninety percent of homicide cases were solved at the
scene, and the detectives had only one chance to do it right. Starting
from the outside and moving in made sure that all the evidence was
as undisturbed as possible and that nothing was missed.

Giannini walked up to the two detectives who were handling the
case, chosen only because their names had been next on the roster.
She knew both men well from her time in Homicide. They watched
her approach curiously, uncertain as to why she was there.

The taller of the two, Mike Gann, had a face permanently set in
sad lines. He was thin to the point of emaciation and always moved
very slowly, as if any sudden action would break something. His partner,
Howie Willis, was a large, jovial, ebony-skinned version of St. Nick,
minus the beard. For some strange reason that Giannini had never been
able to figure out, the two got along quite well—an essential trait for
a homicide team.

"What's up, Lieutenant?" Willis greeted her, the unspoken question from the tone of his voice being, What the hell are you doing
here?

Giannini nodded. "Howie. Mike. I heard this was a mob hit."

Willis looked at her for a second. "The task force taking this?"

Giannini held up her hands. "Hey, I don't know. I just take out the trash for the task force. I'm here because I heard the victim's name and she's in a case file I'm trying to put away downstairs."

"You gotta do major case prints if you want to see the body." Gann spoke for the first time.

Giannini knew that was Gann's way of trying to get rid of her. It was a technique all homicide detectives used to keep the riffraff and straphangers away from their scene. Anyone who wanted to get close to the body was required to get not only their fingers printed, but also their palms, arms—anything that could possibly leave a distinguishing mark that forensics might pick up. It was a large deterrent because the procedure was such a hassle.

"Okay," Giannini agreed. Gann frowned and turned away, going back to his meticulous search of the ground, continuing the grid pattern the two had established.

Willis didn't seem put out by her presence. He was one of the few cops Giannini knew who didn't let his job get to him. He didn't drink, didn't smoke, wasn't divorced, and didn't seem ready to eat the end of his gun. He was a content and reasonably happy man. "Need the particulars?" he asked.

"I'd appreciate it, Howie."

Willis flipped through the notebook in his hand. "The body's over there. We already did our work there, so the coroner's on the way to pick her up. She's lying in one of the overflow tubes. Luckily that one isn't in operation, so it's dry." Giannini could commiserate with him on that. There was nothing worse than a body pulled out of water.

"You know the name. As far as we can tell, cause of death is one shot through the forehead. It's hard to tell how long since she got hit. Not much blood. We haven't found anything yet." He shrugged and grinned. "You can go take a look and you'll know as much as we do. Try not to trip over the murder weapon on the way there if you happen to see it."

"Thanks." Giannini walked to the overflow tube and peered in. Jill Fastone lay on her back, dressed, sightless eyes staring up. Plastic bags were placed over each hand. Giannini knew the detectives had done that to preserve any material that might have gotten under her fingernails during a struggle. The hole just above and between her eyes was black with just a slight fringe of red. Death must have been almost instantaneous. Giannini moved around for a different view—no sign of an exit wound. That meant either a small-caliber bullet or a sub-sonic round, indicating a silencer or a specially modified bullet. The placement of the wound suggested that she had been shot by a pro-fessional. There was no mutilation or special placement or garnish-ment, as there sometimes was with a mob hit—to send a message. The body was simply lying there dead. Giannini peered closely at the wrists—no indication they had been secured. And no sign of a struggle—just the bullet hole.

Giannini stood and looked around. She doubted that Fastone had been killed here. Most likely she was killed somewhere else and dumped. Giannini considered the situation. So Fastone had made it back from North Carolina and been killed. Why? Had she led the mob to the Cobbs and then been killed to remove a witness? If that was the case, it was likely that the mob was still after Lisa. It was hard to tell how long Fastone had been dead.

Giannini walked over to Willis. "I'll give you a call later. I'd like to know when you get an estimate on time of death."

"Sure thing, Lieutenant." Willis smiled and waved. Gann didn't even bother turning around.

Giannini got in her car and sat behind the wheel, trying to collect her thoughts. Lisa's story, the Torrentino file, Jill Fastone's body here in Chicago. Giannini had no idea what the connection was, and that was what troubled her the most. She'd involved Dave in a mess that was growing larger by the minute.

At least Lisa and Dave were safe, she thought. The only link to Dave was herself, and that link was secure.

A shadow loomed in the window, and Giannini started.

Guyton's face was a hard mask. "What are you doing here?"

"Sitting in my car," Giannini replied.

Guyton took in the coveralls, looked up at the crime scene, and then back. "You been over there?"

Giannini knew there was no sense in lying—Gann and Willis could confirm that she'd been there. "Yes."

"Listen, sweetie, you stop sticking your nose in things that don't involve you. This is a task force case and you aren't on the task force. And you aren't on Homicide anymore either. So I suggest you get your little butt in gear and get the hell out of here."

"What's going on, Guyton?" Giannini didn't like having to look up at him through the window of her car.

He leaned an elbow on the door and poked a finger at her face. "We got assholes shooting each other, that's what's going on, and we don't need you fucking things up."

Giannini decided to fish a little. "Fastone was involved with Michael Torrentino for a while. Then she got involved with Philip Cobb, who turned state's evidence and put the Torrentino brothers away for a long time. Now she turns up dead. My question is: Why did she do what she did? And who killed her? The Torrentinos?"

Guyton stared at her for a few seconds, then he leaned over and spoke in a whisper. "Listen, Donna. Don't ask questions, okay? You're not involved, and don't *get* involved, all right? There are heavy hitters in anything to do with the Torrentinos, so back off. For your own sake."

Giannini was surprised by Guyton's sudden change in character; more than that, his sincerity made her nervous. In all the years she'd known the man, he never used her first name; she was shocked that he even knew it. For him to stop threatening and try being nice was totally out of character. What was he hiding? It suddenly dawned on her that beneath his bluster and cajoling, Guyton was afraid, and that truly worried her.

Giannini began to wish she wasn't involved. "All right. Forget I ever asked anything."

As she drove away, Guyton's cold eyes watched her car until it disappeared from sight.

FAYETTEVILLE
30 OCTOBER, 12:56 P.M.

Hammer turned and snaked his hand into his fatigue shirt, pulling out a short-barreled, large-bore revolver. He motioned for Lisa to be quiet and silently made his way to the wall near the front door. She had no idea what had alerted him. Seconds after he was at the door, the bolt slid back and the door started to swing open, only to be stopped by the chain.

"It's Riley," a familiar voice called out.

Hammer reholstered his weapon and slipped off the chain. "How's it going, Chief?"

"It's going," Riley replied as he relocked the door behind him. "Any calls?" He put a small backpack down on a chair.

"Negative."

Riley looked at Lisa. "How are you doing?"

"All right, I guess." She watched as he grabbed a cup of coffee. "What now?"

"Now we call the feds."

Lisa's stomach, having spent the morning churning with a blend of coffee, guilt, fear, and anxiety, kicked into overdrive. "I don't know if that's a good idea. Although it's most likely that they found Philip and me because of Jill Fastone, and I know you think they followed me to the rest area, there's still the possibility that the phone at the Witness Protection end might have been bugged or is at least traceable."

Riley held up a hand. "Don't worry—it's not going to be like last time. Before we make the phone call, there's some preparation we have to do." He reached into a drawer and pulled out a notepad. "We're going to make the call from an unoccupied room in the BOQ on post. That way, if the call is traced, and we have to assume it will be, all they'll find is that room. It will pin us down as to relative location, but Fort Bragg and Fayetteville are pretty big places to go looking."

He wrote on the pad for a few minutes. "This is what I want you to tell the guy on the other end when you make the call."

Lisa took the pad and read. "I'm not sure I understand."

"I'm setting up a personal meeting for you. A meeting where you'll be protected in case the phone for the Witness Protection people is bugged or the call was traced somehow. You just tell the person on the other end what's on that paper and nothing more. Okay?"

"Okay." She put down the pad and Hammer picked it up, reading it himself. He smiled. "Pretty neat, Chief. What do you want me to do?"

"You stay with me. We're going to be the inside protection."

CHAPTER 8

The elevator opened on the second floor of Moon Hall and Riley glanced out, checking the hallway. It was clear. "Let's go."

Lisa Cobb was right behind him, and Hammer brought up the rear. Three halls branched off in varying directions, one to the far right, one half-right, and one half-left. Riley took the far right. With Hammer keeping watch back to the lobby, Riley knelt at the first door and pulled out one of the pieces of equipment he had borrowed from his friend at the counterterrorist committee. A piece of plastic, the size of a credit card, was attached by two thin wires to what looked like a hand-sized calculator. After turning on the small computer, Riley put the card in the electronic lock at the bottom of the door and slowly slid it up. It sensed the access code in reverse. Riley pushed a button and the computer reversed the code, then he slid the card back down. The green light on the lock flickered and they were in the room within three seconds.

Six stories high, Moon Hall stood on a hill overlooking the old post exchange (PX) on one side and on the other side the "Puzzle Palace," which used to be U.S. Special Operations Command (US SOCOM). It was flanked by Hardy Hall, the other guest quarters, a mirror image of Moon Hall. Hundreds of personnel flowed through the two buildings weekly, and Riley figured that calling from here was the safest place possible.

The room they entered was obviously unoccupied—the two beds made and no sign of luggage—verifying what he had learned by calling this room from the lobby phone. He asked Lisa to sit on the bed next to the phone and placed next to her the pad of paper on which he had written the instructions.

She took the phone and dialed the 800 number on the card. The same mechanical voice answered and she punched in the code. This time it was answered on the first ring.

"Yes?"

She recognized the bored voice with the New England accent. "This is Mrs. Cobb. Is this Simon?"

"Mrs. Cobb! Where are you? We sent people to pick you up two nights ago, but you were gone. There were state police all over the place."

"I was attacked at the rest area. It wasn't safe to stay there."

"Are you all right? Where are you now? I'll get people to you right away."

Riley had been leaning over her shoulder, listening to the conversation. He pointed down at the notepad, and she began to read.

"I'll meet you in the parking lot for the old PX at Fort Bragg, North Carolina."

"What?" The voice sounded confused.

"Between six and ten this evening, eastern standard time. The parking lot for the old PX at Fort Bragg. Go through Fayetteville on Route four-oh-one. Get off on All American Freeway to Fort Bragg. When the freeway ends, take a left on Community Access Road. A left on Bastogne. The old PX is on your left. Go into the parking lot and park facing away from the building, with lights off. Every fifteen minutes exactly, starting at six o'clock, turn your lights on for exactly one minute and then off. If it's safe, I'll come to the car.

"You are to put no surveillance on the site—just the one car to make the meet. Any sign of surveillance and I will come out to meet you."

"That's not safe, Mrs. Cobb!" Simon protested. "Why don't—"

"No other vehicles besides the one I meet," Lisa repeated. She continued reading. "If for any reason the meeting is cancelled, I will call you back to rearrange another meeting."

"Wait a second, Mrs. Cobb. Why don't we just come to you wherever you are now?"

"We tried that once," Lisa said, sounding exasperated. "This time we do it my way. Did you get all that?"

Riley started scribbling on the paper: HE GOT IT ON TAPE! HANG UP!

"Good-bye, Simon."

"But Mrs. Cobb, wait—"

Lisa put down the phone and looked up at Riley. "Are you sure they have it?"

Riley nodded. "They not only have it, but they also have this phone number. Time to go."

CHICAGO
30 OCTOBER, 3:10 P.M. CENTRAL TIME

On the eighth ring, Giannini reluctantly hung up the portable phone as she negotiated the Dan Ryan Expressway. Where was he? This was the third time she'd tried Tom's number. Giannini pushed the power-off button and dropped the phone on the passenger seat. Guyton's actions had bothered her, especially piled on top of the missing pages from the Torrentino file.

Trying not to give in to wild speculation, Giannini concentrated on what she did know: Lisa Cobb was safe with Riley. The only link to Lisa was her brother, but Giannini was the cut-out on that, having never told Tom who she was contacting to help his sister. The problem, and the reason she was driving south of Chicago, was that Tom was the most likely point of contact for anyone trying to find Lisa. Lisa and Tom's parents were dead, and they were the only children. Giannini knew it wouldn't take very long for another interested party with the right connections to find out these facts and track down Tom.

Giannini grabbed the phone and dialed a new number—long distance. This time the other end was picked up.

"Hello?"

"Dave, it's Donna."

"Yeah, what's up?"

"I just had a look at Jill Fastone's body."

"What?"

"Someone shot her between the eyes and dumped her body here in Chicago. I don't know time of death, but I'm assuming she was killed after coming back here from North Carolina."

"Any idea who did it?"

"Must have been the mob."

"But I thought she was working for them. I thought she led them to our friend."

"I thought so too. Maybe they just got pissed when they didn't get both of the Cobbs. Maybe they just wanted to get rid of a witness. I don't know what's going on, but this thing is getting deeper by the minute."

"What are you doing?"

"I'm going to talk to Lisa's brother. He's Lisa's only living immediate family and he's the only link between her and me, and subsequently you. I want to make sure he's safe."

"You make sure *you're* safe," Riley replied.

"What about you all?" Giannini asked.

"We've set up a meet for early this evening with the feds, so Lisa should be in the clear by then and I'll be out of it. Don't worry about us; we can take care of ourselves. We'll be leaving in a few minutes to set up our surveillance of the meeting site."

"All right. Give me a call tonight to let me know how it went."

"I'll do that." Giannini put down the phone and drove a little faster.

FORT BRAGG
30 OCTOBER, 5:27 P.M. EASTERN TIME

Riley sat in the corner booth, flanking the front window of the NCO club—Lisa to his right, Hammer on the other side, watching the doors to the bar. Riley's attention was focused on the old PX parking lot across the street. He looked up as a figure approached the table in the dimly lit lounge. Hammer tensed, his eyes taking in the uniform, while his fingers caressed the .44 magnum revolver he had hidden underneath the table. The muzzle was angled up, pointing directly at the newcomer's stomach.

"Master Sergeant Martin," Riley greeted the man without rising. Riley nodded at the empty space next to Hammer. "Have a seat."

Martin slid in, noticing the glasses of water in front of the three people. It was a rather unusual sight in the NCO bar, where the just-off-duty crowd was already raising the noise level with the thud of beer mugs on the tables and the bar. Martin was obviously not comfortable with the choice of meeting location.

"I've got my students waiting over at the ACFAC. I told them everything you gave me this morning. The only thing I didn't tell them—because you didn't tell me—was where we're meeting and what they're supposed to be looking for."

Riley pointed out the tinted window, across Reilly Road. "We've got a personal meeting set up for any time between eighteen hundred and twenty-two hundred. One vehicle in the old PX lot, facing this way. Lights will be turned on for one minute, every fifteen minutes. We're not going to initiate the meet until twenty thirty. I want your people to make sure that no one else is watching the lot during the two and a half hours before we make contact."

"Like who else?" Martin inquired.

Riley shrugged. "Anyone. Even MPs. Watch for static surveillance and also rolling surveillance—they may even use multiple vehicles in rotation. It's most likely that any surveillance will be nonmilitary and not have post decals." Riley pointed. "I want the woods there to the right of the bank covered also. It's a good place to put someone to eyeball the lot. There should be no one in there this time of day. Your men need to be in place by seventeen fifty."

Martin reached into his cargo pocket and pulled out a pair of small handheld two-way radios. He gave them to Riley. "They're set on the proper frequency. My call sign is Eagle One. My surveillance teams are Eagle Two through Seven. Your call sign is Bear One and Two."

Riley flicked on the radios, pressed the send to check for a hiss of static, then turned them off. "One last thing, Top," he said, stopping the master sergeant as he was about to leave the booth. "Make sure you emphasize to your people that if they spot anything, they are simply to call it in. Under no circumstances are they to make contact with anyone they spot. No matter what they see. Is that clear?"

Martin paused and then sank back down on the worn leather seat. "These students are my responsibility, Chief. I'd appreciate it if you would tell me what's going on."

"I can't do that, Top."

Martin wasn't going to be dissuaded so easily. "Then at least tell me if this is real world." He tilted his head slightly toward Hammer, who had remained silent throughout, his eyes scanning the inside of the bar. "Your friend here has been playing with something under the table the whole time I've been talking to you, and I don't think it's his dick."

Riley realized that Martin's request was reasonable. "This is real world. There's a possibility that some armed personnel may show up who aren't exactly friendly to the lady here."

Martin looked at Lisa, then back at Riley. "This some sort of divorce crap or something?" The tone of his voice indicated his displeasure.

"I assure you it isn't anything like that, Top," Riley said. "I can't tell you exactly what's going on for security reasons, but suffice it to say that there's a federal agency involved in this personal meeting, and we're trying to pass this lady over to them. We just want to make sure it goes smoothly. The last time it was tried, the whole thing went to shit and someone died."

Martin's eyes narrowed. He stared at Riley and then Lisa for a few seconds. "Sergeant Major Alexander said to do whatever you asked. He also said I should trust you. That's good enough for me. I'll tell my people to keep their eyes open and their dick out of the wringer if it gets cranked up."

"Thanks, Top."

Hammer watched Martin's retreating back, then turned to Riley. "You sure command a lot of respect around here."

"I've worked with good people," Riley replied.

"Uh-huh" was Hammer's only comment. He glanced at Lisa. "How are you doing?"

She'd washed her clothes at Riley's apartment, but the dark circles under her eyes were a clear indicator that she needed rest. "All right, I guess. I just want this to be over."

Riley tapped his watch. "Another three hours and it should be. I think everything will turn out all right." He ordered another round of soda and water, then looked at Lisa. "If you don't mind me asking, how did all this get started? Donna told me your husband turned state's evidence against the mob, but how did he get in the position to do that in the first place?"

Lisa hesitated for a long time, then spoke. "I think you deserve to know, even though it's not something I enjoy talking about. I only found out what happened after the mob tried killing Philip the first time, as he was coming out of Jill Fastone's apartment. She was the person who brought him into the whole mess."

"What exactly did your husband do for the mob?" Hammer asked.

"He did quite a few things. He was a real estate developer, which meant he handled numerous business transactions involving a lot of money. So he was the perfect conduit for the Torrentino gang: he could funnel their dirty money and make it come out clean. There were a lot of ways he could do that, and a lot of ways he could kick the money back to the Torrentinos—most of the time with a profit." Lisa shook her head bitterly. "With real estate and money, Philip was very smart. It was in other areas that he wasn't so bright. I don't know— I suppose if I had paid more attention, and if things with Melissa hadn't gotten so—"

"Hey," Riley interrupted, "don't try to second-guess what happened. It's done with."

"No," Lisa disagreed. "It's not done with. If it was, I wouldn't be sitting here."

Riley and Hammer remained silent and she continued her story. "Philip did quite a few things for the Torrentinos—most of them illegal. But he started off with things that, while not illegal, were shady, and that's how they hooked him in—besides the presence of Jill Fastone, that is.

"Philip put the names of some of Torrentino's people on his business ledger as sales representatives—giving them the appearance of legitimacy and allowing them to claim that as the source of their income. He juggled the prices of properties he bought and sold and covered the kickback to the Torrentinos in the commissions. It was all very complicated, but Philip had enough of a paper trail to get the Torrentinos indicted and convicted once he himself was caught."

Riley's eyes were scanning the parking lot across the street. "Why did the Torrentinos try to kill your husband in Chicago? That's what started this whole thing. Did he ever tell you?"

"Not really," Lisa said. "Philip never came right out and said it, but I got the impression that it was because of Jill Fastone. I think one of the two of them, or maybe both, took it too far, past what Michael Torrentino could accept."

"You think that's why she showed up in Charlotte?" Riley asked. "That she was really in love with your husband?"

"I don't know—but I think he must have been in love with her. Why else would he have called her?" Lisa said bitterly. "Maybe he was just trying to end it cleanly before he moved on to our new life. Who knows."

Riley shifted his gaze from the window to Lisa. "Jill Fastone is dead. They found her body in Chicago this morning."

Lisa's expression didn't change. "Do they know who killed her?"

"No. Donna said that they suspect the mob."

"That doesn't make sense if she set Philip up for them," Lisa commented.

"It does if she set him up only in terms of being followed down to Charlotte," Riley said. "The strange thing is that you said it looked like they were carrying *two* bodies out of your motel room, right?"

"Yes."

"If that second body was Fastone, why did they—whoever *they* are—take it all the way back to Chicago to get dumped?" Riley's question went unanswered and he switched directions. "If the Torrentinos really wanted to get to Philip and you, they'd keep tabs on those closest to you. For your husband, that would have been Jill. For you, it's your brother."

"Oh, my God!" Lisa exclaimed. "I hadn't thought of that. Is he in trouble?"

"Don't worry," Riley said. "When I talked to Donna a little while ago, she was going to check up on him."

CHICAGO
30 OCTOBER, 4:38 P.M. CENTRAL TIME

Tom Volpe's house was a small two-bedroom "fixer-upper" nestled in a neighborhood of similar lower-middle-class dwellings. Giannini pulled her car into the driveway, relieved to note that Tom's old Mustang was parked there. She had fond memories of cruising in that car north along the shore of Lake Michigan into Wisconsin and to the Upper Peninsula of Michigan.

As she walked up the sidewalk to the front door, she remembered the last time they'd been together—the long drive to the Upper Peninsula, a picnic in the sand dunes that lined the water's edge, and Tom pleading with her to follow him to San Diego and wherever else the navy might send him. Giannini thought it was interesting that she still had her job and he was back in Chicago. He might have been better off accepting her counterproposal that he settle down in the city and go back to school to get the advanced degree in engineering he always wanted while she stayed at her job and supported them. She imagined that idea was too radical even for someone as open-minded as she had thought Tom was. He'd gone into the navy within the month, and that was the last she'd heard of him until the phone call the other day.

Giannini pressed the doorbell and heard the muted chimes ringing inside. She waited a minute, then rang again. She opened the screen door and tried the doorknob; it turned freely and the door swung open. She slipped her right hand inside her jacket and pulled out a revolver.

She slid into the foyer, back pressed against one wall. Her nostrils were immediately assaulted by a strong odor—something she couldn't quite place—that caused a wave of nausea. She darted across to the opposite wall and scanned the front room; nothing there except worn furniture. The corridor split the front of the house—living room on the right, two closed doors, leading to what she presumed were bedrooms, to the left. A swinging door at the end must lead to the kitchen and the rear of the house.

Giannini carefully pushed open the first door. A weight bench and cardboard boxes occupied the floor. She shut the door and moved on to the second door, all the while trying to recognize the smell.

This door revealed a bedroom with a double bed, unmade, in the center, and a bureau against the near wall. She turned and faced the swinging door, then pushed it open with her foot. The stench washed over her. She moved in, propping open the door, and forced herself to keep from gagging at the odor and the sight that greeted her. Tom was secured to a kitchen chair with duct tape around his arms and legs. On his naked chest was a random pattern of round blackened marks. The smell was charred flesh.

"Oh, God!" Giannini groaned and stepped forward. She knelt on the linoleum and checked the vein in his neck—he was dead. His blue eyes were frozen open, his face contorted. Giannini had once seen marks similar to the ones on his chest at a homicide scene: someone had used a blowtorch to elicit information.

A puckered black bullet hole in his right temple indicated how Tom had been finished off by whoever had done this. A rag was tied around his neck, securing a rubber ball in his mouth to muffle his screams. How long had he endured this? Giannini wondered. She had no doubt that he had talked—who wouldn't as the blue flame touched flesh? His skin was still warm; he hadn't been dead long.

She reached into her purse, pulled out her portable phone, and rapidly punched in Riley's number. It rang four times and she heard his voice on the answering machine. She cursed to herself before speaking—maybe he would check the machine from a pay phone.

"Dave, it's—"

A noise startled her, and as she spun around, bringing her gun up, the sap caught her above the left ear. She crumpled to the floor unconscious, phone and gun sliding out of her fingers.

FORT BRAGG
30 OCTOBER, 7:48 P.M. EASTERN TIME

The car had arrived in the parking lot at 1755 and turned its lights on exactly at the hour and every fifteen minutes since then for the designated minute. The car had tinted windows, so it could not be determined who was inside.

Riley pressed the transmit button on the radio Martin had given him and spoke into the small boom mike, his back to the bar. "Eagle One, this is Bear One. Status report. Over."

"This is Eagle One. All my people report in clear. Over."

Riley handed the second radio across the table to Hammer. "I want you to do a sweep of the area on foot. All around the parking lot. Get a feel for it. If you report in clear, we're going to go make the meet."

Hammer nodded and slipped the radio in his fatigue pants pocket. He hid his .44 magnum revolver in the holster under his fatigue shirt and left the NCO club bar. Riley keyed the radio. "Eagle One, this is Bear One. Alert all your units that Bear Two is going to be out there walking around. Over."

"Roger. I'll pass the word. Over."

Hammer departed the NCO club and made his way across Reilly Road, angling away from the old PX parking lot and into the large stand of pine trees that extended from Reilly across to Community Access Road, eighty yards away. In the darkness his camouflage uniform merged with the green and brown background. He worked his way from the edge of the woods facing the parking lot, until he was halfway between the two roads. Then he cautiously moved forward and knelt behind a fallen log, where he could scan the parking lot.

The Fort Bragg main post office was on the far side of the lot, and it was closed for the day. A few cars were pulling up to it every so often as patrons checked their post office boxes. Hammer made a mental note to check the inside of the post office when he made his way around. It would be a good surveillance location.

He spotted two other cars with two men in each one and checked them off—O & I students trying to be surreptitious as they pulled surveillance for Riley. The old post exchange was along the right flank, and nothing was moving there. A pizza place was the only thing open in the long line of stores. On the hill overlooking the parking lot were Moon and Hardy Halls. Hammer knew that Martin had a team in each one, checking the hallways and stairwells for unwanted watchers.

Hammer left the woods and made a beeline for the sidewalk fronting the closed PX. He walked swiftly along the concrete until he reached the pizza place, where he stepped inside. Several soldiers with maroon berets and distinctive AA patches, identifying them as members of the 82d Airborne, were inside, eating or playing the video games. Hammer looked them over and decided they were no threat.

He ordered a Coke and went to an empty table at the front window, checking the scene from this perspective: Riley and Lisa across the street in the NCO club, the car still sitting there, the two surveillance cars with the O & I students, the post office, Moon and Hardy Halls out of sight to the right.

Hammer finished the Coke in a long gulp and threw the empty cup into the garbage on the way out. He crossed the parking lot toward the post office.

The lights were on in the front part of the post office, illuminating the area where the post office boxes were. Hammer was about ready to walk up the stairs to the building when he spied a figure in the far left of the post office box area, peering out into the parking lot.

Hammer spun on his heel and headed across the grass toward Moon Hall. He pulled open the fire door to the staircase on the side of the building and stepped in. Almost immediately footsteps sounded on the concrete stairs above, and two O & I students, looking conspicuous and uncomfortable in their civilian clothes, came clattering down.

"I'm Bear Two," Hammer said, holding up the radio. They nodded and returned to their perch on the third floor.

Hammer slipped on the boom mike. "Bear One, this is Two. Over."

Riley replied immediately. "This is One. Over."

"Abort the meet. I say again, abort the meet. Over."

"Roger. Abort meet. Break. Eagle One, pull in all your little birds and go home. Over."

Martin had been listening in. "This is Eagle One. I copy. Out."

CHAPTER 9

Riley drove down Yadkin Road, negotiating the kamikaze traffic. "Anyone following?" he asked Hammer.

"No sign. I think they're still sitting on their asses waiting for the meet to go down."

"Why'd you call in the abort?" Riley asked. Immediately upon the radio call from Hammer, he and Lisa had slipped out the back of the NCO club. Hammer had met them there, and they'd hopped in Riley's Bronco II and driven away without a word spoken until now.

"I spotted someone pulling surveillance from inside the post office, where the boxes are. He wasn't one of ours, and if he was with the Program, then they weren't following the rules you laid down."

"You sure it was someone watching?" Lisa asked, obviously disappointed. "Maybe it was just someone waiting for a ride."

"It's your life" was Hammer's brusque reply. "You want to take the chance, be my guest."

"All right, everyone calm down," Riley said as he turned off for his town house. "It's better to err on the safe side in something like this," he explained to Lisa.

"Is this ever going to end?" She slumped down in the passenger seat, her face slack with despair.

"The key question is, who was the person in the post office working for?" Riley mused out loud. "If he was additional security laid on by the feds, despite our asking them not to—I think they're very capable of doing that—then we just set up another meet and tell them not to blow it again. But if it was the mob, how the hell did they find out about the meet? We'll know when we call Simon," Riley added as he pulled up in front of his house.

He led the way in the front door. The first thing that caught his eye was the red flashing light on the answering machine. He hit the play-back button as Hammer shut the door behind Lisa. The machine whirred and then beeped.

"Dave, it's—" Giannini's anxious voice stopped in midsentence, then there was the sound of something heavy hitting the floor. "Turn it off," a male voice hissed, then a dial tone sounded. A mechanical voice spoke: "Five-forty-four."

There was a slight pause and the tape came on again, this time with no sound for almost three seconds. The phone went dead: "Five-forty-five." Someone had called, listened to Riley's message, and hung up.

Riley glanced across at Hammer, who returned his look. Lisa sat up straight on the couch where she had thrown herself. Riley flipped open his address book and punched in Giannini's home number—no answer. He quickly dialed her work number—she wasn't in and they didn't know when she would be. Finally he dialed the number for her portable. It rang and rang, with no answer. Riley slowly put down the receiver. His brain was working furiously, considering the entire situation. His emotions were swirling, but he tried to shut down that side of himself.

He made his decision. "Hammer, you and Lisa get out of here. Wherever you go tonight, I don't want to know. I'll meet you tomorrow between thirteen hundred and fourteen hundred out at the airfield at Camp Mackall. I'll drive on the dirt road along the east side of the airstrip. You make the contact if all is secure. If my lights are off, that means I'm doing it under duress, so don't make the contact. Clear?"

Hammer unzipped his jacket and checked his revolver. "Roger that, Chief. Thirteen hundred to fourteen hundred, east side of airstrip. Safe sign is lights on. Contact at my discretion."

"Will someone tell me what's going on?" Lisa demanded, confusion plain on her face.

Riley pointed at the answering machine. "Something happened to Donna Giannini. She tried calling here almost three hours ago and someone interrupted her." Riley didn't add his fears about what form that interruption took. He also didn't remind Lisa that Donna had been on her way to Lisa's brother's house. "Whoever it was tried my number right away, which means they know who I am. I can't get hold of Donna at work or at home and she's not answering her portable phone. She's the only one who knows you're with me. Add in the fact that someone was watching our meeting site, and I think we might be in deep shit."

"But she's in Chicago," Lisa protested. "It's only been a little while since her call."

"The bad guys have phones, too," Hammer reminded Lisa. "As the commercial says, they let their fingers do the walking. We need to get out of here. Once they realize we didn't make the personal meeting, they'll be coming here next."

"But—"

"Listen, Lisa," Riley interrupted her gently. "Donna was the cut-out—the only person who knew both sides. Now we have to assume she's been compromised, which means I've been compromised. So I'm making myself the cut-out. The only way I can contact you once you leave here is during that one-hour block of time tomorrow, and even then you have the option of not meeting me if you think I've been compromised. Hammer knows what he's doing. Trust him."

"But why don't you just come with us?" Lisa asked.

Riley shook his head. "I can't disappear right away. I have to get permission to take time off. Plus, there's some other things I need to do."

"What about my brother? I thought Donna was heading over to his place. Is he all right?"

"She didn't make it there. He's probably fine," Riley said, ushering her toward the door, not wanting to get into that. Hammer had cracked the open door and was peering out. "Now get going. I'll see you tomorrow."

Lisa was too dazed to offer any more protest. She followed Hammer's lead. Riley stood in the doorway and watched as the two drove off in Hammer's pickup truck. He looked up and down the street—all appeared normal. Back inside, Riley went up to his bedroom and pulled his footlocker out of the closet. He opened the combination lock, flipped up the lid, and pulled out the top tray. Nestled in the bottom, wrapped in oilcloth, were various weapons that he had accumulated over the years. Riley wasn't a knife or gun collector—he saw no beauty or art to weapons; they were simply tools that he needed in his occupation.

Riley pulled out the weapons, one by one, and checked their functioning. He already had the .22 High Standard in his left shoulder holster and the 9mm Beretta in the right. He lifted out a Heckler & Koch model

94—a 9mm short-barreled submachine gun available for the civilian market in the semiautomatic mode only. He moved over to his dresser, pulled open the bottom drawer, and reached underneath, feeling with his hand until he touched the small piece of metal taped there. He broke down the H & K 94 and replaced the sear pin that had come with the gun with the one he'd hidden under his drawer. The new sear made the weapon illegal, transforming it into a submachine gun capable of automatic and three-round burst fire.

Riley slapped a thirty-round magazine in the well and chambered a round, leaving it on safe. Next he pulled out a double-edged commando knife and slipped the sheath inside his pants in the small of his back—the one place most people fail to look when doing a body search.

A short, razor-sharp, three-inch dagger went on the inside of his left boot. Riley removed his A-7-A belt and checked to make sure the wire garrote was still in place on the inside of the web material, the metal loops on either end secured in specially sewn pockets, keeping it stretched tight.

Then he dragged a chair back to the closet. Pushing clothes aside, he stood on the chair and felt along the top of the inside lip above the door. He peeled back some heavy tape and removed a money belt, then got down and strapped on the money belt inside his shirt.

Satisfied, Riley went back downstairs. He had lied to Lisa; to be more accurate, he had concealed the entire truth from her. True, he couldn't just leave town without clearing it with his unit. And it was true that the best way to find out what was going on would be to stand fast and confront these people. But the real reason he was staying was reflected in the cold set of his eyes and the efficient way he had prepared his weapons. Underneath all that rational thought, holding him in place like a hard emotional tide, was the echo of Giannini's voice being cut off and something hitting the ground. Whoever these people were, they had hurt, possibly killed, his friend. Riley turned off all the lights and settled down on the floor next to his couch—sub in his lap—to wait.

He tried to focus his mind, but his thoughts kept turning back to Donna. A year ago, Riley had been at a dead end. He had nothing to look forward to, no one he cared about. He felt he had committed himself to the army at age seventeen and gotten screwed in return. Donna Giannini had given him back his life—in more than a literal way. She had entered his world uninvited, in the midst of terror and death, a light that had given him hope for the future. A woman named Kate Westland had touched him in the same way several years before down in Colombia, but he'd let her slip away. He thought he'd become smarter and more aware by the time he met Donna, but apparently not. Once again, he hadn't acted on his feelings.

Riley remembered an old saying he'd heard from Frank Kimble, his first team sergeant in Okinawa, who'd obviously stolen it from someone else: "To know and not to do is not to know." Somehow, he'd assumed he and Donna had plenty of time. Only now, hearing that tape play on his answering machine, did he realize his loss and how little he really knew about the important things.

But there were things he did know, Riley thought. He ran his hand over the cold pressed steel of the weapon nestled in his lap. He knew death—was intimate with it. And death was what was coming; he could feel it. It was all he had left.

FORT BRAGG
30 OCTOBER, 10:00 P.M.

"The car's leaving. Over."

Master rubbed his forehead, wishing the headache that had been building for the past hour would go away. "No sign of the target? Over."

"Negative. They never made contact. Over."

"Shit," Master muttered to himself. What had gone wrong? "Pull back before we get some nosy MP sticking his nose up our ass. Out." He put the mike down on the console desk, picked up a pill, and popped it into his mouth, washing it down with water. The speed snapped through his veins, his skin tightening. He thumped his fist lightly against his lips as he thought.

The secure phone trilled, piercing his concentration. He had it to his ear before he even realized what he was doing. "Master."

"We have some more information for you."

CHICAGO
30 OCTOBER, 9:23 P.M. CENTRAL TIME

Giannini struggled to consciousness, a pounding on the left side of her head defeating that purpose until she realized that it was simply the beat of her heart, pumping blood through swollen flesh. As if realization of the pain was enough, she felt better. She was alive, which in her book made up for anything. She kept her eyes closed and her body motionless and waited for more than five minutes, ears tuned in, skin tuned in, trying to pull out of the air any sense of another presence close by. Nothing.

She cracked her eyelids and saw linoleum gleaming softly in the night light reflected through the windows. A little bit wider and the grip of her pistol appeared. She kept her breathing as relaxed as possible. Thirty seconds. Her right hand snaked out and grabbed the pistol and she rolled to the left, grunting with the pain that splintered through her skull. Her eyes weren't focusing very well, but she could tell that the kitchen was clear. Too clear—Tom's body was gone. Everything looked as if the maid had just been through.

Why had they left her? Giannini felt her stomach twist and flip, and she tensed her arm muscles, feeling the cold plastic of the gun's grip in her right hand. She had to fight the spinning in her head.

She scuttled across the floor until she felt the cabinets against her back. Keeping the gun pointed toward the door leading into the room, she tried to think. Her portable phone was lying not far from where she grabbed the gun. She blinked—there was something flashing on the small screen. She reached out, grabbed the phone, and squinted down at the small white rectangle. "In use" was flashing. Just below, ten numbers were displayed. She grabbed the phone and pressed it to her ear: "Dave! Dave!" The hum of a disconnected line greeted her.

"Oh, shit," she murmured, pressing the off button and then the power button. She rapidly redialed Dave's home number.

FAYETTEVILLE
30 OCTOBER, 10:32 P.M. EASTERN TIME

The ring of the phone half startled Riley, his senses ready for any other sound. He looked at the offending device and considered whether to answer. The second ring echoed through the house. He waited through the third and the fourth.

The answering machine electronically picked up the receiver. "This is Dave Riley. I'm not able to come to the phone right now. Please leave your name and number and I'll get back to you as soon as possible."

"Dave, it's Donna. They have your number. They know who you are! Are you there? Dave?"

Riley uncoiled from the floor and sprinted across the room. He put the sub down on the bar and grabbed the receiver, punching the answering machine's off button at the same time. "Donna! It's me."

"Thank God!" The voice on the other end paused to catch her breath. "Jesus Christ, what a mess. Tom's dead, Dave. I'm at his house. I came here to check on him and he was dead. They tortured him and must have gotten the information about me out of him. But I walked right into them. They didn't even have to look for me. I was trying to call you when someone hit me—"

"I got your message," Dave interrupted.

"What about . . ." Giannini's voice paused. "Is it safe?"

"It's safe," Riley replied. "The meeting was compromised, but we split before anything went down."

"Compromised?"

"Someone was watching who wasn't supposed to be. Might have been the feds just being stupid, but after getting your earlier message, I thought it was the bad guys."

"What do you think now?"

"Could be either. If it was the bad guys, they reacted quickly and followed us onto post, but it's more likely it was the feds being stupid."

"What about you?"

"I was waiting to hear from you," Riley lied.

"You need to get out of there. They know who you are. They got the number off my portable. That's . . ." there was a pause, "God, that's about five hours ago. Get out of there, Dave!"

"Everything's all right, Donna," Riley replied calmly. "Everything's just fine here. How are you? Are you okay?"

"I'm fine. Listen, you've got to—"

"No, you listen." Riley kept his voice level. "You get out of that house and get to somewhere safe. I can take care of things on this end."

Giannini's voice was tentative. "You're sure you'll be all right?"

"I'll be out of here in a couple of minutes," Riley temporized, his mind not at all on his own situation. "I'll contact you through your portable number tomorrow."

"All right. I'm not going to be able to report this without compromising everything, Dave. Anyway, the body's gone and this place looks like it's been cleaned up. I'd have to open up the whole can of worms to my people and I'm not sure that's the best thing to do right now."

"I agree," Riley said. "Until we know who's really behind all this and, more importantly, get our subject under cover, we need to lay low. Are you sure you're all right?"

"I've got a sore head, but I'll live."

"Why didn't they take you?" he asked.

"I'm a cop, Dave. That still makes some people hesitate. Plus, they got what they needed off my phone." She changed the subject. "There are a few people I need to see on this end," Giannini said. "Maybe I can get some answers."

"We could use some," Riley agreed. "You hang onto your portable and I'll get hold of you through that. I won't be coming back to my apartment for a while."

"All right. Call me sometime tomorrow morning. I'll have seen some of the people I need to by then."

"Okay," Riley said. A long silence ensued, each person aware of the other, neither one wanting to hang up. Riley glanced at the clock above his stove and cleared his throat. "Hey, listen, I've got to get going. You take care of yourself."

"You too."

Another pause. Riley's knuckles were white from gripping the receiver. "I'm glad you're all right. I was worried."

"I'm fine."

"Okay. Well, I've got to go. Talk to you tomorrow. Bye."

Giannini's voice was very soft. "Bye."

The phone went dead and Riley slowly put down the receiver. He moved in the darkness to the front window, well back from the crack in the curtains, and settled in to wait.

CHICAGO
30 OCTOBER, 9:35 P.M.

Charlie D'Angelo stared at the two men in front of him as he listened to their report. D'Angelo was in his early thirties, neatly attired in a tailored suit, an expensive pair of designer glasses complementing his businesslike demeanor. He was the antithesis of the "mob boss" look favored by his predecessors, the Torrentinos. His chief subordinates were gathered around his desk, awaiting his reaction to the news the two men brought.

When they were done, he leaned back in his seat. "You left this Giannini woman alive?"

The shorter of the two men—Tony—fidgeted. "She's a cop. I figured we didn't need the heat."

D'Angelo's voice chilled the room several degrees. "But didn't Volpe tell you that Giannini knew who had his sister? And isn't that the information we want?"

"Yeah, but we got the phone number she was trying to call. It's in North Carolina and that's where Jill went."

"Jill's dead," D'Angelo snapped. "And I'm the one who has to tell Mike Torrentino that tomorrow."

Tony swallowed and shuffled his feet.

"And what's this crap about Philip Cobb being dead?"

"That's what Volpe said his sister told him."

"Who the hell would kill Cobb?" D'Angelo wondered out loud. He leaned forward. "Track down who she called. Whoever it is better be able to point us to the Cobbs—dead or alive. If not, cop or no cop, I want Giannini." D'Angelo pointed to the door. "Everyone out."

They all moved except his right-hand man, Roy Delpino. When the door shut behind the last one, D'Angelo kicked his feet up on the desk that used to belong to Mike Torrentino and idly fingered his Harvard ring. "You think they got the truth out of Volpe?"

"They torched him, Charlie. They got the truth."

"If Philip Cobb is dead, that changes things."

"Unless his wife knows where the money is," Delpino noted.

"I don't like it," D'Angelo said. "Something's fishy. I didn't know a thing about Jill going to North Carolina until we tracked down her plane reservations *after* finding her body up here. So did she go on Mike's orders or did she go alone? I don't think Mike is telling me everything."

"Of course Mike's not telling you everything," Delpino said. At D'Angelo's frown, he continued hurriedly. "Think about it. Mike's in jail along with his brother—Louis—and Tony Lorenzo. The only power he has to keep his hand in things here is knowledge. If he gave up his knowledge, we wouldn't need him anymore. Then you'd be the real boss, not just the acting one."

D'Angelo nodded. "He won't give me the names of all the contacts

I need to do business. But I don't understand why he won't level with me about the Cobbs. He wants them a hell of a lot more than I do. It's just business for me. For the Torrentinos, it's personal."

"Maybe he has his own plans," Delpino said. "And if he gets to them—even if Philip is dead—he gets to the money."

D'Angelo swung his feet off the desk and stood. "Well, we'll just have to make sure that doesn't happen."

FAYETTEVILLE
30 OCTOBER, 10:45 P.M.

Hammer checked the rearview mirror one more time and pulled a sharp U-turn in the middle of Bragg Boulevard. He watched behind as he immediately turned right off the main street, drove through one of the countless mobile home parks that lined the boulevard, and then came out onto a side street. "We're clean," he announced. "Nobody following."

Lisa Cobb had been silent ever since departing Riley's apartment, lost in her own thoughts, feeling overwhelmed by everything that had happened in the past forty-eight hours. The pickup pulled in front of a garishly lit bar, the flashing signs boasting GIRLS-GIRLS-GIRLS. "What are we doing here?"

Hammer set the parking brake and cracked open his door. "We need a place to stay, and a buddy of mine runs this place." He jerked his head toward the blacked-out front door, which belched three drunken 82d Airborne troopers. "Let's go. You're safer sticking with me."

Hammer politely held open the front door for Lisa. The interior was dimly lit, and the thudding beat of the DJ's music reverberated through the soles of their feet. The eight-by-eight stage at the far end of the room was currently unoccupied. A scattering of soldiers with high and tight haircuts was intermingled with two tables of long-haired, bearded bikers. Hammer strode directly across the room toward one of the tables. All eyes turned to follow Lisa, the lone woman in the room other than the two half-dressed Korean waitresses scuttling between tables with mugs of beer.

A mountain of a man, black beard streaked with gray, arose from the far end of the table toward which Hammer was heading. He opened his arms wide and wrapped them around the shorter man, lifting Hammer off his feet. When his feet regained the floor, Hammer returned the gesture, lifting the taller man and swinging him around.

Lisa hovered behind Hammer, her eyes flickering about the bar, uneasy with all the attention. She was startled when the tall man bent over and kissed Hammer on the lips with a loud smack.

"Fucking faggots!" one of the GIs at a nearby table yelled out drunkenly.

"Come and get some, asshole," the tall man growled, middle finger extended toward the ceiling.

The GI muttered something and turned back to his comrades. Hammer tapped Lisa on the arm. "This is Jim Lightfoot," he said, pointing at the man who had kissed him. "He's an old buddy from my Vietnam days and he owns this bar."

"Pleased to meet you, ma'am," Jim said, bowing slightly at the waist. He led the way to an empty booth away from the bar and motioned for them to slide in. "Can I get you anything?"

Hammer shook his head. "I need to talk to you and make a couple of calls." He inclined his head toward a staircase behind the bar. "Privately."

"Certainly," Jim replied. He glanced down at Lisa. "You'll be all right. My buddies will make sure you're not hassled. They may not look it, but they're all former Special Operations."

Lisa nodded, having not said a word since entering the bar. Hammer and Jim made their way behind the bar and disappeared up the stairs. The music changed beat, and to a scattering of applause, one of the waitresses discarded her tray and assumed the stage. Lisa sank back in the slashed vinyl seat where generations of America's elite fighting men had sat to watch women disrobe. Blocking out the music and the howls from the other patrons, she held her head in her hands and tried to concentrate, thinking back on all that had happened today. The sudden departure from the NCO club had turned Lisa's upside-down world on its side and taken it for a few spins. She'd pinned her hopes on the meeting this evening, and now she had no idea what was going on.

She suddenly sat bolt upright in the booth. Riley had lied to her— he had to have lied. There was only one way the mob could have gotten to Giannini—through Tom. Lisa stood and walked across the room, oblivious now to the looks. She lifted the receiver on the pay phone hanging to the right of the bar, grateful to hear a faint dial tone. She dialed the operator, one hand pressed over her free ear to block out the music.

"I'd like to make a collect call." She recited Tom's number from memory.

"May I ask who's calling please?"

"Lisa."

"One moment please."

There was a click and then the phone began ringing on the other end. Lisa checked her watch. Tom rarely stayed out this late, especially on a weeknight. By the third ring, the chill in her stomach began expanding.

A large hand reached over her shoulder and slammed down on the hook, disconnecting her. "What the hell do you think you're doing?" Hammer demanded.

"I'm checking on my brother," Lisa retorted angrily.

Hammer poked a stubby finger at her. "*You're* the one who needs checking on, not him."

"Riley lied," she returned hotly. "If they got to Giannini, they most likely got to Tom."

Hammer shrugged. "Yeah, so? What good is calling going to do?" He pointed at the phone. "They can trace a call nowadays in seconds and the other end doesn't even need to be picked up. Did it ring?"

Lisa nodded.

"How many times?"

"Four."

Hammer closed his eyes and counted to five under his breath. "Did you call collect?"

"Yes."

"What name did you use?"

"Lisa."

Hammer counted to ten this time. "Great, just fucking great. So much for hanging around here. Let's go."

He stepped toward the door, but his way was blocked by three soldiers. "What are you doing with the woman, faggot? You giving her a hard time?" asked the one in the middle, pushing himself up to Hammer and poking him in the chest.

Hammer regarded the three for a second. Then without a word he reached forward with one hand, grabbed the back of the GI's head, and jerked it down while bringing up his right knee at the same time. The man's nose crunched on impact, blood splattering over Hammer's pants.

Hammer stepped slightly to the side and propelled the man into the bar, at the same time swinging his left hand in an open palm strike into the chest of the soldier on the right. The man's breath exploded out of his lungs and he sank slowly to the floor, desperately trying to get some air.

Hammer was still moving, even though the third GI put his hands up, indicating he was out of the fight. Hammer grabbed both hands and bent them forward from the wrist, the pain causing the soldier to fall to his knees. Hammer leaned over and whispered in his ear: "Respect your elders, sonny."

Lisa grabbed his arm. "Stop it!"

Hammer paused and looked at her. The soldier was frozen, his face contorted in pain. Slowly, Hammer released his grip and the soldier scurried back a safe distance.

"You didn't have to do that," Lisa cried, shocked at his quick violence.

Hammer looked past her at Jim Lightfoot, who had the first soldier by the collar. "Can you take care of this, Jim?"

The long-haired man nodded. "No sweat. They don't want the cops involved either, do you?" he asked, shaking the soldier.

"No," the man gasped.

"That's no, *sir,* right?"

"No, sir."

Lightfoot smiled. "You see? I got it under control."

Hammer grabbed Lisa's elbow. "Let's go."

FORT BRAGG
30 OCTOBER, 11:23 P.M.

Master opened the drawer and sorted through the contents until he found what he needed. He slipped the leather wallet into his coat jacket and exited the van, accompanied by one other man carrying a metal briefcase. He walked up to the front desk in Moon Hall and flashed the badge inside the wallet. "Agent Watkins, CID," he announced to the startled clerk on duty.

"Yes, sir, how can I help you?"

Master checked his notepad. "What room uses the phone number nine seven six, four two seven six?"

"That's here in Moon Hall, sir, room two-seven-six. Second floor," she added.

"I need a key to get in," Master ordered.

The clerk turned to the computer behind the counter and punched in a code, ran a credit card key through the slot on the side, and handed it over to Master. "The room's not occupied presently."

"I'll return this in a minute," Master assured the clerk, and the two men headed for the elevator on the other side of the lobby. That was one thing he had always liked about dealing with the military: the sight of a badge—a symbol of authority thrust in their faces—and they cooperated without question.

They rode to the second floor and found room 276. Master slid the card down the lock, and the green light flashed. They entered and Master pointed wordlessly at the phone. The technician flipped open his briefcase and pulled out an aerosol can. He sprayed the phone while Master looked around the room. The lever on the inside of the door would also be a good spot, and he indicated so to his man.

Master waited patiently while the man worked, letting the spray settle and then looking over the surface areas for prints. "I've got multiple prints on all surfaces. Only one set that appears to be female—on the phone receiver. Several larger prints on the door."

"Get them all," Master ordered.

The technician picked up a handheld scanner from the case and quickly ran it over all the surfaces, electronically recording the prints. "They're loaded," he announced, checking the small digital display on the back of the scanner. "Ninety-three percent pickup. More than enough to make a positive ID."

"Run them."

The technician looked up in surprise. "From here? We might get traced back once I break into the system."

Master pointed at the phone. "Run them."

The technician shrugged and quickly hooked the modem of the laptop computer into the phone line. On the numeric keypad he punched in a number and then a security code. "I'm in the system," he said. He downloaded the scanner into the computer and typed for half a minute, giving the appropriate orders. Then he settled in to wait. He glanced at Master, who stood gazing impassively out the window into the darkened parking lot. "If someone checks on this run, they're going to get this location, and they'll know the code I entered was misappropriated."

Master shrugged, long past worrying about such minor stuff. This whole thing was threatening to get out of control. He snapped the latex rubber gloves they'd put on during the ride up in the elevator. "We're clean as far as the room goes. I'll dump the ID once we're done here, and I doubt the clerk will remember the name we gave her."

The hard drive on the computer whirred, and the screen came alive with an incoming message.

"The female prints are Lisa Cobb's," the technician announced. His fingers flew over the keyboard. "The clearest ones on the door lever belong to a Riley, David. Chief warrant officer, U.S. Army, SSN 104-56-9246."

Master looked over the man's shoulder at the screen. "Give me more on Riley."

The technician shook his head, nervous about being on the modem that long, but his fingers hit the keys. "Current assignment A Company, First Battalion, First Special Warfare Training Group, Airborne, here at Fort Bragg." The technician glanced up. "He's an instructor in the Special Forces School."

A cold smile crept over Master's lips. "A Green Beanie, eh? That explains some of this shit. Get me an address."

The technician typed and then pointed. "Here in Fayetteville. Off Yadkin Road."

Master noted the street and number. "How about a photo?"

"That's all they have in the fingerprint file. I'd have to access army records to get anything more, and I highly recommend we do that from a secure location."

Master nodded. "All right. I've got enough."

CHAPTER 10

The lights were still on in the upstairs bedroom, which fronted the street outside. Riley sat quietly in the dark downstairs, waiting, weapons close by. His eyes narrowed as a set of headlights pierced the darkness at the corner, then raked across the front of the apartment complex as the car turned in. The headlights went out, and Riley watched the darkened vehicle make its way slowly into the parking lot. It came to a halt fifty meters away, brake lights flashing briefly, front end pointed almost directly at Riley's town house.

He knew the lights in the bedroom were the only thing giving the men in the car pause. He'd left the lights on to give himself a few extra minutes before anyone came crashing through the door. No need to delay the party any longer. He walked into the kitchen, opened the fuse box, and flipped off the power to the second floor, bathing the entire house in darkness. He figured the men in the car would wait about a half hour before trying to come in, if that's what their plan was. The bait set, Riley settled back in the dark shadows and continued his vigil.

CHICAGO
30 OCTOBER, 11:47 P.M.

Giannini flipped through the homicide files; there was no record of Tom Volpe's body being discovered. That meant that whoever had killed him and knocked her out either still had the body or had hidden it. She knew it might never be found. Giannini felt torn, knowing she should report what happened, but not sure how that report would be received and what effect it would have on Lisa's safety.

She realized it was already too late: by not immediately calling in from Tom's house, she'd compromised her professional integrity with the police department. But the events of the previous year, and her close association with Dave Riley, had reinforced one very strong lesson: never act until you're sure what's going on. Overriding all those concerns, though, was the fact that she would have to explain why she was at Tom's house.

Guyton's strange behavior this morning at the filtration plant still bothered Giannini. Besides the obvious problems with Lisa Cobb, there was something very odd going on with regard to the investigation into the death of Jill Fastone and, backing up farther from that, something was not quite right about the whole Torrentino case.

Giannini shook her head in frustration—and then immediately stopped as shock waves of pain radiated through her head. She put down the evening's reports and looked up as the door to the Homicide squad room opened and Howie Willis walked in, eyes still half closed from sleep.

"Hey, Howie, what's new?"

Willis glanced at her. "You're here late—or early." He peered at her more closely. "Do I look as bad as you do?"

Giannini forced a laugh. "No, you look worse."

"Yeah," he said as he sank down at his desk. "Got to get this stuff cleared off so we can go out on the streets in the morning."

"You get the report back on Fastone?"

Willis leaned back in his chair. "You know, strange thing, that case. Seems like a whole bunch of people are interested in what happened. We had Guyton from the task force crawling all over us right after you left yesterday morning."

"It was a mob hit; of course Guyton would be there," Giannini said.

"Uh-huh. 'Cept why'd he tell us not to talk to you? You working for the mob?" Willis asked with a chuckle. "You got the right kind of last name—one of them that ends in a vowel."

"I was closing out one of his old files on the Torrentino case and I found some discrepancies," Giannini explained. "He didn't take that too nicely."

"No, I imagine he wouldn't." Willis looked up at her. "What kind of discrepancies?"

"Nothing I can put my finger on."

"If you put your finger on it, and it pertains to this case, you'll let me know, won't you, Lieutenant?"

"Of course. What about Fastone?" Giannini reminded him.

Willis hesitated for a moment, then pulled a file folder out from one of the many piles on his desk. He slid it toward her. "If anyone asks, you didn't see that. Guyton may be a shithead, but he's a heavy shithead, and I don't need that kind of grief."

"Thanks," Giannini said. She flipped open the folder and quickly scanned the autopsy report. 9mm round. Most likely a subsonic load to work in conjunction with a silencer, which helped explain why the bullet had stayed in the skull. Giannini's eyes widened slightly as she read another reason why the round had acted the way it had. The round was a modified Glaser safety slug. A Glaser round consists of a thin, serrated copper jacket filled with bird shot and sealed with a rounded polymer nose cap. On impact the round ruptures, saturating the inside of the target with the bird shot. In this case, someone had removed the usual number six bird shot and replaced it with larger number four shot. Liquid Teflon had also been added to slow down the dispersion of the shot, keeping it inside the target's body. The modifications spoke of someone who knew what they were doing with weapons and ammunition.

Time of death was estimated between midnight and three in the morning on 29 October. There was little else, except for a short note regarding two small burn marks on the victim's chest. Giannini glanced over the top of the manila folder at Willis, who was laboriously typing at the keyboard of his computer with two thick fingers. "What's with these burn marks?"

Willis paused and glanced up at her. "I asked the examiner that. He said it looked like they were caused by electric current."

"Electric current?" Giannini repeated.

"Yeah. Zap," Willis amplified. "You know, one of those stun guns. Looks like someone zapped her, then finished her off. A stone cold killer, whoever it was. Professional all the way."

"Any idea who the professional was?"

"Nope. The body was dumped and we got no fibers, no rope marks, no nothing. No sign of struggle. It was a very clean job."

"If it was so clean, how come the body didn't just disappear off the face of the earth?" Giannini asked. If someone had gone to such lengths to make sure nothing could be taken off the body and used in a case—other than the bullet—it seemed as though it would have been a lot easier to simply weight down the body and dump it in the lake.

"Good point," Willis conceded. "I guess whoever killed her wanted her to be found."

"A message," Giannini mused. But to whom and for what purpose? Giannini handed back the file. "Thanks, Howie."

She left Homicide and went back to her office. She flipped open her Rolodex and searched for a name and an address. It was time to pay the feds a little visit. Giannini pulled out a card and slipped it into her coat pocket. Then, with a great deal of effort, she managed to shut the door to her tiny office with herself on the inside. She took the chair off the desk, where she'd stashed it, and wedged it up against the doorknob. The feds didn't start work until eight in the morning and she needed some sleep. She curled up on the floor, feet poking into the well of the small desk, leather jacket under her head, and fell asleep within minutes.

CUMBERLAND COUNTY, NORTH CAROLINA
31 OCTOBER, 12:53 A.M.

Hammer pulled up to the old trailer at the end of the dirt road and parked behind it. "Home for the night," he announced. He'd driven down dark roads for the last thirty minutes getting here, the ride in total silence. They'd passed a couple of trailers, then nothing for the last fifty meters. They were at the end of the line.

Lisa took in the decrepit structure and the empty wooded lots surrounding the area. "Are you sure it's safe?"

Hammer was already out the truck door. He leaned back in. "It's safe. We need to get some sleep. We have a lot to do tomorrow." He escorted her inside, and made sure she was settled down in the back bedroom on an old mattress that was lying on the floor. He gave her his poncho liner. "I'll be right down the hall if you need anything. All right?"

"All right." Lisa paused, then asked the question uppermost in her mind: "Do you think my brother is in trouble?"

"Huh? What?" Hammer asked, his mind elsewhere.

"My brother. Do you think he's all right?"

"I have no idea." He seemed to focus back in. "Listen, I'll check on things in the morning, okay? There's nothing we can do now without stirring up a pack of trouble."

She gave a brittle laugh. "Seems like more trouble won't make any difference." She looked at Hammer with her bloodshot eyes, holding his gaze, speaking slowly and firmly. "I want to know about my brother."

Hammer held up a hand. "All right. I'll check with Riley as soon as I can."

She stared at him and nodded. "All right." Her eyes were still on him as she asked another question. "Why did you do that in the bar?"

Hammer regarded her for a few seconds, as if the question had been posed in a foreign language and he had to process it. "We had to leave. They were blocking our way," he explained, as if it was quite obvious.

"You didn't have to hurt them."

"I did them a favor," Hammer said.

"A favor?" Lisa repeated incredulously.

"Yeah. They're young and they'll heal. The next guy they try to mess with in a bar might carve 'em up or put a bullet in their back in the parking lot. They got off easy and learned an important lesson." Hammer pointed at her. "You got enough troubles without worrying about some kids in a bar. Now, get some sleep."

Lisa pulled the poncho liner tightly around her body as Hammer closed the door. The snatches of sleep she'd had over the past few days had been derived from sheer physical and emotional exhaustion. She knew she couldn't face another day without getting some rest. Things seemed to be so far beyond her control that she felt she was outside herself, watching everything going on with a sense of detachment. Only thoughts of her brother, and the danger she'd put him in, made her feel involved in this crazy scenario. As she slid into a troubled sleep, she wondered if it wouldn't be easier to just give up.

Hammer made his way to what once had been the living room but was now a beer can–littered party room. The trailer was a safe house that Jim Lightfoot and his buddies used to escape irate wives or girl-friends, and occasionally the law. Hammer located the phone socket in the wall, then pulled up the wire through the debris until he found the device on the end—an old rotary-dial phone that had seen better days. He picked up the receiver and ensured he had a dial tone, then replaced it. Sitting down in the dark, he stared out into the woods, wondering how Riley's vigil was going.

After fifteen minutes of hard thought, Hammer picked up the phone and began to dial.

FAYETTEVILLE
31 OCTOBER, 1:10 A.M.

The dome light in the car went on for a second and then just as suddenly went out. The slight thud of both doors being shut echoed across the parking lot. Riley watched the two men move across the asphalt, right hands hanging straight down at their sides, the glow of streetlights reflecting off the metal in those hands. Riley stood in the kitchen, slinging the H & K 94 over his shoulder and drawing the silenced High Standard .22. He backed up farther into the darkness, angling so he could watch out the window and also have the front door in his sights. He figured to let them both come in, then take out the trail man with the pistol and try to subdue the lead man without serious injury for interrogation. It all depended on how good they were. The better they were, the more likely he would have to kill them both with the submachine gun.

The men were more than halfway across the parking lot. Riley slipped the safety off both weapons, pistol in his left hand, sub in the right. The two men had their own weapons up now; both held revolvers, which Riley estimated gave him the advantage of superior firepower, in addition to the element of surprise.

As the lead man stepped on the concrete sidewalk that fronted the apartment building, a pair of high-beam headlights reached through the darkness, pinning both men in their glow. The men spun, weapons pointing. A silent strobe of flames spit out from the left side of the car, above the headlights; both men arched back, their bodies twitching from the impact of the rounds that tore through their flesh, not even able to get off a shot in return. As the bodies were still settling onto the pavement the headlights went out and three men sprinted toward Riley's town house, silenced submachine guns cradled in their arms, the man in front also carrying a sledgehammer.

Riley spun and raced for his living room as the front door splintered under the first blow. Extending the metal stock of the submachine gun before his face, Riley exploded through the plate glass sliding doors.

"Hold it!" someone yelled from behind, and a string of bullets churned into the living room ceiling. Riley tore through the makeshift trip wire he'd rigged across the small concrete patio, cans jangling with the pennies inside, and then he was gone into the night.

1:12 A.M.

Master frowned as he pressed the phone against his ear. "But I don't understand."

"It's not up to you to understand."

"What about Riley?" Master asked.

"Terminate all loose ends."

The commo man twisted in his seat, gesturing urgently at the comm link lying on the desk.

"Hold on," Master said into the phone.

"No," the voice replied. "You just do your damn job."

"Shithead," Master muttered to himself as he put down the phone. He picked up the comm set. "Master here."

"This is team two. Target has bolted."

"Goddamnit, I told you just to surveil!" Master exploded.

"We were, but someone else had other ideas. There were two men moving up on the target, and it looked like they planned on terminating. We interrupted and the target split."

Master closed his eyes and rubbed his temples. "Is the scene clean?"

"We've secured the bodies. We're still cleaning the site. So far no official reaction."

"All right. Finish cleaning up and then put the bodies on ice—you know where. Out." Master took off the headset. He went completely still for a minute, then turned to the commo man. "Get me that jerk on the secure line."

The commo man punched in the number and Master waited. The phone was picked up on the second ring.

"Yes?"

"This is Master. I think you'd better hold off on your little plan. We've lost track of your loose end down here."

CUMBERLAND COUNTY
31 OCTOBER, 1:21 A.M.

With a start, Lisa Cobb woke from a dream-filled sleep, her eyes casting about in the dark, trying to orient herself physically and emotionally. Reality flooded back in, pushing out whatever unpleasant images had floated through her dreams. She knew where she was and why she was here, and she realized that the real nightmare was as bad as anything she had been dreaming.

The noises of the woods penetrated the thin windows, the night animals calling out to each other. But it was something else—snatches of a conversation—that had penetrated her unconsciousness. She rolled onto an elbow, the plywood floor creaking under her. Footsteps sounded in the hallway and the door cracked open. She recognized the figure that loomed there.

"Everything all right?" she asked.

"Sure," Hammer said. "I heard you move around—just wanted to check."

"I thought I heard something," she said.

"What?"

"I don't know. Something." Lisa shook her head, trying to concentrate and remember.

"Go back to sleep," Hammer said. "Everything's all right." The door swung shut behind him and she was left in the dark again with her thoughts and elusive dreams.

CHAPTER 11

CHICAGO
31 OCTOBER, 12:49 A.M. CENTRAL TIME

Giannini fumbled in the dark and picked up the phone. "Giannini here."

The dull throb of the dial tone penetrated her ear, its sound adding to her stubborn headache.

The phone rang again, and she put down the desk phone, flipped on the lamp, and grabbed her portable. "Yes?"

"It's Dave."

"Are you all right?"

"I don't know what's going on, Donna, but we're in deep shit. I've got people killing each other to see who can be the first to kill me."

"What?" Giannini asked, trying to clear her head.

She listened as Riley succinctly described the events of the past hour. "Where are you now?" she asked when he came to a halt.

"I'd rather not say over the phone," Riley replied. "I don't know where the hell these people are getting their info, but some of it has to be from the phone lines. It doesn't matter anyway—I'll be leaving here as soon as I hang up."

"You don't have any idea who these people are? Either the ones coming in or the ones who killed them?"

"All I know is that the second group was more professional than the first group." Giannini could hear Riley pause and take a deep breath. "I link up with our friends tomorrow. Then I'm getting us undercover. I haven't figured out where yet. I'll get in touch with you when I do."

"Then what?" Giannini asked.

"Then we solve this," Riley replied. "We stop running, we get our shit together, and we finish it. Right now they've got us reacting constantly. Whoever *they* are—which I'm not too sure of right now."

"Maybe I can help with that," Giannini replied.

"How?"

"I've got several things I need to check on, like I told you earlier. I think I can get some answers."

"It's too dangerous," Riley replied. "Just get out of there and get undercover."

"I remember saying that to someone earlier this evening and that person promising to get to a safe place."

"I won't argue with you," Riley said, accepting the admonishment. "I did that once and learned my lesson. I trust you to do what you think is best. I'm going to keep everyone here undercover, so I guess it's up to you. There's only one thing I want to add, though, that I never said before."

A long silence ensued. Giannini waited. When Riley didn't continue, she finally spoke. "What's that, Dave?"

"Well—I like you a lot, Donna." Riley's voice was low, almost a whisper. "And I don't want you getting hurt." He continued in an uncharacteristic rush of words. "I thought I lost you earlier and I realized I should have told you how I felt a long time ago. And now I have, and now you'd better just take care. Listen, I've got to go— I've been on this line too long already."

"I love you too, Dave."

The phone line went dead.

FAYETTEVILE
31 OCTOBER, 1:51 A.M. EASTERN TIME

Riley put down the phone and moved away from the McDonald's parking lot. He pulled the MP-5 out from underneath his fatigue shirt. Keeping to the edge of Yadkin Road, he began running at a steady pace to the east. Every time a car's headlights appeared from either direction, he'd sprint off the road and hide, either behind parked cars or in the shadows of the businesses that lined the road.

He was crossing the parking lot of one of the innumerable laundromats when a set of high-beam headlights went on from a car parked across the street, pinpointing him with their light.

An amplified voice echoed through the chilly air. "Freeze where you are and drop the weapon!"

The blue stutter of police lights added to the authority of the voice. Blinded, Riley could hear a car door open and a voice repeat the order. He turned and ran, heading for the alley between the laundromat and the next store.

"Halt!" the police officer yelled, taking up chase.

A fence topped with barbed wire enclosed the end of the alley. Riley let the MP-5 hang by its sling as he jumped. The toes of his boots grabbed hold in the chain links. He paused for a second; then, grabbing the top of the fence just below the wire, he did a backflip over the wire and hit the ground with the balls of his feet. After a quick roll he was running again. He spared a glance over his shoulder. The cop was nowhere in sight; he must have headed back for the patrol car.

Riley ran through into the residential area behind the stores, randomly cutting through streets, cursing every time a dog started barking. Twice he spotted patrol cars cruising the street, handheld spotlights searching the night.

Finally, he made it to the overpass that crossed the All American Freeway coming out of Fort Bragg. He climbed over the guardrail, then eased underneath the bridge and hid the MP-5 atop one of the girders. He got back on top of the bridge and continued walking cautiously until he reached Skibo Road, where he took a left. At one of the many trailer courts that lined the road, he found another bank of pay phones. He went to the second phone and dialed information, getting the number he needed.

The phone was picked up on the second ring and the voice sounded alert, used to getting calls in the middle of the night.

"Sergeant Major Alexander."

"Sergeant Major, this is Chief Riley. I need some help."

"What sort of help?"

"I'm at the Evergreens Campground off Skibo Road and I need a ride."

"Be right there."

Riley moved off into the shadows and used the time to consider his options.

FORT BRAGG
31 OCTOBER, 2:20 A.M.

The two bodies were laid out on the steel autopsy tables, their pale skin marred by the black and red puckered holes where bullets had punched through. The air inside the morgue at Womack Army Hospital was an uncomfortable forty degrees and smelled of strong chemicals. The four men gathered around the bodies seemed unaware of the macabre surroundings. This morgue was the same place that bodies from classified Delta Force missions were returned, so strange goings-on were not considered abnormal by the staff.

"Who are they?" Master asked.

The technician had fingerprinted the hands of the corpses and faxed out the ink pictures twenty minutes ago. He stared at his computer screen, his breath visible in small puffs. "It's coming up now, sir." He nodded at the body on the left, an overweight male with long, greasy black hair. "We've got one Victor Lupino. He's got quite a record in the FBI organized crime files. Armed robbery. Extortion. Grand theft auto. Breaking and—"

"Who's he work for now?" Master interrupted the litany.

"Last indication was that he was working for Peter Marrinelli in Atlanta. Marrinelli's the local head honcho for the mob there."

"The other one?"

The technician chuckled. "Bobby aka 'the Snake' Lister."

"Same job description?"

"Yes, sir. Another mob gunman."

"How the fuck did the Atlanta mob get onto Riley?" Master asked no one in particular. "Too many hands diddling with the stew." He stared at the bodies with his pale eyes. "All right. Dispose of them."

One of the men acknowledged that with a curt nod, and the two bodies were wheeled out. Master flipped open the cover on his portable phone and dialed.

FAYETTEVILLE
31 OCTOBER, 2:20 A.M.

"It was my daughter's car, but she's shacked up with a long-haired freak who plays guitar in some rock and roll band, and I told her that if I was going to be paying the insurance I'd be keeping it. Her asshole boyfriend kicked out one of the headlights when he got drunk one night." Alexander was explaining all this as he showed Riley the souped-up Camaro. "I know it isn't exactly the best vehicle for going incognito or whatever, but it's all I got."

Riley eyed the yellow car with bright red flames painted along the hood and sides. "I appreciate your help. You might want to report it stolen to cover your own ass."

Alexander shrugged and glanced up at the night sky. "I don't know what shit you're into, and I really don't want to know. If anyone asks, I'll just say I thought my daughter came by and appropriated it and I didn't report it because I didn't want her to get in trouble."

"Thanks, Sergeant Major."

Riley settled in behind the wheel and drove away from the sergeant major's house, cringing at the racket the mufflers made. His first stop was to pick up the MP-5 from the overpass on Skibo Road. Then he took a chance, driving down Yadkin, past his apartment complex. No police cars with lights flashing; no ambulances; no sign that two men had died there less than a couple of hours ago. Riley frowned in thought as he continued his way onto post. First Lisa's account of a major gun battle on the interstate and now this—both events covered up very efficiently.

He drove to the ACFAC and did a circuit around the building, checking for any surveillance. Other than the cars scattered in the parking lot from students and instructors deployed out to Mackall, there was no sign of life. Riley went in the main entrance and signed in with the guard on duty. He took the stairs two at a time to his office area. From his wall locker he pulled out his field gear and laid it out on the floor.

He packed carefully; on the teams he'd served with he had been known for his packing abilities. He always had the smallest rucksack, although not the lightest. This night, Riley evaluated every piece of equipment and how it would fit into the rudiments of the plan he had worked out in his mind while waiting for Alexander to show up. The rucksack filled up quickly: short sleeping pad; Goretex bivvy sack; poncho liner; camouflage poncho; Goretex rain parka and pants; a fifty-meter length of 10mm nylon rope; climbing rack with assorted nuts, friends, camming devices, and load of snap links; a figure eight, used to help rappel; climbing harness; two twelve-foot lengths of army-issue nylon rope; altimeter; Goretex gaiters; a compact folding saw; and various other items he felt might be useful.

Riley opened the file drawer on the desk and searched until he found the folder he needed. He took out several map sheets and placed them in the protection of his map case, which he put in the top of the rucksack.

Done, Riley took his load back to the car and threw it in the backseat. He drove out Community Access Road onto Reilly Road and entered Fayetteville from a different direction.

He worked his way through the revitalized downtown area to a decidedly less trendy street, lined on both sides with strip clubs, which had just closed down. He rounded the corner and drove up to the back door of one club. Before leaving the car he checked his pistol, making sure a round was in the chamber. He went to the back fire door and entered the building.

"What do you want?" asked a man seated at a desk, his hands suspiciously out of sight beneath the scarred wooden top.

"I need to see Porter."

"Who are you?"

Riley took out his military ID card and placed it in front of the man. "Dave Riley. I'm assigned to the Special Warfare Center."

The man checked the card and then Riley. "How do I know you're not CID?"

"You don't, but Porter can make a few calls and check to see that I'm who I claim to be."

A new voice interrupted from Riley's left. "Yes, but you still could be working for CID."

Riley looked at the newcomer. Porter was a slim, gray-haired man. His left arm was wrapped around a young girl wearing a skimpy swimsuit.

Riley reached under his shirt, pulled off the money belt, and dropped it on the table. "I want to do business. Get rid of the girl."

Porter took in the belt, then jerked his head at the girl. "Get lost." With a pop of gum, she was gone. "Strip," he ordered.

Riley complied, first placing his pistol, then clothes, on the desktop. Porter and the guard observed the accumulation of weapons without comment as the layer of clothes came off. Finally Riley stood there naked. The guard went through his clothes, searching for a mike. "He's clean."

"All right. What do you need?"

Riley reached over to his shirt and pulled out the slip of paper he had prepared at the office.

Porter looked at it, then at Riley. Their gaze locked for ten seconds. "Get dressed. We need to take a ride."

FORT BRAGG
31 OCTOBER, 3:54 A.M.

Three thousand dollars poorer, but better equipped to face the uncertainties of the situation, Riley drove back onto Fort Bragg. He cruised along Chicken Road toward Camp Mackall for five miles, then pulled off onto one of the hundreds of firebreaks that ran through the pine forest. Going in far enough so that he couldn't be seen from the road, he parked the car.

He got out and locked it, then made his way into the trees about twenty meters away. He gathered together a cushion of pine needles, then sank down and threw a poncho liner over himself. The MP-5 was at one side, the pistol on the other. He stared up at the stars visible through the tree limbs and tried to make sense of all that had happened. After ten minutes, he gave up and was asleep almost immediately.

CHAPTER 12

CUMBERLAND COUNTY
31 OCTOBER, 6:23 A.M.

Lisa woke to the gentle nudging of Hammer's hand on her shoulder. "Come on, get up. We've got to get going."

For a brief moment she felt panic, not knowing where she was. She blinked at the sunlight streaming through the broken windows of the trailer and tried to orient herself.

"Let's get some coffee and we'll head over to Mackall. I want to make sure the area is clean before Riley comes out," Hammer said.

Lisa struggled to her feet, the weight in her chest, which she'd grown accustomed to over the past couple of days, settling back in place. "All right."

Hammer led the way out to his pickup truck, Lisa following wordlessly. At a quick-stop he bought them both cups of coffee and plastic-wrapped cinnamon rolls, then continued the drive in silence. Lisa ate the meager breakfast and sipped at her coffee, watching the low-lying North Carolina countryside slip by. They passed a sign indicating they were entering a military reservation, and soon came to a triangular intersection. Hammer veered to the left.

Lisa finally spoke. "What are we going to do once we link back up with Riley?"

Hammer shrugged. "I don't know. That's sort of up to him."

"Don't you have any ideas?" Lisa asked. "Riley's last plan didn't work very well."

"It worked quite well," Hammer contradicted calmly. "You're still alive, aren't you?"

"Why can't we just drive into a town and go to the nearest police station and ask for their protection?" Lisa demanded.

Hammer turned onto a dirt road. "You can. In fact, you could have before you ever linked up with Riley, but you didn't. Is that what you want to do now?" he asked, sparing her a quick glance.

Lisa sat back in the worn vinyl seat and stared out the windshield. After a long silence she answered. "I don't know what I want anymore. Everything I had is gone—my old life, my husband. Even the new life they promised us seems to be gone. Everything has gotten so complicated so quickly."

"That's the way it goes sometimes," Hammer said. "We don't control as much of our lives as we like to think we do." He made a left onto another dirt road. "We could go to the cops, but since we don't really know what's going on, they certainly won't either. Proving your story won't be easy. And going to the cops will advertise your location—something that hasn't worked well so far. Let's wait and see what plan Riley has come up with." He paused for a second, then asked. "Who's this Donna Giannini that Riley keeps talking about?"

"She's a friend of my brother's. I called my brother and he got her involved, and then she got Riley involved in all this."

"She's in Chicago?"

"Yes."

"How come she's doing all this checking on stuff. What does she do for a living?"

"She's a homicide detective with the Chicago Police Department."

That caught Hammer's attention. "How does Riley know her?"

"I don't know."

"Hmm" was Hammer's only comment.

They broke out of the trees into a large open field stretching as far as they could see to the left and right. The trees on the far side were more than three hundred yards away. A dirt runway was in the center, surrounded on both sides by high grass and scrub vegetation.

"This is the airstrip," Hammer announced. "Let's find a place to sit and watch."

FORT BRAGG
31 OCTOBER, 7:30 A.M.

The parking lot outside the ACFAC was packed with the cars of students and instructors. Riley left the souped-up Camaro and made his way across the lot, passing a formation of students preparing to board the "cattle cars" to go out to a range. It was possible the building might be under surveillance by whoever had been outside his house the previous night, but Riley doubted that anything would happen with so many witnesses around. And if they were watching, that was fine with Riley, because he had a plan for dealing with anyone curious enough to follow him.

He entered the building and went to the A Company area. Major Welch was in his office, surrounded as usual by stacks of paper. Riley knocked on the open door and entered.

"Chief, what's up?"

Riley shut the door and took the chair across from his commander. "Sir, I've got a problem and need to burn some leave time. I've got forty-five days saved up; I only need to take about a week, though. My team is off cycle right now and everything's covered, so that won't be a problem."

Major Welch put down his pen. "You mind telling me what kind of problem?"

"It's personal, sir."

Welch accepted that without comment. "Anything I can help with, other than giving you leave?"

"No, sir. I can take care of it."

"You have a leave form?"

Riley slid the form, which he'd taken out of the admin clerk's desk, across to the major.

Welch picked up his pen and scrawled his signature in the indicated block, then handed back the form. "You need any help, you be sure and give me or the sergeant major a call, okay?"

"Thank you, sir."

At least now he wouldn't have the army after him for being AWOL, Riley reflected as he left the building and returned to the car. He drove out of the parking lot and headed for Chicken Road to go out to Mackall, checking his rearview mirror constantly. There was no sign of anyone following. After passing the intersection of Chicken and Plank Roads, he proceeded another three miles until he went over a slight rise in the road. He immediately slammed on his brakes and pulled off to the right, parking the car facing the road along a firebreak. He checked his watch and waited for ten minutes, MP-5 at the ready. Nothing. Satisfied, Riley restarted the car and continued on his way.

7:45 A.M.

"Master here."

"We spotted Riley on post at his workplace."

"What's his present location?" Master asked, indicating for the van driver to get them rolling.

"He's heading west."

"Is he tagged?"

"Yes."

"How long was he at the academic facility?"

"About ten minutes."

"I'm on my way." As the van moved out, Master dialed.

The phone was picked up on the first ring. "Yes?"

"This is Master. We relocated Riley. He'll probably link up with our target."

"Good. Make a clean sweep of it, then close this thing down. No more fuckups."

Master didn't bother responding. He pressed the off switch on the phone.

CHICAGO
31 OCTOBER, 7:45 A.M.

Giannini entered Guyton's office without knocking and took the seat directly across from him, the cluttered desk separating them.

"What do you want?" Guyton asked irritably, closing a file.

"I want some answers."

He snorted. "What makes you think you got a right to ask me questions?"

Giannini leaned forward. "Don't fuck with me, Guyton. Something smells real bad around here and I think you're part of the stink."

"Don't come in here with that attitude," Guyton warned, getting up out of his chair and dwarfing Giannini as he leaned over his desk.

"Who was Fastone working for?" Giannini asked bluntly.

Guyton blinked. "What?"

"I was at Lisa Cobb's brother's house yesterday. Someone worked him over with a blowtorch and then killed him."

Guyton sat back down slowly. "I didn't hear about that."

"That's because I haven't told anyone. Someone sapped me over the head, and when I regained consciousness, the body was gone."

"You should have reported it."

"No," Giannini shook her head. "I don't think so. Not until I find out what's going on."

"I don't have to tell you nothing," Guyton said.

"Why'd Fastone start having an affair with some suburban real estate developer who had no links to the mob?"

"Hormones, I guess," Guyton said with a forced laugh.

"Bullshit. You still don't get it, do you? Someone's after the Cobbs. And that someone may be after all those who had anything to do with the Cobbs, and that puts you pretty damn high on the list."

"Hey, I didn't do nothing wrong," Guyton said.

"What *did* you do?" Giannini asked. When Guyton didn't answer, Giannini pressed home her attack. "Right after I leave here, I'm going to the feds and I'm going to make some noise."

Guyton let loose a genuine laugh this time. "Noise about what? You don't know shit."

"I know there are pages missing from the Torrentino files. I know that someone is going after the Cobbs and they don't care who they have to kill to get to them."

"The Cobbs are safe. They went under in the Program," Guyton said.

"Then who killed Fastone? Who killed Tom Volpe, Lisa Cobb's brother?"

Guyton didn't answer.

Giannini tried another approach. "Tell me about Fastone."

"What about her?"

"She set up Philip Cobb, didn't she? She was working for Torrentino when she got involved with Cobb, wasn't she?"

"Of course she was working for Torrentino," Guyton said finally. "Any idiot—except Cobb, that is—could have figured it out. He had no idea who she was when she sashayed into his life."

"Torrentino blackmailed him with the affair?" Giannini asked.

"I suppose. I don't really know, and it didn't really matter. Maybe Cobb just wanted to make some big money. Whatever his reasons were, he started working for the Torrentinos. He was washing more than two million a month for them through his firm, helping make them legitimate while getting dirty himself."

"His kid was dying," Giannini spat out. "It ever occur to you he might have needed the money?"

"Everyone needs money, Giannini. Not all of us go to the mob for it."

"Why'd they try to hit him if he was worth a couple of million a month to them? The file makes it sound like Michael Torrentino was pissed 'cause Cobb was screwing Fastone, but if he set up the whole thing, that doesn't hold water."

Guyton stared at Giannini for a long time. She returned the stare. Her mind sorted through the facts, coming again to the pieces that didn't seem to fit. Suddenly she sat bolt upright. "You son of a bitch!" she exclaimed. "Torrentino didn't try to kill Cobb in Chicago. You set it all up, didn't you? That's why the investigation into the attempted hit was so skimpy in the files and there were pages missing! The two supposed hit men, the cop just happening upon them in time to break it up, the whole thing—you planned it, didn't you?"

"Not me," Guyton said. "The feds. O'Fallon and his guys from the task force thought it up. I just gave them a little help. And that's why your threat of going to the feds doesn't bother me."

"You're a cop, for God's sake!"

"And he was a goddamn criminal!" Guyton returned hotly.

"You're supposed to uphold the law—not bend it to fit your needs." Giannini paused to get herself under control and back in focus. "Cobb never knew he was set up? Not even after the trial?"

"No."

"Jesus Christ," Giannini muttered. "The poor bastard got it coming and going."

"He was a crook, Giannini. He took a slice of that two mill every month. The Torrentinos didn't make that money selling cookies door to door. Cobb deserved what he got. Hell, he deserved to go to fucking jail. He got off scot-free as far as I'm concerned."

You don't know the half of it, Giannini thought. "Was Fastone cooperating with you and the feds?"

"No. She was still working for Torrentino."

"Then who killed her?"

Guyton looked troubled. "I don't know."

"Maybe she wasn't working for Torrentino," Giannini mused. "Maybe she got involved with Cobb at Torrentino's urging in the beginning, but then she came up with a better idea. Maybe she was on her own at the end."

"What are you talking about?" Guyton asked.

"It looks like a professional hit," Giannini said, getting back to the known facts.

"Yeah," Guyton agreed reluctantly.

"Was she after Cobb?" Giannini asked.

"What do you mean?"

"The Torrentinos had to have a contract out on Philip Cobb after what he did to them. If Cobb didn't know Fastone had set him up, they still might have used her to get to him, figuring Cobb might try to contact her some way."

"Maybe," Guyton conceded. "But why kill her then?"

"Because I think they got to Philip Cobb and killed him," Giannini said, watching the surprise flit across Guyton's face.

"Cobb's dead? How do you know?"

"I've got my own sources," Giannini said. "Maybe Fastone led them to him; he was killed, then they killed her to tie up loose ends. Or maybe she was on her own and they followed her."

"Either way, it's over," Guyton said.

"No, it's not over," Giannini replied, standing.

"What do you mean?"

"How'd you break Cobb? How'd you get him to think the Torrentinos were after him?"

"He was scared," Guyton said.

"Yeah, but he must have had a reason to be scared," Giannini returned.

"He was screwing the boss's girl—that's a damn good reason."

"Maybe," Giannini said as another piece of the puzzle turned over in her head. "Or maybe Cobb was doing something *else* that he wasn't supposed to, and he was afraid the Torrentinos had found out about it."

"Do you know something else?" Guyton asked.

Giannini wasn't in the mood to answer questions—not when she had so many of her own. "Who's doing the work for the Torrentinos on the outside? Who's the acting boss?"

"Charlie D'Angelo."

Giannini turned to the door. Guyton stepped out from behind his desk. "What's going on, Giannini? What do you know?"

"I don't know nothing," Giannini snapped back over her shoulder. "All I do know is that your little setup has already cost at least one innocent person his life, and the game isn't over by a long shot." She slammed the door behind her.

CAMP MACKALL
31 OCTOBER, 8:45 A.M.

Riley parked just inside the gate to the Nicholas M. Rowe compound. Two MH-47 helicopters squatted like large green grasshoppers outside the compound gate on the large helipad, their motionless dual rotors drooping halfway to the ground.

Riley tried the Selection and Assessment shack first. S & A was the cadre that ran potential Special Forces students into the ground on a daily basis. The few people in the shack didn't know where the crews were for the helicopters. Walking out the door of S & A, Riley scanned the compound and spotted what he was looking for. Two 292 antennae were jury-rigged on the south side, poking up above the buildings. Riley tracked the wires from the antennae into a building.

Two NCOs were sitting in front of a bank of radios, monitoring a Q-course Phase 13 exercise. On the far side of the open bay building, several men in flight suits were lounging about on a row of cots. Riley made a beeline for one of the men; there were four dots on the silver bar pinned to his maroon beret, which protruded from a side pocket.

Riley nodded at the higher-ranking warrant officer. "Hey, Chief, how's it going?"

The man's name tag identified him as Chief Warrant Officer Prowley. "All right."

Riley glanced at the map pinned to the corkboard on the wall. "You flying missions for Phase 13?"

"Yeah, we got six exfiltrations tonight."

"Uwharrie National Forest?"

Prowley nodded. "Four of them. Two in Pisgah."

"You out of Fort Campbell?"

"Yep." Prowley still hadn't moved from the cot.

"When do you head back there?"

"Tonight, after we bring the last load back here."

Riley sat down next to Prowley and pulled out a 1:250,000 scale map of North Carolina and Tennessee. "Listen, I'm with A Company, First Battalion, and we've got a last-minute tasking to run an escape and evasion mission for one of our deployed teams. I was wondering if you all could help us out tonight."

Prowley looked at Riley, then glanced a few cots over to where an officer lay sleeping, a maroon beret covering his face, the gold leaf of a major's insignia gleaming on the 160th Task Force's cloth shield. "I don't know. The major might not be too keen on it. You know how the army works. Got to plan taskings half a lifetime in advance and all that."

"Yeah, I know," Riley said. "But I got this one dumped on me by my major, and he isn't the sort you want to go back to and say you couldn't get something done."

Prowley nodded in commiseration. "I know how that goes. What's the mission?"

"Three pax, myself being one of them. Pickup at the helipad here when you drop off your last load, and drop us off here." Riley pointed at the map. "It shouldn't be too much out of your way, and it would really help me out."

Prowley looked at the location. "That's pretty much on our flight path back. I guess we could do it. You have a landing zone there?"

"No." Riley smiled at the pilot's look of concern. "Don't worry. We'll get off your bird."

CHICAGO
31 OCTOBER, 9:50 A.M.

"Jesus, Giannini, I could get in big trouble if someone sees me with you," the man in the black leather jacket whined, eyes darting about the deli. He was in his midtwenties, and his dark hair was slicked back, complementing the sunglasses he wore to give him an authentic punk look. Giannini wondered if he'd simply copied the crime shows on TV or if the crime shows copied real life.

"You'd have been in bigger trouble if you hadn't seen me, Nickie. You owe me."

"But people are talking about *you,*" he said, taking a nervous drag on his cigarette. "I about shit when you called me—and calling me at the *club*—Jesus, Giannini, what are you, nuts?"

"Which people are talking about me?" Giannini asked. She'd selected Nickie because he was the only contact she had who had connections with Charlie D'Angelo. She'd called him at the "club," one of the local hangouts for mob-affiliated people, and pretended to be a girlfriend. She really didn't care if the ruse had gone over or not. "What are they saying?"

"They want to know what you're poking your nose into."

"What happened to Jill Fastone?" she asked bluntly.

"Ah, geez, Giannini! We don't even mention her name around Charlie. Mikey's steamed and he's letting Charlie know. Charlie is supposed to take care of things and now Mike's girl ends up dead." Nickie shook his head solemnly. "Bad fucking news."

Giannini frowned. "Any idea who killed her?"

Nickie leaned forward and lowered his voice. "Listen, I owe you for getting me off that bust, but this is heavy shit. We're dealing with the boss, and if he finds out I'm talking to you, my ass is history."

"I'm not wired, Nickie. This is personal—not business; it won't ever come up in an official capacity. If you don't talk to me, I've got some people I could talk to about things you've told me in the past. And you and I know they won't like it."

"Aw, shit." Nickie stubbed out his cigarette. "All right. I was at the clubhouse when they found out about Jill's body being discovered. Charlie about blew a gasket. He wanted to know what the hell was going on. It's been real strange ever since the trial. Some people are saying that Charlie isn't seeing eye to eye with Mike about some things."

"What things?"

"Ah, I don't know, Giannini."

"Philip Cobb," Giannini prompted.

Nickie blinked. "Yeah—that's something that's bugging the crap out of everyone. How'd you know that?"

"I'm not stupid," Giannini spat out. "What's the story on Cobb?"

"The word's been out since the trial that whoever found Cobb and did him would be a rich person—at least that's the word from Charlie. Charlie talks to the Torrentinos every day on the phone from prison, so I guess that's what they want too.

"We were all looking for Cobb, but Jill—she apparently got a line on him in Georgia or someplace like that down in cracker land. And she went off to do him but didn't tell nobody. Then she shows up dead in Chicago." Nickie shook his head, his limited thinking abilities already strained by what he was relating. "It didn't make no sense—the feds wouldn't have done that. Now Mike wants to know who done Jill. And he still wants Cobb. More than ever."

"Philip Cobb? Or his wife?"

Nickie shrugged. "Both. But mainly the guy." He paused. "But there's also a rumor that maybe Jill got to Philip Cobb and killed him."

"Where'd you hear that?"

"Just heard it," Nickie said evasively.

"Fastone went down there to kill the Cobbs?" Giannini asked, trying to figure out all the angles to this maze.

"Yeah. At least that's what we all think," Nickie amended.

Giannini sat back in her seat. "What about Tom Volpe?"

A mask slid over Nickie's face. "I don't know nothing about that."

She wanted to know more, but she was too confused by what she already did have. "How much is the contract on Cobb up to?"

"Five hundred thousand."

She whistled lightly. "Shit, they are pissed, aren't they? That's a little high, ain't it?"

"Cobb put Michael away for a long time." Nickie looked at her, then leaned forward. "But there's more than just Mikey being pissed. Word I hear is that Cobb got some money that belongs to the Torrentinos squirreled away somewhere. A lot of money."

"What's a lot of money, Nickie?"

He licked his lips. "I'm hearing rumors of a couple of mill. That's what really burned Mikey's ass—he didn't know about it until after they went to trial. Not only does Cobb put Mikey away and walk free, but he walks away a rich man with our money. Now you know why Mikey wants Cobb so bad."

Giannini frowned. Something wasn't making sense here. "Any word of a freelance professional trying to horn in on it?"

"Uh-uh. Charlie's keeping this in the family." Nickie looked around. "Listen, I really got to go."

"All right." Giannini didn't watch him leave. She sat at the small table for almost ten minutes, lost in thought.

CAMP MACKALL
31 OCTOBER, 1:12 P.M.

Lisa watched the vividly painted Camaro bump its way along the east side of the airstrip from the perch Hammer had chosen for them in a tree on the west side. "The lights are on," she noted.

"Yeah, but that ain't his truck," he muttered in return.

"What do we do?" she asked.

"Right time. Right place. Right signal," Hammer recited. "Let's hope it's the right person. We let it go by once—see if anyone's following."

The Camaro passed by and then disappeared out of sight at the far end of the airstrip. Five minutes later it reappeared on the same road, heading in the opposite direction.

"All right," Hammer said. He pulled out a survival mirror from his pocket and angled it, reflecting sunlight at the car's windshield. Ten seconds later the car came to a stop, then turned and headed across the dirt strip directly for their position. Hammer tapped Lisa on the shoulder. "You stay here."

He slipped down to the ground and took up position behind some deadfall, thirty yards away. He pulled his revolver out of its shoulder holster and cocked it. The car passed between several trees and came to a halt near the tree in which Lisa was hidden. Hammer steadied his aim on the windshield.

The driver's door opened and Riley stepped out, MP-5 at the ready, looking about. Hammer put his thumb on the hammer, and slowly let it ride forward before standing. "Yo!"

Riley turned. "Where's Lisa?"

"I'm here," she called out as she clambered down to the ground. "What do we do now?" she asked as she came over.

"First, we get this car undercover," Riley said.

"My truck's about forty yards that way," Hammer said, pointing. "In a depression that you couldn't find unless you practically walked on top of it. That car should fit. Think you could have picked something a little more conspicuous?"

"I didn't have the opportunity to be choosy," Riley replied, his sense of humor gone.

Once the vehicles were in place, the three gathered at one end of the pit. It was about forty yards long by twenty wide and could be entered only on one end by car. The dirt walls were about eight feet high and ranged in slope from vertical to sixty degrees. The marks of backhoes and bulldozers were evident throughout the area.

"Looks like some engineer unit dug this thing for a training exercise a while back," Riley commented.

"I found it when I was working for F Company six months ago," Hammer said. "One of the points for the land nav course is about a quarter mile to the west."

Lisa reached out and grabbed Riley's sleeve. "What happened to my brother?" Riley's brief pause struck home. "He's in trouble, isn't he?" Lisa continued, her heart pounding. "You said he was the link to Giannini, and if they got to Giannini—that means they got to him."

"Giannini's all right," Riley said. He looked at Lisa, trying to think of a gentle way to say what he knew. Then he simply said it. "Your brother is dead."

Lisa leaned back against the hood of the car for support. "How?"

"Someone got to him—Giannini got there too late. He was dead when she arrived at his house, and whoever killed him knocked her out and got my number off her portable. I think that's how they tracked us to Fayetteville and the drop."

Hammer stepped forward. "What's the plan now?"

"We wait," Riley said, opening his rucksack and pulling out his small stove. "Anyone for some coffee?" He glanced up at Lisa and saw the look on her face. He was not used to dealing with civilians, and realized he was being too matter-of-fact. "I'm sorry about your brother."

She seemed dazed. "It's all come apart, hasn't it? From the very beginning my life was doomed to failure. I should have known my place and kept to it."

Riley wasn't sure what she meant. He stood. "Why don't you lie down in the car and get some rest. You've been through a lot."

He escorted Lisa to the back of the Camaro, and she numbly climbed into the cramped backseat. Riley put his poncho liner over her, then stood awkwardly, looking down at her for a while before returning to his stove.

"What are we waiting for?" Hammer asked Riley as he walked up.

"We wait to talk to Giannini and hopefully find out what's going on."

"What's she doing?"

"I'm not sure," Riley replied as he lit the stove. "I got attacked last night at my apartment, so the meeting must have been blown. Like I said, they must have traced me from my phone number off Giannini's portable phone."

"You were attacked?" Hammer repeated. "What happened?"

Riley related the events of the early morning. When he was done, Hammer was shaking his head. "It doesn't make any sense. How come there were *two* sets of people outside your apartment? And why did one group kill the other?"

"I don't know," Riley said. "But whoever the second group was, they're extremely well organized. They didn't hesitate to fire at me once they busted through my front door. And a few hours later there was no sign of the cops at my place, and nothing in the paper or on the radio this morning about two bodies being found."

"The same as when she was attacked on the freeway," Hammer noted, nodding toward the car.

"Yeah," Riley said. "We need to go deep under until Giannini comes up with something to get us out of this mess."

"Any idea where we should go?" Hammer asked. "I'm not too sure hanging around here is the best idea."

"I've got us a way out of here that can't be traced, and we'll be going to a place where someone could hide out for years without getting spotted."

Hammer was intrigued. "Where?"

Riley smiled grimly. "You'll see."

CHAPTER 13

The young flunky in the three-piece suit was not impressed with Giannini's police ID or her rumpled appearance. "Captain Donnelly normally requires people to have appointments to see her. She's a very busy person," the young man added, snapping open a file folder.

Giannini glanced past him at the door with Donnelly's name on it, then back at him. "This isn't a normal situation."

"I suppose it might not be, but since you won't tell me what it is, I really can't—"

Giannini didn't let him complete the sentence. "You go to your boss and you whisper in her ear the name Philip Cobb."

The young man looked startled for the first time. He got up and disappeared. In thirty seconds he was back with the district supervisor for the Federal Witness Protection Program. Donnelly towered over both of them in her high heels. She extended a hand to Giannini. "Chris Donnelly."

"Donna Giannini, Metro Homicide."

Donnelly gestured toward her office. "Why don't we go inside and talk?" She led the way, shutting the door behind Giannini. The office was on the eighteenth floor and had a superb view of downtown Chicago. An L-shaped desk dominated one side, the front portion empty except for a neat stack of file folders. A computer, screen glowing, sat on the short side of the L along with three phones.

"I think I work for the wrong people," Giannini commented, taking in the office.

"Working for the federal government does have its advantages," Donnelly admitted. She took her seat and steepled her fingers. "What about Philip Cobb?"

Giannini was tired of sparring with people. "He's dead."

Donnelly didn't blink. "How do you know that?"

"I got a phone call from his wife, who saw his body."

Without a word Donnelly turned to her computer and her fingers flew over the keys. After thirty seconds of tapping, she paused and waited. Finally she shook her head. "I'm afraid your information is wrong. I'm showing a green status on the Cobbs—both Philip and Lisa."

"What's that mean?"

"It means both are alive and healthy and under no threat." Donnelly turned from her computer. "So what kind of game are you playing, detective? I don't appreciate people coming in here with stories."

Giannini was taken aback. She didn't know for sure that Philip Cobb *was* dead; she only knew what Lisa had told Riley. She did know that Tom Volpe was dead, but that wasn't information she felt like spreading to the feds right now. It was confusing enough; she needed to keep others out of the loop as much as possible. Could Lisa have been mistaken about Philip? And what did Lisa know about Philip's hidden money that Nickie referred to? She wished she knew Lisa Cobb better. What was real here?

Giannini tried a different approach. "What about Jill Fastone?"

"Who?"

"The woman who set up Philip Cobb with the Torrentinos. Her body was found here yesterday."

Donnelly shrugged. "I didn't know that, and quite frankly I don't care. Is that what you're here for? To try and get a line on Philip Cobb for your investigation into Fastone's murder? Is that why you're giving me this story about Cobb being dead?" Donnelly stood. "You can leave now, and you can be sure I will be in contact with your superiors. The Witness Protection Program is a highly classified operation, and we don't appreciate people trying to interfere. There are proper procedures to be followed if you desire information, and coming to my door and trying to trick me into releasing information is not one of them."

"Wait a second," Giannini protested. "I'm not sure exactly what's going on, but I was called by Lisa Cobb, and she said that her husband was dead and people were trying to kill her. She called me from North Carolina two nights ago."

For the first time Donnelly's professional composure cracked slightly. "North Carolina? What did she say?"

"She said someone had killed her husband and that they were trying to kill her," Giannini repeated.

"Who is 'they'?"

"She assumed it was the mob. Jill Fastone showed up at the motel where Lisa and her husband were."

"Where's Mrs. Cobb now?"

"I don't know."

"You don't know?" Donnelly glanced over her shoulder at the computer screen for reassurance. "If something happened to the Cobbs, we'd know about it. They most certainly would not have a green status. And since you don't know where Lisa Cobb is—that's if your story has any truth to it—then I think you're fishing for her location. I can save us both a whole lot of time by telling you that I don't know where she is now and I can't find out."

"I don't need you to find out where she is," Giannini said. "She's with a friend of mine right now. As a matter of fact, what I want is to get her back in your program. My friend's had some people take shots at him, and we'd all feel a lot better if you people had her in your protection."

"But she *is* under our protection," Donnelly said, acting as if she were dealing with an idiot.

"Can you double-check that? Who in the Program knows where she is?"

"The district manager for whichever district picked up the Cobbs, and four people at our headquarters in Washington." Donnelly turned to her keyboard one more time. After a minute she looked at Giannini. "I've double-checked as you requested and the information is the same— the Cobbs are alive and well."

Giannini stood abruptly. "I'm sorry to have wasted your time."

FORT BRAGG
31 OCTOBER, 2:50 P.M.

"Master here."

"Terminate the targets."

Master frowned. "I thought we—"

"You aren't paid to think. Do what I tell you. Immediately."

"I only have a surveillance team near them now. I'll need some time to put together an assault team."

"Terminate now. Your surveillance team can do it. There will be a bonus."

The secure connection went dead. Master glanced at the analyst. "What's the location of the target?"

"Camp Mackall. Holding steady about a klick off this airstrip," he said, pointing at a map.

"What about our surveillance?"

"Three kilometers away. Holding."

Master checked his watch. He could be out to Mackall in forty-five minutes. Why were they in such a rush to terminate all of a sudden? He called the surveillance team leader.

CAMP MACKALL
31 OCTOBER, 3:12 P.M.

Lisa was still in the back of the Camaro wrapped in guilt and sorrow beneath the poncho liner. Hammer was seated on the tailgate of his pickup truck, whittling away at a stick. Riley took another sip of the coffee he had just made and glanced about. The sun was a quarter way down in the western sky, glinting through the pine trees surrounding their hiding place in the depression. He slung the converted MP-5 over his shoulder and put down the canteen cup.

"I'm going to take a look around."

Hammer nodded, his knife not missing a slice.

Riley moved out of the depression along the way they had driven in, walking slowly, taking the opportunity to be by himself and try to clear his head of all the contradictory and confusing events of the past two days. He sincerely hoped that Donna could come up with something. He planned on driving by himself to Camp Mackall just after dark and calling her from one of the pay phones there.

Riley reached the spot where the dirt road opened onto the edge of the airstrip and turned right, skirting the tree line. He paused as he heard the faint mutter of an engine. Climbing a nearby tree, he peered out over the airstrip. A van with darkened windows was rolling slowly along the dirt road on the near side of the clearing, coming closer to Riley's position. There was no Fort Bragg sticker on the windshield, but Riley knew that didn't mean much, because many civilians drove through the open reservation. He was more interested in the four antennae poking out of the roof. Subtracting one for the van radio and one for a car phone, that still left two extra.

The van slowed as it drove past Riley and then stopped at the trail junction where Riley had just come out. The side door slid open and two men stepped out. They wore wraparound sunglasses and long, dark brown raincoats. Most alarming to Riley, though, was that they sported French-made FA-MAS assault rifles with laser sights on top and silencers on the end of the incredibly short barrels. They moved smoothly and silently from the van down the trail, covering across each other's front.

Riley let them get out of sight and then swiftly climbed down from the tree. He poked his head in the van, muzzle of the MP-5 leading—it was empty. He then quickly traced the steps of the two men. When he caught a glimpse of them, fifty meters ahead, he ducked into the concealment of the trees. The two were focused on what lay ahead of them. Riley silently made up ground, moving through the trees like a wraith, closing to within twenty yards. Then ten. Five.

One of the men paused, head cocked, some sense alerting him, and Riley committed himself, sprinting forward. He smashed the folding stock of the submachine gun into the head of the man on the left, dropping him. As the man on the right was wheeling around, bringing his weapon to bear, Riley swung the MP-5 by its barrel. The stock hooked under the barrel of the FA-MAS, ripping it out of the man's hands. The shock of the impact tore the MP-5 out of Riley's hand, and both weapons flew off into the brush.

The man glared at Riley, hand half reaching for the pistol in his shoulder holster; then he paused, seeing Riley's hand frozen in the same position. Abandoning that effort, the man leaped forward, lifting his right knee as if to kick, and then just as swiftly snapping his left foot out in a front kick directed toward Riley's face. It was a basic feint and move, which Riley had seen thousands of times in the dojo. He reacted instinctively, moving to his right, out of range of the kick, and snapping a turn kick into the man's midsection with his right leg, using the man's momentum to double the effect of the kick.

The man's breath exploded out of his lungs as he doubled over, but he continued the movement and rolled, coming to his feet and spinning around, the raincoat flying open. Riley didn't wait for his opponent to get set; he fired off a left turn kick in the direction of the man's face, which missed. Riley continued with the vector of the kick and spun, right arm extended, smashing a back fist into the side of the man's head. Riley grabbed the dazed man's hair with both hands and pulled his entire body down, slamming his knee into the man's chest. Riley repeated the movement four times, feeling ribs snap under the pounding of his knee.

Riley saw a red dot waver unsteadily across the man's back, then disappear. He whirled, keeping his hold on the man, and the burst of rounds ripped into the hapless man's back, the silencer on the FA-MAS making a whisper of noise. Riley fell to the ground, the body still between him and the gunman, the raincoat half wrapped around his own body.

Ten feet away, the first man shook his head, trying to get a clear picture of the target. Blood streamed down over his face from the wound caused by Riley's butt stroke. The man fired a second burst, the rounds again tearing into the human shield Riley kept between them.

Maintaining his hold with his right hand, Riley drew the High Standard .22 from inside his shirt and fired, his bullets passing through the man's third burst. Firing as fast as he could pull the trigger, Riley saw that his rounds were having no effect even though they were hitting center of mass in the chest. He raised the barrel slightly and put the next four rounds into the man's head, one of the bullets splattering the left eye and killing him.

Riley dropped the bloody shield and got slowly to his feet. He ripped open the man's raincoat. Sheets of Kevlar body armor were attached with Velcro to the inside of the raincoat, which explained why the bullets hadn't gone through the body and hit Riley. He searched for a pulse and felt a faint one. Despite the armor, one of the rounds had torn through the man's neck, and blood was spurting out—an arterial wound. Riley took a deep breath, then slammed the edge of his right hand into the man's neck, crushing the cartilage. With a brief gurgle and a froth of blood at his lips, the man died.

Riley sank back on his haunches for a minute, motionless. Then he moved, searching the bodies for any sort of identification, finding nothing. There was no sign of who they were or where they were from.

Leaving the bodies, Riley ran back down the road to the van and climbed inside. He scanned the interior, searching for anything that might be useful. The entire left wall was crammed with electronic equipment. Riley recognized some of the devices; others were quite foreign to him. He spotted a small glowing screen with an acetate overlay of a map of the immediate area. A small bright dot showed on the screen, slightly off center. There were no documents inside the van.

Riley took a portable phone from its charger next to the driver's seat and stuck it in his thigh pocket. He grabbed a small backpack and loaded it with magazines for the FA-MAS rifles from an open footlocker. Then he left the van and returned to the bodies, secured both rifles along with his MP-5, and made his way back to the depression.

Hammer was still seated on his pickup, whittling, and Lisa was asleep in the back of the Camaro. Hammer glanced up at the two weapons in Riley's hands; he looked past him, then back. "What happened?"

"We had some visitors."

Hammer sprang to his feet and caught the FA-MAS Riley tossed to him, followed by three full magazines.

"Time for a little upgrade in firepower." Riley went over to the Camaro, got down on his knees, and looked under the front bumper.

"What happened to the visitors?" Hammer asked.

"They're about a hundred meters thataway." Riley pointed. "Both dead. Their van is at the edge of the airstrip."

Hammer fingered the bullpup automatic. "Pretty fancy hardware." He watched Riley carefully. "What are you doing?" he asked as Riley moved around the side of the car, looking underneath.

"They tracked us here electronically. The only time I figure they could have put a bug on me was when I left the car in the parking lot outside the ACFAC." Riley glanced up. "Unless of course they bugged your car, but I don't see how they could have done that." He reached underneath the right wheel well and felt around. "Here we go," he said, pulling out a small black plastic box with a three-inch wire antenna. He put it on the ground and smashed it. "Time to get out of here." He glanced in the back window of the car—Lisa was still asleep. "We need to leave the car at the compound so the sergeant major doesn't get in trouble, then we'll use your truck to move out."

"To where?" Hammer asked.

"We'll hole up in the woods until tonight, then I've arranged further transportation." He jerked a thumb at the car. "Don't tell her about our visitors—she's got enough shit to deal with right now."

Hammer nodded.

Riley walked over to Hammer's pickup truck and sat down on the tailgate for a second. Hammer was cleaning up the area, loading the gear. He glanced over at Riley, who still hadn't moved. "You all right?"

Riley lifted his hands and looked at them as if they weren't even part of him. They shook slightly. His gaze was directed at the hands but his eyes didn't seem to be seeing them.

Hammer frowned. "Hey, Chief, you okay?" He walked over and laid a massive paw on Riley's shoulder. "Listen, partner, we got to get out of here."

Riley's eyes refocused and he stared at Hammer, then nodded slowly. "Right."

Hammer finished his sweep of the area. "You say you left their van on the edge of the airstrip?"

Riley nodded.

"I'm going to move it under some cover. Might give us a bit more time when whoever they work for comes looking for their people. Then we clear out."

Riley nodded, his mind elsewhere. Hammer jogged out of the clearing toward the airstrip.

CHICAGO
31 OCTOBER, 2:43 P.M.

Giannini spotted the tail within two blocks of leaving Donnelly's office. Two men in a black El Camino. Whoever they were, they weren't very good. They ran a red light amid a cacophony of car horns in order to keep her in sight.

The key question she asked herself was whether she'd been tailed to the meeting with Donnelly or whether the tail had started there. The answer to that question was critical, especially in light of the information Donnelly had just given her.

Giannini glanced down at the steering wheel as she drove up State Street, the El Camino four cars back. Her knuckles were white, and she could feel a small bead of sweat trickle down her back. She was scared, and she knew she had good reason to be. Five hundred thousand dollars worth of scared—besides messing with someone who had enough influence to fool with the Witness Protection Program's computers.

She considered simply going to police headquarters, but that might be jumping out of the proverbial frying pan into the fire. She wondered how much Guyton knew about the case that he hadn't told her. If the mob was offering five hundred grand for Philip Cobb, that meant that whatever he had hidden was undoubtedly a considerably larger amount—Louis had said a couple of million. She'd known good cops who went bad over a lot less. This thing was much bigger than she was, and she felt very alone and exposed. She braked at a light and glanced back. The tail was now two cars back.

Giannini made up her mind. She worked her way out of the Loop toward the south side of Chicago. After fifteen minutes she ended up in a less-populated area of warehouses. The tail was very conspicuous now, which led Giannini to believe that whoever was following her either didn't care that they had been spotted or were so bad they didn't realize it.

She suddenly spun the wheel hard left, turning into a narrow street, and then immediately slammed on the brakes. The street was deserted— a connector alley between two larger roads. It was lined with dumpsters and wooden pallets—the debris from the backs of the stores in the buildings on either side. Giannini leaped out of the car, drew her revolver, and waited. The nose of the El Camino appeared around the corner twenty feet away. The driver stopped quickly when he realized he had gone too far in to back out easily.

"Get out of the car!" Giannini yelled, muzzle pointed directly at the dark windshield. There was a long pause, then the driver's door opened. Her friend Nickie stepped out, hands held high.

"Tell your buddy to get out, too," Giannini said, feeling slightly relieved.

The passenger door opened and a taller punk version of Nickie unfolded from the car.

Giannini kept the gun up as she approached them. "Why are you following me?"

Nickie smiled nervously and shrugged. "Oh, come on, Giannini. You know why. I didn't mean no trouble. But you know—I had to. D'Angelo would have had my ass if I had a line on the Cobbs and didn't follow it up."

"Put your hands on the hood of my car," she ordered, waving with her gun. The two trooped over and assumed the position.

Giannini shifted the aim of the revolver and fired, the .44 magnum Federal Hydra-Shok round tearing through the thin metal of the hood of the El Camino as if it didn't exist and continuing through the engine block before ending its path in the asphalt. She fired twice more, ignoring Nickie's screams of protest.

"Jesus, Giannini! You didn't have to do that! That's my wheels!"

Giannini walked over and stuck the warm muzzle into Nickie's back. "You want to see what else I'm going to do?"

Nickie's eyes grew wide. "But—but—"

"Get out of here." Giannini suddenly realized that Nickie was looking past her.

She whirled as a Lincoln Town Car came roaring down from the other end of the street. With a screech of brakes it came to a halt thirty feet away on the other side of her car. Both front doors swung open and a man jumped out of each. The one on the right had a sawed-off shotgun; the one on the left had a semiautomatic pistol.

Giannini snapped off a shot in their direction, then dove behind Nickie's car. Nickie and his friend sprinted for the far end of the alley and were gone. Giannini heard the roar of the shotgun and the splatter of pellets against the metal of the car. She peered under the car, searching for any sign of approaching feet.

She had two rounds left in her revolver. She debated briefly whether to break open the cylinder and reload, or to take her chances with two shots against two opponents. She heard movement to her right and twisted her head. She couldn't see anything, but she knew that at least one of them was trying to outflank her.

"Give it up, Giannini!" a voice yelled out. "We only want to talk."

"Right," Giannini muttered to herself. She edged around the El Camino, listening carefully for the sound of footsteps in the garbage-encrusted street. There was the slightest rustle of an old newspaper; Giannini popped up, muzzle of her .44 magnum leading. The man with the shotgun was caught halfway between the far wall and the car, the weapon at his hip. They both fired at the same time. The shotgun pellets bounced harmlessly into the bricks ten feet above Giannini's head. Her round was more effective, hitting the gunman in the right shoulder and spinning him completely around, shotgun flying out of his hand.

The other gunman fired off two rounds, one of them smashing the windshield of the El Camino, the other whistling harmlessly down the alley as Giannini regained her cover behind the car.

"Jesus, I'm hit," the shotgun man cried out.

Giannini's confidence level was higher now that the shotgun was out of the picture. She knew that most people were notoriously inaccurate with handguns at ranges greater than ten feet. Unlike the movies, it took a lot of practice to get good with a pistol and be able to hit what you aimed at. She flipped open the cylinder to her magnum and pocketed the empty casing and one good round. Her hands moved efficiently as she removed the speed loader from her blazer pocket and loaded six new rounds with one movement.

"We can stay here all day for all I care," Giannini called out. "I radioed for backup. They should be here any minute."

"Get me out of here!" the wounded man cried out.

Giannini heard the scuffle of feet. She rolled right, coming to a halt on her stomach, arms extended, revolver aimed straight ahead. The man with the pistol was scuttling along the far wall, pistol pointing at the El Camino. He fired as fast as he could pull the trigger, covering his movement toward his partner.

His aim was somewhat better this time and Giannini felt, as much as heard, a round crack by, less than a foot away, over her head. She squeezed the trigger, feeling the gun buck in her hand. Her first round hit low, catching the gunman in the thigh, doubling him over. Her second round caught him in the chest as he sank to the pavement, punching the body back against the wall, where it came to rest, legs splayed, lifeless head lolling back against the bricks.

"Jesus Christ!" the wounded man screamed. He pulled a small-caliber revolver out of a waistband holster and began firing wildly as Giannini stood up. She snapped a round off at him, killing him instantly.

She ran to her Mustang and got in, then carefully edged around the Town Car and drove out the far end of the alley. She made her way to the Dan Ryan Expressway and headed south. It was time to circle the wagons.

Several blocks away Nickie and his friend finally stopped running. They'd heard the firing and now the distant sound of sirens.

"Damn, man, you think they killed her?" his friend asked. "I didn't sign up to be part of no cop killing. They said they just wanted to talk to her."

"I guess she didn't want to talk to them," Nickie said. He tapped the envelope full of hundred dollar bills the men had given each of them. "I don't know about you, but I'm getting the fuck out of town."

CAMP MACKALL
31 OCTOBER, 4:15 P.M.

The two bodies lay on top of the pine needles, sprawled as they had died. Despite the chill in the air, flies buzzed about, lighting on the bloody flesh.

Master leaned over and looked at the empty eye socket where a bullet had torn through. The impact of three more rounds showed on the front of the man's face. Master slowly ran a gloved hand along the lifeless cheek, then withdrew it. He glanced over at the analyst, who was crouched by the other body. "Well?"

"I can't tell. There's blood around his mouth. The armor stopped most of the rounds. He's got a wound in the neck that nicked the artery, but I'm not sure that's what did him in. Looks like he got hit in the neck with some blunt object. I guess that's what killed him."

Master straightened and looked around. Two other members of his team appeared over the lip of the depression, weapons at the ready. "Two vehicles," the lead man announced. "Tire tracks come in and go out." He held up a mangled piece of metal and plastic. "The bug from Riley's car." The man jerked a thumb over his shoulder. "The van is parked about four hundred meters that way—it's been ransacked."

"*Two* vehicles?" Master repeated.

The analyst cursed. "We've lost them."

Master shook his head. "No. We'll find them." He looked down at the bodies. "We'll find them," he promised.

CHAPTER 14

FALLS CHURCH, VIRGINIA
31 OCTOBER, 5:00 P.M.

"What's the status?" the man at the end of the table asked. He was seated in a high-backed chair, his face hidden in the shadows cast by the track lighting on the bookcase behind him. The glare illuminated the other three people seated in the room.

"We've got seven bodies and two major incidents we've had to clear up," the lone woman said. She held up a three-and-a-half-inch disk and waved it at the others. "Now we have Chicago querying the status of the Cobbs."

"It's getting out of control," the second man whined. "We need to get out while we can."

"Get out? *Get out?*" the man growled. His face was heavily lined— the price of years of decision-making—and his hair was white. The faint trace of a scar ran from below his left eye to his neck. He slapped his palm on the tabletop and glared. "There is no getting out, Simon." His voice returned to normal. "What does Chicago know, Ms. Jamieson?"

"Donnelly ran an initial status on the Cobbs in her local file, Mr. Getty. Of course she got a green. Then she double-checked, running the request to Lodestar. Again she got green."

"And?" Getty prompted.

"And nothing. Donnelly's satisfied. She thinks Giannini was trying to dig up something on the Fastone case for the locals."

"That's not good," the third man spoke. He pushed his round spectacles farther up on his nose. "We don't want them to push on Fastone."

Simon leaned forward. "If that idiot Master hadn't—"

Getty raised a hand and Simon immediately fell silent. "Master doesn't know everything and doesn't need to know more than he already does. We can't change what has happened. We must focus on the situation as it is and decide what to do next." He rubbed his scar briefly and then looked at Ms. Jamieson. "Summarize the loose ends."

"Three. Lisa Cobb, of course. This army man, Riley. And now Detective Giannini of the Chicago police."

"Options?" Getty inquired.

"There are no options," Ms. Jamieson replied. "We have to terminate all loose ends."

"Do it," Getty said. He focused his hard eyes on Simon. "I want you to go down there and take personal charge of this mess."

INDIANAPOLIS, INDIANA
31 OCTOBER, 5:55 P.M.

The signs flashed by and Giannini fumbled with the map with one hand, trying to make the decision between I-65 south off the beltway or I-74 east. She made her choice and let the split for I-65 go by, driving to the next exit, where she got on I-74.

It had taken two hours for her hands to stop shaking after leaving Chicago. She'd killed a man years ago during a bank robbery, but it hadn't been as quick and brutal as the exchange in the alley.

Less than three minutes onto the new route, her portable buzzed. She punched the receive button. "Hello?"

"It's me," she heard Riley say. "What do you have?"

"Well, hello to you too," she said dryly. "I got a whole lot of trouble is what I have." Giannini told him about the ambush in the alley.

"Are you all right?" was Riley's first concern.

"I don't feel too hot, but I'm all right."

"Are you being followed?"

"No, I'm clean."

"So you think these two men were from the mob?" Riley asked.

"I'm sure of it. My little friend Nickie must have set me up after I talked to him this morning. There's a hell of a lot more going on here than meets the eye." She quickly relayed all she had found out since the last time they talked: the money Philip Cobb supposedly had hidden, the fact that Philip Cobb had been set up by the feds, and the puzzling fact that the Witness Protection Program listed the Cobbs as being safe and sound.

"There must be a mole in the Program if someone's manipulating the computer," Riley commented when she was done. "That's bad."

"No shit, it's bad," Giannini retorted, feeling the stress of the last forty-eight hours and her near death. "It means we might not be able to get help from them like we hoped. Donnelly thought I was there fishing for information on Fastone's murder. I'm sure she's already called my department, and they're just looking for an excuse to take my badge. The fact that I just left two bodies lying in an alley means they can have it. As for the mole, it doesn't have to be someone in the Program messing with the computer. If you have the proper code words, you can access pretty much any system over the phone lines."

"I don't understand something," Riley said. "If the mob is after Cobb not only because he put away the Torrentinos, but also because he stole a lot of money, why'd they kill him? Seems like they'd want him alive."

"We don't know he *is* dead," Giannini said. "We only have Lisa's word on that."

"How much do you trust Lisa?" Riley asked.

"I don't know her at all, really," Giannini admitted. "I trusted her brother," she said, emphasizing the past tense.

There was a long silence, which Giannini bore as long as possible before she felt compelled to speak again. "Well? What now?" She glanced reflexively in the rearview mirror. "I'm on the road heading in your direction. The feds are certainly going to be checking up on me, and the Chicago PD might well find out about what happened in that alley if they find Nickie or his friend. I figured it was time for me to get the hell out of Dodge before the next big gunfight."

"I don't know what to do," Riley replied. "We're getting out of town and going undercover for the time being. We had our own little incident here not too long ago." He told her of the attack by the two men in the van. "I guess you ought to join us and we can try to figure out something. This has gone beyond what I can deal with right now. These people are using top-notch equipment, and sooner or later the group with superior firepower is bound to win."

"Where are you heading?" Giannini asked.

"The Smokies," Riley said.

"Where can I link up with you?"

"You know where," Riley said. "Remember when we went there? The place where we had that talk? I'll be keeping an eye on it and I'll see you there. You're going to have to walk in from the main road."

Giannini didn't hesitate. "Yeah, I know where you're talking about. I figure it will take me about another eight hours or so of driving to get there."

"There's no rush. We won't be on the ground until sometime early in the morning. Try to make it there tomorrow after it's light."

"All right."

"I'll see you then. Be safe."

CAMP MACKALL
31 OCTOBER, 5:57 P.M.

Riley put down the receiver and glanced around the entrance to Camp Mackall. The MH-47s still sat on the landing pad outside the gate, awaiting their night missions. A group of students were practicing on the rappelling tower set in the tree line, sliding the sixty feet down to the ground on nylon ropes. Satisfied the area was still secure, Riley picked up the receiver and called Sergeant Major Alexander, informing him that his daughter's car was in the parking lot and that he had left the keys at the Selection and Assessment committee shack.

On time, Hammer pulled up in his truck and Riley slid in next to Lisa. "Giannini's on her way down," he said as Hammer drove them away from the camp to the new hide site, six miles away.

"She meeting us here?" Hammer asked.

"No. We're taking a ride tonight to get us away from here." Riley pointed at the dirt road that ran behind Mackall. "Let's head out there and wait for dark."

FORT BRAGG
31 OCTOBER, 7:23 P.M.

"Anything?" Master asked.

The analyst didn't turn around. "I'm getting a message in from Virginia."

Master got out of his chair, crossed the small space separating them inside the van, and peered over the man's shoulder. "What do they want now?"

"They're sending someone down to take charge."

"Shit," Master muttered. "That's all I need. Anything else?"

The analyst tapped the keyboard for a few seconds. "They've added another name to the target list."

"Who?"

"A Donna Giannini. Chicago police."

Master went back to his chair and sat down, massaging his temples. "A cop? Why?"

The analyst read the information as it came in. "She's connected to Lisa Cobb. Apparently she's the one who got this Riley fellow involved and she's been checking on the situation."

"So that's why they're sending someone down—they're afraid of losing control," Master mused. "If she's Chicago PD, why are they telling us? That's out of our area."

The analyst turned and looked at Master. "They got a contact on her using her portable phone less than two hours ago. They bounced it back through the relay towers and she was somewhere around Indianapolis when she took the call."

"Indianapolis?" Master drummed his fingers on the chair as he considered this fact. "Anything on the conversation?"

"Not yet, sir. The computer was logged on with the call and location. It will take them some time to access the tapes and get the conversation."

"Where was the number she was talking to?"

"You can't trace the other end," the analyst explained. "We could only find where the call went from landline to radio and get the mobile's approximate position."

"All right." Master flipped open a road atlas and looked at the Indiana map. "She's heading south, at least. That means she's coming closer to us. So all the players are coming home to roost. The question is: where?"

CAMP MACKALL
31 OCTOBER, 7:45 P.M.

Riley, Hammer, and Lisa Cobb were off the western edge of the Camp Mackall reservation, about two miles from the Rowe Training Facility. Riley handed Lisa a canteen cup of hot noodle soup and then sat down

on the ground, his back against his rucksack. Lisa was sitting on the
tailgate of Hammer's truck, alongside the owner, who had his knife
out and was whittling again.

"You said your husband worked for the Torrentinos, laundering money,"
Riley opened the conversation, uncertain how to proceed.

"Yes," Lisa answered, the canteen cup paused halfway to her lips.

"Did you know anything about it before the police showed up at
your door?"

"I told you I didn't." Lisa's voice was cold.

"But didn't you wonder where your husband was getting his money?"

"My husband used to make very good money in his business. I didn't
look at his books."

"But . . ." Riley hesitated for a second. "Did your husband—after
everything came out in the open—ever talk about money he had hidden away?"

Hammer stopped whittling and swiveled his head to look at Lisa.

"What do you mean, 'money he had hidden away'?"

"I mean exactly what I said," Riley replied. He gestured about. "We're
out here with our asses on the line because someone wants you dead,
but it appears that it's more than simply a case of the mob wanting
revenge. Giannini found out there might be a lot of money involved—
money that your husband skimmed or stole or whatever. Someone just
tried to kill Donna." Riley's irritation was clear in his voice. "I want
to—scratch that—I *need* to know what the hell is going on. Is there
something you aren't telling us?"

"I don't know what you're talking about," Lisa said, her body stiffening.

Riley couldn't accept that. There were too many unconnected pieces
of the puzzle. "Your husband called Fastone, right? Or at least that's
how you think she ended up down there in Charlotte."

"Yes."

"And you're pretty sure it was his body you saw outside your motel
room door?"

"Yes."

"So maybe Fastone got the location of the money," Riley reasoned
out loud. "Or maybe the two of them were in on it together and they
had a plan."

"I don't know what money you're talking about," Lisa repeated.

"Giannini says it's probably a couple of million dollars—money that your husband stole from the Torrentinos. That helps explain a lot of the shit that's been coming down lately. It also helps explain why Fastone was killed—one less person to know about the money."

"But it don't explain why they're still after her," Hammer said, pointing at Lisa with his knife.

"No, it doesn't," Riley acknowledged. He looked at the young woman long and hard in the waning light. "Unless, of course, your husband was killed before he told them the location of the money and they think you're the only link to it. If you have anything to tell me, do it now, before it's too late."

"I've told you everything," Lisa insisted.

Riley looked from her to Hammer, who shrugged and went back to his whittling. He stared at Lisa until finally she broke the eye contact. "All right, then," he said, not sure what to believe anymore.

CHAPTER 15

CAMP MACKALL LANDING PAD
31 OCTOBER, 11:22 P.M.

They could hear the two helicopters long before the blacked-out sil-
houettes appeared, hovering low over the tree line to the west of the
landing pad. The choppers had been active for the past three hours,
running exfiltration missions, and they'd dropped off the last load of
students ten minutes ago. They'd circled for a while before coming
back—as per the plan Riley had arranged with Chief Warrant Officer
4th Class Prowley.

"Ready?" Riley asked, placing a reassuring hand on Lisa's shoulder.

She nodded, her face tight with anxiety. She was dressed in a loose-
fitting pair of jungle fatigue pants and shirt that Riley had stolen off
one of the drying racks outside the tin shack barracks on the compound.
His lightweight jacket was zipped up tightly around her neck, and her
short hair was stuffed under a black watch cap. Anyone looking closely
would be able to tell she was female, but that didn't particularly bother
Riley; women were often used on special operations exercises. What
worried him was someone finding out she was a civilian. The army
had rules about civilians on military flights. He'd given Lisa strict orders
not to talk to anyone aboard the aircraft. Riley had helped her buckle
on a combat vest with two canteens on top of the jacket, the bulky
black vest helping to mask her slight figure.

The lead helicopter settled down, blowing dust about; the second
remained airborne a few hundred meters off. Riley led the way around
to the left side of the bird, toward the rear where the back ramp was

settling down. Hammer followed them, carrying his own small back-pack of gear.

Riley ran up the back ramp, threw down his rucksack and submachine gun, and settled Lisa in one of the nylon web seats that lined both sides of the cargo bay. In the dim glow of the red night lights, he buckled Lisa's safety strap, waving off the crew chief who had come over to help.

"You got everyone?" the crew chief yelled in Riley's ear.

"Yeah," Riley replied, giving a thumbs-up.

The crew chief mumbled something into the boom mike in front of his lips and, with a waver, the helicopter lifted, the back ramp still open to the night air.

The MH-47 was the special operations version of the venerable CH-47 Chinook, which had seen extensive service in Vietnam. Using a powerful tandem rotor configuration, the helicopter was able to carry a large load of troops long distances under adverse weather and visibility conditions. The interior of the cargo bay was large enough to hold a couple of cars or almost forty troops.

Like all other special operations aircraft, the MH-47 flew close to the earth, and Riley could see the tops of trees flicker by a few feet below the bottom of the rear ramp as they headed off to the west. He looked around the interior, noting the contents. A small pallet sat in the front middle of the cargo bay and held the crew's kit bags and luggage. Along the left bulkhead, a thick rope was tied down, its length tripled back on itself.

Riley made his way to the cockpit, where both pilots were seated, arrayed in a futuristic ensemble of night vision goggles, flight helmets, and sterile flight suits. He recognized Chief Prowley, with his hands on the controls to the right. The copilot was watching the complex array of instruments and relaying their readings to Prowley, who was dividing his time between looking at the terrain outside through the enhancement of his goggles and watching the small TV screen set in the control panel to his left front. The screens showed the terrain ahead; a computer adaptation made it look like high noon outside.

Riley grabbed a headset off a hook on the cockpit ceiling and placed the cups over his ears to listen.

"Got that microwave tower at eleven?" the copilot's voice crackled over the intercom.

"Roger," Prowley replied. "That's checkpoint two. How's the time?"

The copilot glanced at a map covered in acetate, then the glowing red time display. "We're plus four seconds on checkpoint two."

"Sounds good. How's it going, Chief?" Prowley said, finally acknowledging Riley's presence.

"All right," Riley replied. He hadn't spoken before, not wishing to distract the pilots from their task of flying, especially this close to the ground.

"So how are you getting off at your target?" Prowley asked.

"Two degrees to the left," the copilot interrupted, his eyes still intent on the instruments. In response, Prowley banked the helicopter slightly.

"I see you have a fast rope rig in the rear," Riley answered. "You don't mind if we use it, do you?"

"No, but we need to keep it. Can't be dropping off two thousand dollars worth of equipment on an unauthorized mission. The crew chief will have to winch it back in after we let you off, which means we'll have to be on station about forty seconds."

"That's no problem," Riley said. "What's time on target?"

"We've got two hundred forty miles to your drop-off point," the copilot answered. "We're going low level the whole way, so that will slow us down a bit." He consulted the grease-pencil numbers on the map. "TOT at zero-one-four-seven, give or take a few seconds."

"Okay, thanks," Riley said.

"What's this thing here, right next to where you want us to drop you?" Prowley asked, nodding at his partner, who held the map and pointed at a symbol on the paper.

"That's a tower, about fifty feet in height. You can use it as your reference point to find the place to drop us."

"Why not simply put you down in this parking lot?" the copilot asked. "We could set down there."

"It should be closed this time of year," Riley said, "but I don't want to take any chances on security. The opposing force on this exercise might have gotten the park people to open it," he added, trying to keep up the image of a training exercise.

"I'm going to put that tower right in front of my windshield when I let you all out," Prowley said. "Does it have anything on top of it, like a radio antenna?"

Riley concentrated, trying to remember. "I don't think so, but I can't guarantee that."

"We'll take it slow and careful then," Prowley said as he returned his concentration to piloting the helicopter.

Riley took off the headset and made his way back into the cargo compartment. Hammer was lying down on the far side. Riley leaned over to look at him—from all he could tell, his partner was asleep. He stepped across to where Lisa sat, her eyes wide open.

"Ever flown on a chopper before?" Riley yelled in her ear, trying to be heard above the whine of the two turbine engines.

She shook her head.

Riley didn't bother to ask if she'd ever rappelled before. He had not planned on giving her the good news until they were airborne— past the point of no return. He was glad the fast rope was on board; if it hadn't been, his plan was to use the nylon rope he had in his pack and standard-rappel out off the back ramp. That would have been much more difficult for Lisa, to say the least.

"Listen," he yelled in Lisa's ear. "When we get to the mountains, the helicopter isn't going to be able to land. We're going to have to use that to get off." He pointed at the thick rope. "That's called a fast rope, and it's very simple to use." He proceeded to explain how it was employed. Her eyes grew wider as the helicopter made its way west across North Carolina, leaving the flatland of the seaboard behind.

POPE AIR FORCE BASE, NORTH CAROLINA
1 NOVEMBER, 12:10 A.M.

The unmarked Lear jet touched down and swiftly braked to taxiing speed. Master watched it approach from his position in front of his command van. He was reflexively squeezing a climbing ball in his left hand, the effort causing the muscles in his forearm to ripple.

The jet's hatch swung open and a small set of stairs descended, down which a young man in a three-piece suit bounded. The man had thinning blond hair and clear-rimmed spectacles; he carried a large briefcase in his left hand and a smaller one in his right. He put down the small one and extended his right hand as he came up to Master, but the older man ignored it.

"You're the guy I talk to in Virginia?" Master asked.

"Yes, I'm here to—" Simon began.

"Shut up," Master ordered, cutting him off, his eyes glinting dangerously in the glow of the airfield landing lights. "This is *my* operation and these are *my* people. You got anything to say, you say it to me, but otherwise you keep the fuck out of my way."

Simon positioned the small briefcase between them. "It might be your people and your operation, but it's *our* money. So far, *your* operation hasn't gone very well. That's why I'm here—to make sure it does." With that, he turned and climbed into the van, Master following, eyes glinting furiously.

As soon as the side door slid shut, the vehicle began moving. Master, seated in a swivel chair, waited a few moments to calm down before turning to face Simon, who was in one of the fixed chairs bolted to the floor. "Do you have the conversation this cop Giannini had?"

Simon opened his briefcase and pulled out a laptop computer. He turned it on and slipped in a three-and-a-half-inch disk, while handing a copy to Master's analyst. "The transcript is on the disk. She was talking to Riley. They set up a meeting in the Great Smoky Mountains."

"Where in the mountains?" Master demanded.

Simon gestured at the disk. "They didn't say. See for yourself."

Master turned and looked at the computer screen as the analyst scrolled up the conversation. When Master had looked at all of it, he turned back to Simon. "Do you have anything on Riley?"

"I've got records on him—including his black file, or at least what I could get access to; it wasn't complete. He's been involved in several classified operations." Simon scanned the screen. "In eighty-nine his Special Forces team got involved in an operation on mainland China during the Tiananmen Square riots. The pages are missing as to what the operation was or its purpose, but based on the security codes it was very high level. In ninety-one he was part of the covert raids the DOD and CIA launched into Colombia to destroy the cocaine-processing plants there."

"I heard about those missions," Master said. "Go on."

Simon shook his head. "There's some reference to a domestic operation last year in Chicago, but we couldn't get access to what happened. All we know is that's where he met Giannini—she was involved in it also."

"Domestic?" Master repeated with a frown. "How the hell was some SF guy involved in a domestic op?" When Simon didn't answer, he leaned forward. "Give me his two-oh-one file."

Simon passed him the manila folder and Master scanned the officer record brief (ORB). The acronyms told him all he wanted to know about his adversary.

DOB 08/12/59
BIRTHPLACE- NEW YORK
SEX/RACE- M/WHITE
NUMBER DEPENDANTS- 0
RELIGION- N/A
MARITAL STATUS- SINGLE
HEIGHT/WEIGHT- 67/150
EDUCATION- ASSOCIATES DEGREE
AWARDS AND DECORATIONS-
    AAM (army achievement medal)- 04
    ASR (army service ribbon)- 01
    ARCOM (army commendation medal)- 03
    MSM (meritorious service medal)- 02
    Ranger Tab
    SF Tab
    Master Parachutist Badge
    Expert Infantry Badge
    Foreign Jump Wings—Thailand, Panama, Republic
      of Korea

Schooling: Infantry One Stop Unit Training 1977; Airborne 1977; Ranger School 1979; Special Forces Qualification Course 1980; Jumpmaster School 1981; Malaysian Tracking School 1982; Republic of Korea Mountain Commando School 1983; Special Operations Training 1985; Special Forces Operations and Intelligence School 1986; Special Forces Warrant Officer School 1990; Nuclear Weapons Safeguards School 1990.

"A fucking airborne, ranger, hero," Master said out loud. "Let's see where he's been." He looked at Riley's assignment history, which was listed in reverse order, with the most current assignment at the top.

    93/08 1st Special Warfare Training Group, Fort Bragg—
          Instructor/Writer
    93/04 Walter Reed Holding Det.—Convalescent leave

92/10   5th Special Forces Group, Fort Campbell—Detach-
        ment executive officer
90/07   7th Special Forces Group, Fort Bragg—Detachment
        executive officer
90/03   Warrant Officer Accession Course—Student
89/07   Walter Reed Holding Det.—Convalescent leave
88/02   Special Forces Detachment Korea—Detachment
        operations sergeant
84/02   7th Special Forces Group, Fort Bragg—Detachment
        senior engineer
80/06   1st Battalion, 1st Special Forces Group (forward),
        Okinawa—Detachment junior engineer
80/01   Special Forces Qualification Course—Student
77/08   82d Airborne Division, Fort Bragg
77/02   One stop unit training, Fort Benning

"You don't know why he was in the hospital twice, do you?" Master
asked.

Simon shook his head. "All we know is the first one coincides with
the mission into mainland China and the second one with whatever
happened up in Chicago."

"So he wasn't kissing babies wherever he was," Master said. "He
got shot up, or blown up, or tripped over his own feet and hurt himself. Given what he's done here so far, and looking at these records,
I'd say we've got ourselves an M-1, A-1, badass hero." Master leaned
back in his chair. "We'll have to play this one tight."

He flipped open his atlas. "The Smokies are a big area to go looking in, but we'll get them." He looked down at the full-length photo
of Riley dressed in his class A greens, which was clipped to the inside of the folder. "And this time you won't get away, Mr. Riley," he
whispered to himself.

KNOXVILLE, TENNESSEE
1 NOVEMBER, 12:20 A.M.

Giannini checked into the first motel she found off the interstate, paying
cash for her room and signing a false name on the registration card.
She didn't think the subterfuge was worth the effort, since the sleepy

clerk barely spared her a glance before disappearing into a back room
to go back to sleep. She'd wanted to continue on to the rendezvous
point, but Riley had said to show up in the daylight, so she figured
that Knoxville was as good a place to stop as any.

Her room was in the rear of the motel, and she parked her car right
in front of the door. After putting on the chain, securing the dead bolt,
and closing the curtains, she lay down on the bed, fully clothed, with
her revolver at her side ready for use. She was almost certain she hadn't
been followed, but after her last conversation with Dave, she wasn't
going to take any chances. The muted roar of trucks rumbling down
the highway echoed through the room as she closed her eyes and waited
for sleep to come, trying to keep her mind from wondering what the
daylight would bring.

CHAPTER 16

GREAT SMOKY MOUNTAINS
1 NOVEMBER, 1:37 A.M.

"Ten minutes!" the crew chief yelled. "Give me a hand with this," he added, tapping Riley on the shoulder.

Together, they secured the looped end of the fast rope to a bolt in the roof of the helicopter, just ahead of the back ramp. For the past hour, the ride had gotten increasingly hair-raising as the Piedmont gave way to the foothills of the Smokies. As they worked, they could feel the extra weight as the pilots added power to gain altitude up the southeastern slopes of the mountains.

The crew chief kept the bulk of the fast rope in place by wrapping a loop of cargo strap around it. Riley pulled on his rucksack and secured it by buckling the waistband tight around his hips. Hammer did the same with his backpack. They cinched down the slings on their weapons and secured those over their shoulder. Riley then took his twelve-foot length of sling rope and slipped it through snap links on the front of his combat vest, one on each shoulder. He tied off open loops on the two free ends and stuffed the slack in empty ammo pouches on each hip, securing the Velcro fasteners on top.

"You ready?" Riley asked Lisa.

She nodded. She was clenching and unclenching her hands nervously. The open ramp right next to them, the high-pitched whine of the turbine engines, the trees going by just below—all combined to make a frightening scene. Riley had seen trained military men verging on panic in similar situations.

"You go right after Hammer. Just hold on tight and slide. All right?" Riley peered at her, making sure he got eye contact.

"Hold on tight and slide?" she repeated, incredulously. "That's it?"

"That's it," Riley said.

"Five minutes!" The crew chief grabbed a monkey harness off the wall and buckled the straps around his body. He then hooked the end of the tether into an O-bolt on the floor of the helicopter. He played out the slack, walking toward the back ramp, and then cinched down the line to prevent him from falling out the back. He opened up a plastic case, pulled out a set of night vision goggles, and slipped them on.

Riley peered out the back. The terrain below had changed in more ways than its topography. The lights of civilization had been left behind. Riley assumed that a small glow to the left rear was the town of Cherokee, North Carolina. Beyond that there was only the darkness of the forest. Riley edged his way closer to the ramp and, grabbing the ramp's hydraulic lift, peered out. High ridges loomed like black walls on either side. The helicopter was still going up the valley, heading toward the crest.

"Two minutes," the crew chief yelled.

A sudden swing to the left caught Riley by surprise, and his fingers tightened on the metal in reflex. Lisa fell to the floor; Hammer leaned over and lifted her to her feet, wrapping one arm around her and the other around a metal strut along the side of the aircraft. He was yelling in her ear, trying to get her to focus on the upcoming event.

The black walls on either side had disappeared. The helicopter was now flying on top of a ridge, moving to the southwest, barely twenty feet above the highest treetops. Riley peered down: he occasionally could make out a black opening below where a two-lane road also followed the ridgeline. They were right on course.

"One minute." The helicopter was slowing. A large open area passed by to the left, about a hundred yards away. Another two hundred feet up in altitude and a quarter mile to the southwest, the pilot brought the craft to a hover.

The crew chief threw out the fast rope, then leaned over to make sure it was touching the ground forty feet below in a small clearing surrounded by tall trees. "Go!"

Riley took Hammer's place holding Lisa, and nodded his head toward the ramp. Hammer reached out and wrapped both massive arms around the rope. His teeth glinted in the glow of the red lights. He shouted "Later!" as he stepped off the ramp and slid out of sight.

"Grab it tight," Riley advised Lisa unnecessarily.

She pulled the rope in tight to her chest and moved her feet back until she could feel the edge of the ramp under her sneakers. The cold night air swirled in the back ramp, chilling her, and the whine of the engines combined with the thunder of the massive blades overhead. She looked at Riley and he nodded. Lisa froze. "I can't!" she screamed at him.

The crew chief gestured downward, "Go! Go!"

Riley had been prepared for this. He pulled the loops on the sling rope out of the ammo pouches, then hooked each end into the snap links on the shoulder of Lisa's vest, the fast rope now locked in between them. He grabbed her upper arms. "On three."

"No!" Lisa screamed back.

With a deep breath, Riley slid sideways until his feet were also on the edge of the ramp. "Two!"

"Please don't," she begged.

He stepped back, pulling Lisa with him. Their weight pulled them away from the ramp, and the thick, soft rope raced through between them. The impact with the ground was surprising, but not as hard as Riley had feared it would be. They stood still for a moment, savoring the feel of land beneath their feet.

"Let go!" Riley yelled over the noise of the chopper, grabbing Lisa's hands and prying them loose from his jacket sleeve. He popped the ends of the sling rope loose from the snap links on her vest and stepped back. He waved up at the black silhouette of the helicopter, knowing that the crew chief could see him clearly through the night vision goggles. He then unslung the silenced FA-MAS and made sure it was ready for action.

The fast rope lifted slightly and then more quickly as the helicopter gained altitude. In thirty seconds the sound of the aircraft was a distant mutter to the northeast, and then there was silence. Riley looked around. The observation tower that had so concerned Prowley was to their front. They were standing in a small clearing at the base of the long curving concrete ramp that gave access to the tower. Weatherbeaten pine trees crowded up on all sides.

"This tower is the highest point in the Great Smoky Mountains National

Park. We're on top of Clingmans Dome right now," Riley informed Lisa and Hammer. He pointed off in the darkness to the left. "The Appalachian Trail runs along the ridgeline and is off in that direction a hundred meters or so." He gestured in the opposite direction. "We'll go this way about two hundred meters and then bed down for the rest of the night. That ought to be far enough away from the trail and the tower so that even if someone heard the bird and comes to investigate, we'll be all right."

With that, he turned and led the way into the dark woods. Lisa followed directly behind him, her right hand on his rucksack, letting him guide her through the woods. Hammer took the trail position, allowing a little distance between himself and Lisa, his own FA-MAS ready for action.

KNOXVILLE
1 NOVEMBER, 3:45 A.M.

Giannini awoke, slightly better for her couple of hours sleep. Leaving the key in the room and the door unlocked, she went out to her car and started the engine. Riley had said to arrive after first light, but Giannini didn't feel comfortable waiting. She wanted to get there and enjoy the relative safety of being with Riley. Thirty seconds later she was on the interstate.

GREAT SMOKY MOUNTAINS
1 NOVEMBER, 3:55 A.M.

Riley scanned the surrounding woods, holding his eyes slightly off-center to use the night-vision portion of the retina. He could hear the slight rumble of Hammer snoring and the uneasy movements of Lisa Cobb's troubled sleep, but he tuned those out. He could swear he had heard something. He shook his head: he was tired, having not slept in quite a while, and he must have dozed off.

Shifting position, Riley pulled in the collar of his heavy-duty parka, feeling a chill run through his bones. It was coid up here, the lateness of the season combining with the altitude to drop the temperature into the midthirties. He settled down, leaning back against his ruck, and closed his eyes. As he drifted off to sleep, his last conscious thought was to wonder where Giannini was.

PIGEON FORGE, TENNESSEE
1 NOVEMBER, 4:43 A.M.

It was the off-season, and the middle of the night, and for that Giannini was grateful. Pigeon Forge, besides being home to Dolly Parton's theme park, Dollywood, was the outlet shop, motel, gift shop capital of Tennessee, and traffic on a normal summer day was usually at a standstill along Route 441. She passed a museum advertising Buford Pusser's "death car" and an indoor skydiving building, where participants could hover in a stationary position above an updraft. She felt a long way from Chicago and wondered what on earth she was doing here. Between what had happened at Tom Volpe's house and the events of a few hours ago, she knew her life would never be the same. The only thing certain about the immediate future was the obvious fact that it was going to be very dangerous.

She looked up, beyond the clusters of neon signs. The tops of the Smokies disappeared into a bluish gray haze highlighted in the moonlight. The steep tree-covered slopes beckoned ominously. It was rough terrain, and the road she was on—441—was the only one that cut through the park, connecting Tennessee with North Carolina.

She passed the turnoff for Dollywood, and then Pigeon Forge was behind her. Gatlinburg—the last stop in civilization this side of North Carolina—was next. Giannini took the bypass, circling the town to the west, going under the massive cables that carried the tram out of Gatlinburg into the nearby mountains. The four-lane road narrowed down to two lanes, and the terrain closed in on both sides. The Sugarland Visitors' Center was at the border of the park. Signs flashed in her headlights, warning of possible road closings in case of bad weather. The red metal barriers were open this morning, though, and Giannini passed through.

As she entered the park itself, the clouds closed in like a ceiling, totally blocking out the stars and moon. The weather report on the radio called for intermittent clouds all day with the possibility of a storm late in the evening or early the next day. Route 441 was now called the Newfound Gap Road; Giannini's destination lay almost halfway along the road, astride the Tennessee–North Carolina border. It was fifteen miles from Gatlinburg to the Gap, and negotiating the winding road that often switched back on itself to climb the steep slopes gave Giannini time to reflect on the last time she was here.

It had been in the late spring. She'd driven down from Chicago to see Riley, and they'd agreed to meet in Knoxville. She'd felt tentative about the trip. The only other times she'd visited Riley he'd been laid up in his hospital bed recovering from the wounds he'd received in the Chicago mission. He'd called shortly after he arrived at Fort Bragg and started his new assignment. She could tell he was nervous and uncertain—something that surprised her given the confidence and self-assurance he'd displayed when they had worked together. It hadn't really occurred to her at the time that in calling her and arranging the "date," Riley had been entering uncomfortable, unfamiliar territory.

Driving down for that trip she had also experienced a bit of nervousness, but that had changed to irritation when she met Riley and discovered his plans for the weekend. She had envisioned a nice hotel and a romantic dinner, but instead Riley had handed her a backpack. They were going camping in the mountains.

She'd hidden her disappointment and gone along with the plan; to her surprise, the effort was more than worth it. The city girl discovered that she loved the quiet serenity of the trails and the spectacular views that would suddenly appear as they crested a ridge or hilltop. They spent two days walking a loop that started and ended at Newfound Gap. The last day—on the way back—they stopped at the Clingmans Dome observation tower. It was there that Riley finally touched her— moving tentatively behind her and taking her in his arms. And this was after spending two nights sleeping in the same tent, inches apart. The lack of physical contact was Giannini's second surprise of the weekend. Like the first, it initially bothered her; then, as time went by, it became something she appreciated. After two nasty divorces and a job that put her in contact with cops and criminals all day long, Giannini was used to being on the defensive. She was pleased by the respect Riley showed her, and his willingness to have patience. It was a welcome change.

When Riley told her to meet him at the place where they had "that talk," she knew immediately what he meant. They'd spent four hours on the observation tower and Riley had opened up to her, talking about his life and the things he'd done, and she found herself doing the same.

It was a special time—one of those interludes in the hectic craziness of their everyday lives that both had cherished afterward.

Giannini shook her head as she took a hairpin turn. It had also been a time they had not been able to repeat due to the demands of their jobs. No, she corrected herself, she might as well be honest: she had not made the effort to see Riley because the relationship scared her. She realized she felt closer to him—after that one weekend—than she had to any man, and it made her feel vulnerable. She had told herself that she didn't want to get involved with a man whose job could easily take him halfway around the world on a moment's notice and could get him killed just as quickly. And now, Giannini thought to herself, she was the one who had put this man in danger. She wished she had made more of an effort to be with Riley instead of always finding excuses.

As the road made its way up toward the Gap, the oak-hickory forest gave way to spruce and fir trees, part of an ancient forest that extended along the back of the Appalachians from Maine to Georgia. The cloud cover was only a few hundred feet overhead, reflecting a faint glow from her high beams. On the left side a steep mountain stream tumbled over rocks as it raced down the hillside. On the right, the terrain took off steeply, angling up at almost a sixty-degree slope into the darkness. Giannini had yet to see any other traffic on the road, which would soon be closed for the winter.

The road slid into the clouds, and wisps of gray flew past like ghosts in the bright light. Giannini slowed further. The road went through a short tunnel and then looped back on itself, crossing over the roof of the tunnel.

The car punched through the gray clouds, and Giannini was surprised by a patch of moonlight that splashed across the windshield and then just as quickly disappeared behind higher white clouds. The road leveled off, and then the parking area for Newfound Gap appeared. Giannini passed the lot and drove toward the intersection of the Gap road with the Clingmans Dome access road. It was there she found the first obstacle. A red metal pole was locked across the tar road, denying access. Giannini turned around, drove the hundred meters back to Newfound Gap, and left her car in the parking area there.

She now remembered Riley saying she would have to walk in; at the time she had assumed he meant from the Clingmans Dome parking area. She got out of the car and checked the map posted on the wall of the small shelter.

"Goddamn," she muttered when she saw it was seven miles from Newfound Gap to Clingmans Dome. She went back to her car and opened the trunk, replacing her flats with the sneakers she used at murder scenes. She also grabbed the set of coveralls, having a feeling she might need them. Leaving the car behind, Giannini slipped under the metal barrier and set off up the road.

CHEROKEE, NORTH CAROLINA
1 NOVEMBER, 7:15 A.M.

While Giannini was making her way to the park from the north, Master and his men had driven up from the south. Two vans were parked in the lot behind the Oconaluftee Visitors' Center awaiting his instructions. Master was currently seated in his van beside the driver as they negotiated the streets of Cherokee.

"There," Master ordered, pointing to the left. "Pull in there."

The driver did as ordered, rolling onto the gravel in front of a small round building whose walls consisted mostly of glass. Two helicopters sat in the field behind the building; the sign in front advertised "Mountain Flights, Inc."

Master had ignored the presence of Simon for the entire ride across North Carolina, and he continued to do so as he stepped to the back of the van. He pulled open a drawer and thumbed through various IDs until he found what he needed.

"Wait here," Master ordered Simon as he put his hand on the door latch.

"Where are you going?" Simon asked, fingering his attaché case.

"To get an idea of what we're up against here. Riley picked the Smokies for a reason, and the more I know about the area, the better chance I have of figuring out where they'll be." Master stepped out of the van and entered the building. A man seated behind the counter waved at him, continuing his conversation on the phone. The man was burly with long, dirty-blond hair tied behind his neck in a ponytail. Master walked over to a large three-dimensional model of the mountains, which was set up on a table in the center of the room. Color-coded fiberglass tubes arrayed over the terrain showed the routes the helicopters flew and how much the various excursions cost.

The man hung up the phone. "How can I help you this morning? Looking for a ride through the mountains?"

Hammer flipped open the ID case he'd chosen. "I'm Lieutenant Loggins with the Alcohol, Tobacco and Firearms Agency."

The man looked at the ID, then at Master for a second before sticking out his hand. "Jim Ferguson."

Master nodded toward the helicopters out back. "You the pilot?"

"One of them. It's kind of slow this time of year and we alternate days off."

Master turned his attention back to the map board. "You know this area pretty well?"

Ferguson shrugged. "I fly over it. I haven't been on the ground much except for driving through. But, yeah, I guess I know it pretty well. What do you need?"

"We're looking for some fugitives and we think they might be hiding out in the park," Master said.

Ferguson whistled. "It's a damn big park."

"If *you* were planning to hide out, where would you go?"

"These people driving a car?"

Master paused and considered the question. They'd spotted the Camaro parked at the Rowe Training Facility. The sergeant major who'd come to pick up the car had professed ignorance, and Master had ordered his men to back off—they had made enough of a scene already around Fort Bragg. There was still that other set of tire tracks leading away from the spot where the two men had been killed. Master could think of no other way they could have gotten up here. "They got here by car, but we think they're on foot now."

Ferguson looked down at the model. "Like I said, it's off-season here and the whole park is pretty empty, but the least traveled area is here"— he pointed at the southwest corner of the map—"down by Fontana Lake on the North Carolina side. The Tennessee side is much more active."

"Where could they leave a car down there?"

"Pretty much anywhere. You can check with the park rangers. There's a ranger living down there right along Route 28. If someone's in that area, it's likely he'll know."

Master looked at the large area the map covered and considered Riley's background. "What about up in the mountains?"

Ferguson's finger waved through the air tracing the roads around the perimeter of the park. "You have a heck of a climb to get any height." He pointed at a black line bisecting the area. "Newfound Gap Road cuts right through and there's a parking area here." He pointed at a small black space high up in the mountains. "There's a lot of trails in this area, and you can go off in any direction and disappear within a hundred yards."

Master was silent for a minute, ignoring the fidgeting of the pilot. He couldn't even be certain that Riley was here yet, but the odds were he was. Giannini had to be en route, because the transcript indicated she was not to arrive until after daylight. He wanted to catch them all together and end this thing. If he could spot her moving in, he might be able to follow her. He suddenly looked up. "We need to hire you for the day."

Ferguson blinked. "I run three hundred and fifty an hour." He eyed Master suspiciously. "And I need half that up front."

Master reached into his jacket pocket and pulled out a wad of money, peeled off two thousand in hundred dollar bills, and handed them over. "Get your bird cranked up."

Master turned and strode out to the van. Getting inside, he looked at Simon. "What do you have on Giannini?"

"I've got an outline of her file and—"

"I need a description and what kind of car she's driving."

Simon irritably flipped over a few pages. He'd come down here expecting to be in charge and was none too happy about the way he'd been treated since getting off the jet. Despite that, there was something in Master's eyes that told him to hold any complaining until he was safe in the cocoon of his Virginia office. "Here's a fax of her photo, and she's driving a 1988 red Mustang GT."

Master looked at the photo and then at the analyst. "All right. I want Surveillance One to head down to the vicinity of Fontana Lake. Check for Giannini's car. She should be coming in soon. Make sure they talk to the park ranger for that area. Have Two and Three head up to Newfound Gap and station themselves there. I'm going to look over this area from the air. I'll take a portable with me to maintain commo with you at this location."

"Yes, sir."

Simon raised a hand as Master turned to leave. "What do you want me to do?"

"I already told you that—stay out of my way." Master stepped out of the van and scanned the panorama of tree-covered mountains. You have to come out sometime, he thought, and when you do, I'll be waiting.

CHAPTER 17

GREAT SMOKY MOUNTAINS
1 NOVEMBER, 8:20 A.M.

"You stay here with Lisa," Riley ordered as he checked the functioning on the FA-MAS rifle. He pulled back the charging handle and replaced the slightly damp cartridge that had been in the chamber all night.

"Roger that, Chief," Hammer replied. He was rummaging through Riley's rucksack. "What are you going to do?"

"I'm heading up to the tower to look for Giannini. She should be here this morning."

"Then what?" Lisa asked. The few hours of sleep on Riley's quarter-inch-thick sleeping pad had not provided much rest. Her hair was disheveled, and dark shadows under her eyes showed her weariness. "Do we just hide up here forever?"

"I don't know," Riley said. "As far as we can tell, someone's tapped into the computer at the Witness Protection Program. That explains a lot, but we don't know who that somebody is, and until we do we're making stabs in the dark." Riley spread his arms helplessly. "I don't know what to do next. I tried to outsmart these guys and it almost got my head blown off. All I know is that the next step is to get Donna Giannini here with us. Then we can sit down and figure out what to do without having to worry that someone's ass is hanging out in the wind."

"I know what *I'm* doing next," Hammer said cheerfully. He looked at Lisa. "How about some nice warm nectar of the gods?" he asked, holding up Riley's portable stove and some instant coffee. He started pumping the primer on the stove without waiting.

"I'll be back by noon," Riley said, touching Lisa on the arm. "We'll figure out something then."

Lisa watched him leave and then turned her attention to Hammer, who was concentrating on the task at hand. "You don't seem very concerned about all this."

Hammer chuckled and shook his head. "I don't worry about things I can't control." He looked up at her. "Bullshit is part of every job description in the army, and a long time ago I learned to go with the flow."

He peered in the canteen cup on top of the stove to check the water. Then he looked at her and his expression became serious. "Listen, I spent three years fighting a war that no one even talks about anymore. A war that some assholes in Washington started and then pissed away. If that wasn't bullshit, I don't know what was."

"But you stayed in the reserves, or else you wouldn't be here," Lisa noted.

"Not at first. I got out as soon as I returned to the States, and I swore I'd have nothing to do with the army ever again." Hammer's eyes took on a distant look. "I got back and bought a Harley, first day after I outprocessed. I took all that money I hadn't spent for three years sucking shit in the jungle and I hit the road." He laughed. "Hell, I can't even remember half the things I did or the places I went. I was high, I was drunk, I was so fucking out of it most of the time I could have *killed* people and I wouldn't have known. And the funny thing is, I wanted to kill someone. I wanted a face that I could look at and say: 'Hey, you, motherfucker, you're the one that caused my buddy Juke Taylor to get his guts blown all over the place. And you're the one that sent Team Hawaii out one day and they were never heard of again and the only reason I wasn't with them was because I was down in Nha Trang getting an infected tooth pulled.'

"I looked at everyone and thought, Maybe you're the *man*." Hammer's voice hadn't raised a decibel as he spoke. "And that I could just blow the *man* away and it would all be square. Payback.

"It took me a year and a half to figure out that that was bullshit too, and that the civilian world ain't no different. The man is us." He poked a finger at his own burly chest. "I don't have the answers, and I don't really ask the questions anymore. You got to look out for number one, lady—especially now." He seemed surprised at his own outburst and slightly embarrassed at the need to make it. "Ah, well, enough speech making. Let's have some coffee."

"Why is Riley risking his life for me?" Lisa asked. "He doesn't even know me."

"Because a friend asked him for help, and that's all the reason he needs." Hammer reached down to his cargo pocket and pulled out his tired-looking beret with the unauthorized personalized monogram sewn on the inside liner. "Probably because Riley believes in what this represents. The men I'd served with wearing this were the only thing that counted to me back then. We had honor with each other, and in this day and age that isn't a word people think too much about. But I guess Riley still believes in it. Maybe he'll learn better some-day." Hammer looked at her hard and quickly changed the subject. "Is what you told him true? You don't know nothing about the money?"

Lisa's face was tight. When she answered, her voice sounded weary. "I didn't know what my husband was into until the police showed up at my door. And all I learned, I learned from sitting in court listening to Philip testify. Nothing ever came up about him having a lot of money. Obviously, I didn't know him very well, did I?"

"But you might have an idea where he would have hidden it," Hammer said. "You know, maybe a bank account he didn't disclose to the feds. Hell, he could have kept it in cash and buried it in the backyard."

"I don't know anything about it," Lisa insisted, starting to get angry.

"Well, you can tell Riley and me that story," Hammer said calmly as he poured her some coffee. "But if these people get hold of you, they ain't gonna buy it."

8:40 A.M.

Riley skirted the wood line to the north of the Clingmans Dome tower and trail. By doing so he also avoided the Appalachian Trail, which runs along that side. The vegetation consisted of red spruce and bal-sam fir trees, many of which had been blown down by the fierce weather that often lashes the top of the mountain. The Dome is the highest point along the two thousand miles of trail, and the second-highest point on the East Coast of the United States, topped only by nearby Mount Mitchell.

A six-foot-wide tar path led from the parking area to the Dome, three-quarters of a mile to the east of the observation tower. Riley had considered getting off the helicopter in the parking lot, where the chopper would have been able to land, but he had chosen instead to come directly to the Dome for two reasons: he hadn't been certain that the parking lot was clear of trees along the side for a landing; and, on the off chance that the access road wasn't closed for the season, he felt that rappelling in on top of the Dome would be more secure than landing in the parking lot.

He expected to meet Giannini coming up the path, so he moved to a position on the side of the hill where he could look down along a straight section of the path, into the empty parking lot. Riley settled down behind an uprooted fir tree and got comfortable. The temperature was in the low fifties, and the dark clouds scurrying by not far overhead threatened bad weather later in the day.

He heard the helicopter long before he saw it. The sound of the blades was trapped between the high ground and the cloud cover. Riley pulled out a small set of binoculars from the butt pack of his combat vest and scanned the surrounding area. The aircraft was coming closer, and Riley edged along the log until he was under the cover of an upright tree. Still he could see nothing.

The helicopter roared by less than thirty feet above the treetops, coming from Riley's rear. He froze, not even daring to look up as it banked, and then he caught his first glimpse—a Bell Jet Ranger with "Mountain Flights, Inc." painted on the side. The bird did another loop around the Dome, then headed for the parking lot, following the access road to the east. Riley focused the binoculars on the helicopter and caught a glimpse of the two men seated inside—a pilot wearing a soft cap backwards with a headset, and a man in the copilot's seat, map in his lap. Riley twisted the ring on the middle of the binos and the man's face jumped out at him. Riley lowered the glasses slightly— an FA-MAS rifle with silencer and laser sight was propped against the side of the man's seat, leaning against the glass panel on the door. Riley felt a chill race down his back. They were here. He didn't know how they had found out and arrived so quickly, but the critical thing was that they had done it.

Riley slowly relaxed and refocused his attention on the parking lot and path, unaware of the figure flitting through the trees behind him, slowly moving up on him.

8:43 A.M.

Master shook his head; it was as he expected. They would never find anyone on the ground from the air, and there was a hell of a lot of ground to hide on. He unfolded the map the pilot had given him and consulted the information printed at the top. There were eight hundred square miles of wilderness, most of it in extremely rugged high country. Master's estimation of Riley went up a notch.

As the helicopter passed over Newfound Gap Road, Master's feeling of despair evaporated. A red Mustang GT was parked in the lot, along with three other vehicles. He could see several people scattered about. Whether Giannini was among the tourists was impossible to tell from the helicopter.

"Hold here!" he ordered Ferguson. Master quick-dialed on his portable phone, making sure the earplug was in place so he could hear over the sound of the engines and blades.

The other end was picked up immediately and the voice rasped in Master's right ear. "Surveillance One."

"This is Master. What's your location?"

"Thirteen miles along the Newfound Gap Road."

"What's your ETA at the Gap?"

There was a brief pause. "Ten mikes."

"I've got what appears to be Giannini's car in the lot. There are also—I count five personnel there. Approach unobtrusively and see if Giannini is one of them. Also keep your eye out for Riley or Lisa Cobb. If you clear all the people, I want you to check the Mustang's plates when you get there and confirm. If it is Giannini's car, secure the area. Also run the plates on the other cars that are parked there."

"Roger."

Master redialed, calling his other vehicles down in the visitors' center and ordering them up to the parking lot in Newfound Gap.

"How much fuel do you have?" he asked Ferguson.

"About two hours' worth."

"All right. Let's check out this area."

8:45 A.M.

The sound of a branch snapping jabbed into Riley's consciousness. He rolled left, ignoring the pain as a stub of the tree he was hiding behind tore through his parka and into his side. He swung the muzzle of the FA-MAS, his finger light on the trigger.

"Whoa!" Giannini yelled, holding her hands clear of her body, .44 magnum in the left hand. "I think I had the drop on you there," she added.

Riley cursed. "Damn, Donna, you should know better than to sneak up on me like that." He checked his watch. "How long have you been here?"

"Since five-thirty this morning."

Riley stood, and absently felt the small wound on his side. "I told you to get here after daylight. We could have walked into each other in the dark, and that—"

"Yeah, well things happened to change the plan," Giannini interrupted. "What did you do to your side?" she asked, walking up to him.

"It's nothing," Riley said.

"Right," she said, reaching out and unzipping his jacket. "You manly men—it's always nothing." She reached under his fatigue shirt and peered at the scratch. "You're right—it's nothing." She dropped the shirt and looked him in the eye. "Well, are you just going to stand there or what?"

Riley shifted from one foot to the other, feeling slightly foolish, draped as he was with weapons and looking somewhat grungy from his night under the stars. He reached forward and gave her an awkward hug.

"I drive all the way from Chicago and that's all I get?" Giannini asked. She grabbed his arms and wrapped them around her. "Hold me!" The bantering was gone from her voice. "Hold me tight."

8:50 A.M.

Lisa heard the voices the same time Hammer did. They both froze and looked at each other. Hammer put his finger to his lips, signaling for her to be silent, then picked up his rifle. He slid silently out of camp, heading in the direction of the sound. Lisa stayed in place for a few seconds, then followed, having no desire to stay alone in the middle of the woods.

She tried to move as quietly as possible, but less than ten feet out of the campsite she brushed against a branch. Hammer whirled and gestured for her to go back. Lisa shook her head firmly. Hammer again pointed back and Lisa again refused. Hammer rolled his eyes and shrugged. He continued downslope.

The voices grew closer—a man's and a woman's. Lisa crept up right behind Hammer's left shoulder and peered over. Through the trees she could make out a trail cut across the mountainside about thirty feet away, the ground well worn. Whoever was making the noise was coming this way from the left. Hammer slipped the barrel of the silenced rifle over a low branch of the tree he was hiding behind.

A woman appeared first, a large backpack towering over her head. Her long blond hair flowed over the shoulder straps, and she wore brightly colored, loose-fitting pants and a worn plaid shirt. She was laughing and looking over her shoulder. Coming up the trail behind her was a tall young man with an even larger backpack. Lisa watched as the barrel of Hammer's rifle tracked the two. Her chest constricted as she saw Hammer's finger curl around the trigger. The two campers were now directly in front, oblivious to the death that had them in sight.

Hammer's finger tightened on the trigger, even as the girl let out another laugh.

"No!" hissed Lisa.

The muzzle moved to the right, centered on the man's head, and stayed there until the two disappeared around a bend in the trail. Hammer slowly pulled the weapon back in and turned to look at Lisa with a blank expression.

"You were going to kill them, weren't you?" Lisa said quietly.

Hammer shook his head absently, as if his mind were elsewhere, and without a word led the way back to the campsite.

9:12 A.M.

"It's Giannini's car, but she's not in the area."

Master peered down at the ground, then up at the clouds, close above the blades of the helicopter. He spoke again into the portable phone. "How about the other vehicles?"

"Negative on them. Tourists."

"Hold," Master ordered. He dialed the number of his own command van. "Put Simon on."

Master grimaced as the voice he had grown to hate came on. "Yes?"

"You call your boss back in Virginia and you tell him to get this road closed."

"What?"

"I want your boss to call the fucking National Park Service and close the Newfound Gap Road in the Great Smoky Mountains National Park," Master enunciated. "Got it?"

"Yes, but I think—"

"I don't give a shit what you think, what you feel, what you fucking suppose, or anything," Master snapped. "Just do it." He hung up and glanced at Ferguson, who had not been able to hear the conversation above the sound of the aircraft and was concentrating on flying. Master recalled his men below: "Clear me a landing pad at the end of the parking lot and mark it."

CHAPTER 18

"What happened to my brother?"

Lisa's first question for Giannini didn't surprise Riley. On the way to the campsite he'd told Giannini that Lisa didn't know how her brother died. Giannini took Lisa gently by the arm and led her a short distance away to break the grim news.

"So what now?" Hammer asked quietly.

Riley watched Lisa react to the news, throwing herself into the comfort of Giannini's arms. "I don't know. We've run as far as we can, but we can't stay here forever."

He told Hammer about the attack on Giannini in Chicago. He also told him about the helicopter—Hammer had heard it—adding in the fact of the weapon.

"So they know we're here," Hammer summarized. He glanced at the two women. "They probably followed Giannini somehow. Maybe they bugged her car, just like they did to your car at Bragg."

"How they got here doesn't matter," Riley said. "What happens now is what's critical. I could hear the helicopter hovering down near Newfound Gap for quite a while."

"They'll find Giannini's car, then," Hammer replied.

"What really bothers me," Riley said, "is that we've got more people after our ass than I can count and I'm still not sure who they are."

"If they're nearby, why don't we find out?" Hammer suggested.

Riley frowned. "What do you mean?"

"I've got something—"

Hammer was interrupted by the two women rejoining them. There were tears on Lisa's face, and her look indicated she was many miles away, experiencing a new grief.

Riley did the formalities of introducing Giannini to Hammer. She smiled crookedly at the older soldier. "So you're stuck on this bus to nowhere too?"

"One big happy family," Hammer acknowledged.

"Let's talk this out," Riley suggested. He sat down on his rucksack, and the others got as comfortable as they could on the ground. The sun was completely covered by clouds now, and the gray weather only deepened the gloom around the small circle. "All we have is the phone number to the Witness Protection Program, but we have to assume it's been compromised. The Program is still showing a good status for Lisa and her husband, and we know that's bullshit, so not only is the phone number compromised, but we also have to figure that someone has access to the Program's computer system. That says to me it has to be someone on the inside."

"But is that someone working for the mob?" Giannini asked. "From what you told me, you had *two* groups of people outside your town house."

"Maybe both groups were working for the same people," Lisa suggested. She felt numb, but was trying to focus on the conversation. "I'm sure that the Torrentinos offered a lot of money for my husband's whereabouts."

"Half a million dollars," Giannini said. "But my source in the mob told me there were no freelancers involved. I don't know who hit me in the alley, but I assume they were working for Charlie D'Angelo, because they found me through my contact, Nickie. That means they ultimately were working for the Torrentinos."

"Not necessarily," Riley said. "It might be that—"

"If you'd let me finish what I was gonna say," Hammer broke in, "I might have a way we can find out who's after us without having to yap our jaws all day." He reached into his fatigue pants pocket and pulled out a small plastic case with a four-inch metal antenna. "I took this out of the van at Camp Mackall. I say we turn it on."

"What?" Lisa exclaimed. "Are you crazy? I thought the whole point of coming up here was to hide out."

"We may not be hiding as well as we'd like," Giannini said. "My car is parked down at the Newfound Gap lot, and it won't take them long to find it if they're flying around here in a helicopter."

Riley had been silent, considering the bug in Hammer's hand. "I say we turn it on."

Lisa looked at him as if he'd grown another head. "Are you both going nuts?"

Riley spoke calmly, in a low voice. "I hope they—whoever the hell they are—don't know we're up here. But we haven't had much luck so far. *Every* place we've gone *or* been, they've shown up eventually. And usually when we didn't expect them to. If they are here looking for us, then I say we invite them at a place and time of *our* choosing for once."

Giannini nodded. "Hell, yeah. I'm tired of running."

Riley reached into his cargo pocket, pulled out the topographic map of the area, and spread it on the pine needles. "I think we have some work to do."

CHICAGO
1 NOVEMBER, 10:00 A.M.

Charlie D'Angelo looked at the newspaper report of the two men murdered in the alley before throwing the paper into the wastebasket next to his desk. His chief subordinates were gathered around his desk, awaiting his reaction to the news.

Charlie drummed his fingers and thought for a few seconds before speaking. "Gentlemen, the situation concerning the Torrentino brothers is most unfortunate and I sympathize with their desire to see justice done." He pointed at the wastebasket. "But the price is getting out of control. We had a one hundred thousand dollar contract with these two gentlemen, half paid up front, and not only was the work not completed, but we have also lost our initial investment." He twisted his Harvard ring. "In economics that is called 'sunk cost'—an investment that cannot be recouped. The key is that you cannot throw good money after bad." He could see a few frowns crinkle Neanderthal foreheads as they tried to follow what he was saying.

"In other words, we pissed away fifty grand and got nothing in return. We've been offering a half million for the Cobbs—or shall I say our associates the Torrentinos have been offering a half million. But we must realize that that money is also *our* money." D'Angelo shrugged. "If we get a line on these people and can do them, fine. But we can't waste any more resources chasing them down."

"What about the two million Cobb skimmed?" one of them asked.

"Also sunk cost," D'Angelo said. He checked the faces surrounding him, looking for signs of protest, for still-strong tendrils of loyalty to the jailed former bosses. He saw none. "Good. Let us move on, then."

The men moved out—all except Roy Delpino, who sat down across the desk from D'Angelo and lit a cigar. "So what's the real story?"

D'Angelo leaned back in his chair. "The real story is that this is turning out to be a big pain in the ass and a waste of resources. Just like I said."

"The Torrentinos are going to be pissed," Delpino observed.

"Fuck the Torrentinos," D'Angelo replied with a cold smile. "I control things now and I'm tired of taking orders from prison. The Torrentinos are history."

Delpino frowned. "You're going to give up on the money?"

"Philip Cobb is dead."

"What?"

"Cobb's dead. Fastone's dead. The only one who might know the whereabouts of the money is Cobb's wife."

"How do you know all this?" Delpino asked.

"A little bird told me," D'Angelo said. "And no, I'm not giving up on the money. I have an inside line on Cobb's wife and we shall soon see what she knows." He pointed at the door. "But we certainly don't need all those assholes to know that, now do we?"

GREAT SMOKY MOUNTAINS
1 NOVEMBER, 11:30 A.M.

"Newfound Gap Road has been closed to incoming traffic," Simon reported to Master as he put down the portable phone. "The park rangers have the gates manned to allow traffic that is already on the road to depart."

Master was seated in his swivel chair, eyes focused on the pictorial map of the Great Smoky Mountains National Park taped above the communications console. Simon's words buzzed in his head and were noted, then he went back to pondering the map. He had three of his men up in the helicopter, searching to the east and west of the Newfound Gap, taking particular note of the trails in the area. The problem was that the spruce and fir trees covered much of the ground, making observation poor.

Master's left forefinger tapped on the console for several minutes, irritating the other occupants of the van, none of whom dared say a word. Finally he turned to Simon. "We need to consider pulling out."

Simon's surprise was evident. "What?"

Master lifted his forefinger slightly and indicated the map. "They could be anywhere. I assume they're on foot, but even then, given a twelve-hour head start they can be anywhere in"—he closed his eyes in thought, then opened them—"about a fifteen-mile circle of where Giannini's car is." He grabbed a red pen and a ruler and roughly traced a circle of that scale around Newfound Gap. "This is some of the worst terrain for searching I've ever seen. We're not going to find them from the air, not unless they are especially stupid—and given their actions so far, I don't think we can count on that. Even on the ground, my men could walk by within twenty feet of them and miss them.

"We need to consider pulling back and waiting them out. They have to come out sometime. Riley will go AWOL in a week. Giannini is already AWOL from the police department."

"What about—"

Simon was interrupted by the analyst's startled yell. "Sir!"

Master turned. "What?"

The analyst pointed at one of his computer screens. "One of our tracking devices has been activated."

"One of our search teams?"

"No, sir." The analyst tapped on the small keyboard in front of him. "Transponder code indicates it's one of the ones that was on Surveillance Two's van."

The van out at Camp Mackall, where the two men had been killed. Master's eyes narrowed. "And it just got turned on?"

"Yes, sir."

"Location?"

The analyst placed an acetate overlay of the topographic map on the screen. "Right here."

Master noted the location, then marked it on his paper map with a red pen. It was a white area, indicating open terrain—a rarity in the park. Andrews Bald was written across it in small black letters.

"What does it mean—the tracking device being turned on?" Simon asked, bewildered by the exchange.

Master stared at the map. "It could be Mister Riley inviting us to a party." He picked up the portable phone. "And I believe we will accept the invitation."

CHAPTER 19

Something about these ATF people bothered Ferguson. He tried to put his finger on it as he banked the Jet Ranger around Mount Kephart and headed for The Sawteeth, a set of jagged peaks running along the spine of the mountains. He'd worked with law enforcement officials before on various missions over the park—mostly Drug Enforcement Administration agents searching out marijuana fields in the more remote areas of the park—and these guys were different.

The first thing that struck him was that they paid in cash. Anyone who had any dealings with the government knew that you had to have forms filled out in triplicate to get any sort of reimbursement—and that was only after a long wait. Ferguson had about dropped his teeth when the man pulled out a wad of cash and forked over the money. He'd also noted the strange-looking automatic weapon the man had brought on board; it didn't look like government issue. Another thing was that after dropping off the head agent in the Newfound Gap parking lot, these other three had climbed on board and they were armed to the teeth with very high powered gear.

"Fly along that trail," the man to Ferguson's left ordered.

As he complied, Ferguson wondered why ATF agents would need silenced weapons—for that's most certainly what those odd-looking rifles were. Ferguson felt the roll of bills sitting comfortably in the breast pocket of his flight suit and relaxed. Whoever these guys were, they had paid and they had badges—that was good enough for him.

189

Something caught Ferguson's eye. "Your phone is flashing," he said over the intercom to the man sitting in the copilot's seat, who'd identified himself as Rivers.

Ferguson couldn't hear the conversation, but it electrified Rivers. He flipped closed the phone, opened his map, and began looking for something. He turned to Ferguson. "You know where Andrews Bald is?"

"Yeah. Other side of Newfound Gap Road. It's about the only clear place up here—other than the parking lots—where I can set down, so we have it marked on our maps as an emergency landing field."

"Drop us off there, then go back to Newfound Gap Road and pick up the rest of your money from"—he paused for a second—"Lieutenant Loggins."

Sounded good to Ferguson. He would be glad to get rid of these guys. He increased throttle and pulled up on the cyclic as he reversed course.

12:10 P.M.

Andrews Bald was one of only two balds in the Smokies. On all the other hilltops, natural growth had overwhelmed the open areas with forest. The Park Service had designated Andrews, along with Gregory Bald farther to the west, as experimental research subzones. Because of that, the hilltop was maintained as an open area with the present plant life. It was also one of the few places in the park where a person could get a view unrestricted by trees as far south as the Nantahala Mountains.

The Forney Ridge Trail ran from the parking area below the Clingmans Dome tower for two miles to Andrews Bald. That was the route Hammer and Riley had taken to get to their present position on the northeast side of the Bald, overlooking the bushes and grasses that sloped down to the forest on the far side of the Bald, where the terrain dropped off precipitously into Flat Top Gap.

"Hear it?" Hammer asked. "OH-58," he added, giving the term for the military version of the Bell Jet Ranger. "In Vietnam I could always tell what kind of chopper was coming just by the sound."

"That's what I saw flying around," Riley said. He felt a surge of adrenaline kick through his system as the probability of his fears being confirmed grew higher.

The aircraft came in high from the east, headed directly for the open area. The pilot pulled pitch as it descended, the skids touching down lightly about a hundred yards away from the tree line in which Hammer and Riley were concealed. Three armed men dressed in black hopped off, and the aircraft lifted and was gone.

While two of the men pulled security lying on the ground, facing east and west, the third man put a metal briefcase on the ground and flipped open the cover. He knelt over it, took a bearing, and then closed it. He gave an order Riley couldn't hear, and the men were on their feet.

The three men moved professionally toward the north side of the open area, to the hard-packed earth of the Forney Ridge Trail—about thirty yards to the right of Riley's position. The three moved in a triangle, lead man pointing due north, the others covering the flanks.

"Same weapons," Hammer noted quietly, spotting the FA-MAS silenced rifles held at the ready by each of the men.

Riley didn't reply. He slowly put down his own rifle and picked up the two plastic clackers that lay by his side.

12:12 P.M.

Master handed the money to the pilot and didn't wait for the bird to take off. He sprinted back to his command van and jumped inside.

"Let's go!" he ordered. The driver threw the vehicle in gear and they roared off onto Newfound Gap Road, almost immediately squealing to a stop at the locked gate at the Clingmans Dome road. Master opened the passenger door and steadied his Glock 10mm against the open window frame. He fired one shot, the round ripping apart the gate lock.

"Go," he said, and the driver nosed open the gate, then accelerated down the road. The other two vans, holding the rest of Master's team, followed.

12:13 P.M.

The three men were less than ten feet from the trail and forty feet from Riley when he squeezed the clacker in his right hand. The crack of the claymore mine was deafening, followed immediately by the sound of thousands of steel ball bearings whirring through the air. The three men immediately hit the ground, one of them firing a wild burst.

Riley had taped the mine to a tree, angling it upward at sixty degrees to ensure that no one would get hurt. It was a firepower message, which he now followed with a verbal one.

"Leave your rifles on the ground and stand up with your hands behind your heads, fingers interlocked!" he yelled. "I've got another mine aimed right at your faces!"

There was a brief pause, then a silent fusillade of bullets ripped through the air above Riley and Hammer. Hammer peered over the thick log he was hiding behind and shook his head. "I told you they wouldn't surrender."

Riley didn't repeat his request to the three men. He squeezed the clacker in his left hand. The claymore, which was secreted in the high grass less than ten feet from the three men's position, exploded. The steel balls scythed through the grass and ripped into human flesh. The point man took the center brunt of the arc of death, his body tossed almost a yard by the simultaneous impact of hundreds of the pellets. The man on the left died as his face was peppered by the steel, both eyes punctured. The third man caught the blast on his left side. His arm was almost severed, but his body armor caught the majority of the explosion and he clung to life, rolling with the blast.

Riley and Hammer stood, then moved out of the security of the trees toward the carnage. The sound of the mines going off still echoed in their ears, and the smell of explosive filled their nostrils. Covering across each other's front, they came upon the bodies. The wounded man held up his blood-covered right hand in supplication as a froth of blood flowed over his lips. Hammer fired twice, the impact of the rounds throwing the man's head back into the dirt and blowing brain matter all over the ground.

"We needed him to talk!" Riley snapped.

"He was dead meat, but he was ready to take one of us with him," Hammer replied calmly, as he ensured the other two men were dead by the expeditious manner of putting a round through each of their heads. He looked up at Riley. "This was just the first wave. There'll be more. You can talk to them if you like."

Riley began searching one of the bodies as Hammer did another. Riley frowned at the ATF badges pinned to the front of the black body armor, and for a brief moment the bottom fell out of his gut. Had they just killed three law enforcement personnel? He quickly slapped down the pockets, searching for some other form of ID. Other than the gold badges, there was nothing else on the bodies.

"ATF?" Riley asked Hammer as he wiped off his bloody hands on the vest of the man at his feet.

"As good as any cover," Hammer said. "After Waco, everyone recognizes the letters." He pointed down. "They got no IDs though. There ain't no way a cop goes out all duded up for World War III without carrying an ID." He kicked the mangled metal case, holding up what used to be a working electronic tracker. "Plus they came in on the signal. They're the bad guys, and pretty damn well-equipped bad guys."

"But we're no closer to finding out who they are," Riley added. "Let's get back to Lisa and Giannini." He cut the transmitter from the back side of the tree, where he had taped it, turning it off before slipping it into his pocket. As Riley disappeared up the Forney Ridge Trail, Hammer reached down and pulled one of the badges and a portable phone off the lead body. He checked the phone to see if it still functioned, then put it in the cargo pocket of his fatigue pants.

1:23 P.M.

Master moved down the trail, years of civilized living slipping away with each step he took. He was back in the jungle, walking point, in a cross-border mission. With slight hand gestures, he deployed his men as they approached within a half mile of Andrews Bald. He held up his left hand clenched in a fist, and the signal was passed down the line, each man freezing in his tracks. Master slipped the portable phone out of the slot on his combat vest and quick-dialed the team he had sent into the Bald by helicopter.

"Come on, assholes," he muttered, as the phone rang and rang. He'd been out of contact with the team for an hour and a half now, ever since ordering them in. They should have called in an initial entry report right after landing, but there had been nothing. The ringer on the phone could be turned off—and usually was in situations such as this—but the phone put out a noticeable vibration when a call was incoming. Additionally, a small light could be activated to signal a call. His team should be answering.

Master had considered going to the Bald in the helicopter—it would have been the quickest way—but he had vetoed the idea. The pilot had already seen enough. Master didn't want him in on whatever was happening on the Bald.

Master pointed to the left of the trail, and two men moved out there, twenty feet to the flank. A gesture to the right, and that side was covered. Master and the four remaining men took the center path. It was slow moving through the thickly wooded terrain, but Master had long ago learned the value of doing things the right way. When live ammunition was involved, you didn't get a second chance.

The nine men dipped down through the saddle formed by Andrews Bald and Clingmans Dome, then moved two hundred feet up the slope of Andrews Bald itself. The terrain was wooded until they got to the southwestern slope, and Master halted his men fifty feet short of the open area. He moved his flanks forward to provide security, then slowly walked forward himself, carefully scanning every tree and bush. He halted at the tree line and peered out into the open area.

The three lumps of flesh that had been his men lay not far ahead. Master studied the way the bodies were sprawled, what little he could see of their wounds, and the blackened arc of cut grass, and he knew immediately what had happened. Still he didn't move. He ordered his flank security teams to move around the wood line, clearing it. Finally, when that was done, he moved forward.

He stared down at the three bodies while one of his men checked their wounds. "Claymore, sir."

"I know that," Master snapped.

"Each was finished off with a round through the forehead."

Master's estimation of his opponent went up again. Obviously Riley could do what had to be done.

"Police them up," he ordered. "We're going to have to haul them out."

His men looked none too pleased, but no one protested. They broke out ponchos from their butt packs and began putting together makeshift stretchers to carry out their dead.

A vibration on Master's chest informed him that his phone was ringing. He pulled it out and flipped it open.

"Master here."

He listened to the voice on the other end without comment, then hung up. His voice was ice cold as he turned to his men. "Dewar, Kramer, you come with me. The rest of you get the bodies back up the trail to the van."

Without explanation, Master turned and led the way back toward Clingmans Dome.

1:30 P.M.

Riley's report on the ambush had been succinct, and Lisa and Giannini were lost in their own thoughts. He'd left Hammer down by the trail leading up from the parking lot to pull security. He had a feeling things were going to get hairy real soon.

Giannini concurred with Hammer's assessment of the men's identity. "They weren't ATF, Dave—not without IDs and not acting the way they were."

"I'm past the point of worrying about who these people are," Riley said. "Somehow, some way, they followed us. If we couldn't shake them by coming here, I don't know what to do."

"If Hammer hadn't wasted that wounded man, we might have some answers," Giannini noted.

"He was still armed," Riley told her. "I gave them a chance to surrender, and I showed them that they had just stepped into some deep shit by blowing the first claymore. You can't give a fellow much more warning than that."

"Let's just go to the police," Lisa said. "We . . ." She paused as Hammer stepped into the campsite and walked up to her.

"What are you—" Riley began and then halted in surprise as Hammer lifted his .44 magnum, pressed it against Lisa's forehead, and cocked the hammer. In his left hand, he held a claymore clacker, the handle already pressed *down*.

CHAPTER 20

GREAT SMOKY MOUNTAINS
1 NOVEMBER, 1:32 P.M.

"Don't do nothing foolish now," Hammer warned. "Put your weapons on the ground, slowly, and do it with your off hand—which in your case, Riley, means your right—or we get a close look at the lady's brains."

"What the hell do you think you're doing?" Riley asked, his hands carefully away from his sides.

Hammer dug the barrel of the gun into Lisa's skin, causing her to cry out. "Do as I say."

"Bullshit," Riley replied. He drew his 9mm and pointed it at Hammer, who edged slightly sideways, placing Lisa between them. Giannini followed Riley's lead, the two of them aiming at the man from a distance of twenty feet.

"Not bullshit," Hammer said calmly. He lifted his left hand, which held the clacker. "I've got the last mine you brought aimed right at this clearing from the tree line. As you can see, I rewired the clacker: I let *go* of it, and we're all Swiss cheese." He smiled grimly. "I know how you were trained—never surrender your weapon in a standoff, and always take down the bad guy. But in this case, you take me down, you take all of us down."

Riley kept the bead directly centered on the part of Hammer's head that he could see. He tried to gain some time. "Why are you doing this?"

"That's not important right now," Hammer said, his voice cold. "What *is* important is you put down your weapon in the next ten seconds, or I blow her fucking brains out."

Riley glanced at Giannini, who shook her head helplessly. Slowly, she put down her revolver at her feet. Riley looked at the clacker and traced the wire to where it disappeared into a bush. He returned his gaze to Hammer and looked into his eyes for almost five seconds. Hammer's finger tightened on the trigger.

"All right, all right," Riley said. He put down his 9mm at his feet.

"The silenced twenty-two in the other shoulder holster," Hammer said. Riley complied.

"The boot knife and the one in the small of your back and your combat vest."

The arsenal at Riley's feet grew.

"Step away—this way—a few more feet." Hammer guided Giannini and Riley away from their weapons. "All right. Hold it. Now face-down on the ground, hands behind your back."

Riley and Giannini did as they were told. Hammer released Lisa, the imprint of the gun barrel bright red against her temple. "In the middle pocket on the outside of my backpack you'll find some electrical tape," he instructed her. When she had the black roll in her hand, he told her to tape Riley and Giannini's hands behind their backs. She did Riley first, and Hammer counted each loop out loud, ensuring that Riley's wrists had at least ten wraps. Lisa then did the same with Giannini.

When Lisa was done, Hammer took the tape from her and wrapped the clacker handle shut, then taped Lisa's hands behind her back.

Riley twisted himself into a sitting position. "You mind telling me why you're doing this?"

"Oldest reason there is," Hammer answered. "Money."

"I told you I don't know anything about any money," Lisa protested.

Hammer laughed. "Well, first off, little lady, I don't believe you. But second, even if you don't, I'll still make something off this mess."

"What do you mean?" Riley asked.

"Enough questions," Hammer said as he gathered all the weapons and stuffed them into his backpack, along with Riley's combat vest. "Everyone on your feet. We got a little trip to make." He waited until everyone was standing, then gestured with the muzzle of the FA-MAS. "We're going down to the trail, then to the observation tower. Now, if you want to be stupid you can try running for it, but I don't think you'll outrun the muzzle velocity of my rifle. So let's not be stupid, okay?"

CHEROKEE
1:40 P.M.

Jim Ferguson paused in midbite as a silver Mercedes pulled into the lot fronting his office. A man wearing an expensive leather jacket got out and came inside. "How much for an hour over the mountains?" he asked, looking over the display map.

Ferguson glanced at the car, the man's Rolex, then at the safe where he had put the money from this morning, and said a short prayer of thanks. Today was most certainly turning out to be his day.

"Five hundred."

The man smiled and peeled off five crisp one hundred dollar bills. "My wife and I spent our honeymoon down here thirty years ago," he said as Ferguson took the money. He pointed at the map. "Fly us up along the high part of the mountains, all right?"

Ferguson nodded and grabbed his kit bag. "We'll be ready to take off in five minutes."

GREAT SMOKY MOUNTAINS
1:45 P.M.

The trip to the Clingmans Dome observation tower had been made in abject silence, everyone lost in their own thoughts and fears. Riley was so confused with the whole situation that he'd made the decision to simply focus on the most immediate problem—getting out of the present predicament. Hammer had directed them up the long winding ramp to the tower, and now the three of them were seated with their backs against the three-foot-high concrete wall that made up the outside of the tower.

The concrete walkway came into the twenty-foot-wide tower from the west. In the center of the platform, a six-foot-wide column extended upward, holding a mushroom-shaped concrete roof that covered most of the platform, leaving only the outside three feet exposed. Hammer was standing, peering down the trail that came up from the parking lot. He'd piled Riley's combat vest and the weapons on the far side of the center column from the prisoners.

Riley probed underneath his belt with his fingers and slowly began working free the garrote he had there. Giannini, sitting next to

him, could tell he was up to something, and she started talking, trying to distract Hammer.

"You said you were going to make some money whether or not Lisa
knows where her husband's money is hidden. What did you mean by
that?"

Hammer seemed to be considering whether he should answer, then
apparently decided he had nothing to lose. "You people are pretty
naive, you know that?" He gestured at Riley, who halted his movements momentarily. "What are you, some kind of knight in shining
armor, coming to the aid of the damsel in distress? Who the hell do
you think has been after her all this time? Who do you think wasted
her husband?"

"It was the mob, wasn't it?" Giannini asked, confused. Riley slipped
a finger under the ring on one end of the garrote and popped it free.
Hammer's words echoed in his head, and for the first time he knew
the answer to Hammer's questions. He wanted to kick himself for not
realizing it sooner. It all clicked into place: the high-power equipment,
the phone lines tapped, the message on the marshal's computer in Chicago.
All the "what" pieces now fit. The only thing he didn't understand
was the all-important "why."

Hammer pulled a portable phone out of his fatigue pants pocket and
gestured downhill with it. "The mob!" Hammer laughed. "They only
got in the way of these guys, and when they did, they were eliminated."

"The two men at my house," Riley said, doubling up the wire of
the garrote, the rough edges cutting his fingers as he bent it.

"Yeah—the first two, they were mob. The others—they weren't."

"You told them we were up here?" Riley asked, holding his body
still and using his fingers to create a sawing motion at his wrists.

"I didn't have to," Hammer said. "She did—using one of these,"
he added, waving the portable at Giannini. "I just used this one to check
in, and our friends are on their way here as we speak."

"How'd you know what number to call?" Riley asked.

"Redial," Hammer answered, thumb over one of the buttons. "I figured
those guys we wasted had to be talking to one of their buddies."

"Will someone tell me what the fuck is going on?" Giannini exploded, frustrated with the conversation flitting above her head. "If it
wasn't the mob, who the hell was it? Who are these 'others'?"

"I just want to know how you're affiliated with these people," Riley
asked, ignoring Giannini for the moment, trying to buy time and also
get what could be important information.

"I'm not," Hammer said. "I work for myself. Whoever pays the most gets my services. Right now we're in a curious position. I'm not sure who should get that honor.

"The fellow who's coming up the hill," Hammer said, "we call him Master. He's a freelancer. Does shit jobs for anyone with the dough to pay—DEA, DIA, CIA, any of the alphabet soup. I knew him from my time in CCN-North, and we've kept in touch over the years. It's not too bad." Hammer smiled. "Only have to work a couple of months out of the year, doing what I was trained to do, and then coming on active duty for a few weeks every year to get brought up to speed on the latest special ops stuff." He looked at Riley. "If you'd been a little smarter, I might have let you in on it."

"Our government!" Giannini whispered, shocked, as it all sank in. "These people are working for the government?"

"Ain't it a bitch?" Hammer said cheerfully as he pushed redial on the phone. "Of course, I've worked for the mob too at times."

1:51 P.M.

Master halted his men on the near side of the Clingmans Dome parking lot and gestured for Dewar and Kramer to cross and clear the far side. He waited in the security of the downslope, out of sight, until one of them gave a yell, indicating it was safe to cross. He checked his van on the way across to make sure it hadn't been tampered with. The other two vehicles were gone, taking the bodies of the ambush victims out of the area. Master joined his men at the building holding the rest rooms for the area.

"No sign of anyone?" he asked.

"No, sir," Kramer answered. "Area's clear."

Master frowned. The asset had said to meet here. The phone buzzed on his chest and he flipped it open. "Yes?"

"You there yet?" the voice on the other end asked.

"I'm at the rest rooms near the Clingmans Dome parking lot," Master answered. "Where are you?"

"Up the hill," the voice said. "In the tower. Come up the path; I can see anyone moving cross-country, so don't try that or I'll put you in a world of hurt and you won't get your door prizes."

"Why don't you just terminate them? I'll give you standard pay plus a ten thousand dollar bonus," Master said.

"Two reasons. One is I kind of like them and don't feel like doing 'em. But more importantly, the young lady here might be worth a couple of million dollars alive. I also hear that some people in Chicago are offering half a mill for her."

"Don't screw with me," Master threatened. "You know the way the game is played. I've got a contract, and you are either part of my side of the contract or you're on the other side."

"Don't get a bug up your ass. Just come on up like I said and we'll talk this over like the gentlemen we are." The phone went dead.

Master turned off his phone and slowly counted to ten before speaking. "Kramer, our targets are in the observation tower on top of the hill." He pointed to the spot where the path curved up and out of sight. "I want you to get the sniper rifle out of the van, then move around to the right and try to get an open shot. It's imperative that you stay concealed. Keep an open mike on the FM so you can hear what's going on." He grabbed Kramer's arm as he went by. "You never worked with Hammer—the fellow up there—but he's good. You won't get a second shot."

"Yes, sir."

Kramer walked to the parking lot, opened the weapons locker on the floor of the van, and extracted a Heckler & Koch PSG1 sniper rifle. He slung the weapon and the carrying case for its tripod over his shoulder, then he disappeared into the woods and made his way uphill. Master pulled out the small boom mike and the earplug for the small FM radio concealed in an upper pocket on the back of his combat vest, and made sure he had commo with Kramer. Then, with Dewar following fifty yards behind, out of sight, Master began walking up the path.

1:55 P.M.

Riley had heard Hammer's side of the conversation and redoubled his efforts to get loose. As he worked the garrote back and forth, the coarse wire was slowly cutting through the electrical tape. It was also slicing the flesh on Riley's wrists and hands. He could feel the blood flowing across his skin. The pain was sharp and Riley used it to keep his focus.

"How are you connected with these people?" Giannini asked.

Hammer was moving around the tower, peeking over the edge and checking all directions. "I've worked with them at times. Most of 'these people,' as you call them, have some sort of special ops background.

Where else can you get such well-trained people who are used to doing shit jobs?" He glanced at Riley. "Correcto-mundo, buddy?"

Riley ignored Hammer. He looked over at the fourth member of the group, who had not spoken since they'd arrived here. On the other side of Giannini, Lisa was slumped against the wall, head down, and he wondered if she'd fainted.

"It's kind of funny," Hammer said, "but it was pure chance that I was in the right place at the right time. I didn't know what was going on either until I spotted the surveillance in the post office at Bragg when we tried to turn her over."

"That's why you terminated so quickly," Riley noted. "You recognized someone."

"Yeah," Hammer said, his attention now totally focused on the surrounding terrain. "I called my control from the trailer the other night to find out what was going on. They told me to hold—they wanted to get you all together, and now they have."

"But you helped kill those men earlier today," Giannini said, not bothering to hide the disgust in her voice.

"Risks of the job," Hammer said. He glanced over his shoulder, then back to the outside world. "I wasn't in charge of the situation and we were all split up. Also, the information about the money her husband hid away and the mob's contract changed the complexion of everything. I made another phone call to some of my mob connections and found out that someone in Chicago is offering five hundred grand for the little lady, so I ended up with a little bit of a dilemma."

He pointed at Riley. "If I'd taken you down alone up at the Bald, then Master would have wanted to take control, and I couldn't allow that. Besides, you held the clackers—I didn't do a thing."

"That's why you shot the wounded man," Riley noted. "You didn't want him to talk."

"Partly," Hammer acknowledged. "But the bottom line is that as long as I have the lady here, I've got options."

Riley glanced at Giannini; she rolled her eyes and shook her head. He's nuts, she mouthed silently.

Hammer chuckled. "You both are so stupid. Don't you know it's all a game and you got to not only learn the written rules, but also the unwritten ones? There's a whole 'nother world out there beyond the gray. It's all black and you're in it now. We make up our own rules, and the number one maxim is survival of the fittest."

"I still don't understand why—" Giannini began, but a gesture from Hammer stopped her. He squatted down, just barely peering over the concrete.

"That's close enough," he yelled.

"There's no negotiation," Master's voice carried clearly in the cool air. "Give over the targets."

"They didn't give you background on the woman, did they?" Hammer called out.

"Enough to do the job."

"You don't know about the two million her husband hid away or you wouldn't have wasted him in Charlotte. And you don't know about the half million contract put out by the mob in Chicago or you might have entertained a competing bid," Hammer said.

"There are no competing bids," Master replied calmly. "I do my job as contracted. Cobb was a criminal and was dealt with accordingly."

Hammer glanced at Giannini and Riley and winked. "How much does it cost the Program for each person they hide away? A hundred grand a year? Multiplied by all the years they got left? And how much are they paying you on the contract?"

"I don't know how much it costs them," Master replied. "I don't really care."

To the west of the Dome, Kramer unfolded the tripod and connected it to the bottom of the barrel hand guard. He set down the tripod and made sure the legs were secure. He was as close as he could get to the tower without being spotted—about a hundred yards away, hidden among the trees. The walkway made its 180-degree curve less than fifty yards from his position. He leaned his cheek against the guard on the stock and looked through the scope, confirming what he had feared when he first spotted the tower. He keyed his FM radio and spoke into the mouthpiece.

Master was standing on the tar walkway, less than a hundred feet from the tower. He couldn't see Hammer or any of the prisoners, and when Kramer's voice came into the small receiver in his ear he wasn't surprised at the message.

"I can't get a clear shot unless they stand up. I can't see any of the targets, and if I move any closer I'll be spotted. I do have some clear space along the walkway if they try to come down."

"Hold position," Master whispered into the radio. "Break, Dewar, double-time down to the van and bring up the two-oh-three."

"Roger," Dewar replied from his hidden position around the curve farther down the path.

"So what's the average life expectancy?" Hammer yelled to Master. "You got to figure that in ten years the Program saves a million on each person that really disappears. With the Cobbs you were looking at two for the price of one." He shook his head. "I don't think we're making enough on this deal."

"It's not just the money," Master replied. "It's the concept."

Hammer turned to Riley and Giannini and lowered his voice. "You'll like this—I've heard it before."

Riley wondered about all the talking—something wasn't right. Why was this Master fellow stalling for time? Riley glanced down the walkway, half expecting to see some men sneaking up on them. His hands were now entirely drenched in blood but he continued the awkward sawing motion.

"What's the concept?" Hammer called out.

"The idea that criminals should be rewarded simply because they agree to testify to save their ass. You know what I mean, Hammer. We served our country and it spit in our face, yet these people break the law and then get rewarded for it."

"He's got a point, don't you think?" Hammer said to his prisoners.

The blood-covered garrote slipped out of Riley's fingers and fell to the floor behind him. He put both palms together and pressed—he could feel some give.

"I don't think—" Hammer's next words were cut off as the sharp crack of an explosion sounded close by. He popped his head up and peered out. The smoke from a grenade round floated by.

"Again!" Master hissed, as Dewar popped open the grenade launcher barrel slung underneath the M-16 frame. As soon as Dewar had fired the first round, Master joined him. Both were hidden on the far side of the path from the tower, on the beginning of the downslope leading to Forney's Creek. The expanded cartridge slipped out and Dewar rammed home another high-explosive (HE) round.

Five miles to the west, flying five hundred feet above Silers Bald, Ferguson saw the puff of smoke on Clingmans Dome and wondered what it could be. His trip with the couple who'd arrived in the Mercedes had started in the west, and he was working his way east along the spine of the mountains. Whatever the smoke was, he would see shortly.

"Son of a bitch!" Hammer exclaimed, hitting the deck. "Guess they aren't going to negotiate."

"Why the hell did you even try?" Riley said.

Hammer looked at him. "Because I thought Master would be reasonable, and I'm tired of working for peanuts. If I get this to go down, I could retire and be done with this crap. Guess that's not going to be possible."

Hammer stood, hands held up. "All right, Master. You've got—"

The 7.62 x 51mm round entered just under Hammer's left eye, glanced off the cheekbone and tore through his mouth, and exited through his right jaw. The impact threw him against the concrete wall, then he toppled to the floor.

Riley heard the report of the sniper rifle even as Hammer's blood splashed over him. He made one final surge with the tape and the last strands parted. With the knife from Hammer's combat vest, he sliced through Giannini's and Lisa's bindings. Then he scuttled around the deck, keeping low, to the pile of weapons and gear; he threw on his combat vest, resecured both his pistols and his FA-MAS, and handed Giannini her revolver.

"He's still alive," Giannini said, kneeling next to Hammer.

Riley slid next to his former partner and checked the wound. Hammer's eyes followed him above the bloody mess the round had made. They all flinched as another HE grenade exploded, this one against the outside of the concrete wall; the concussion made their heads ring.

Hammer muttered something, spitting out blood, broken teeth, and splintered bone. Riley ripped open the field dressing from Hammer's vest and reached up to wrap it around the man's head. A bloody hand came up and grabbed his arm in a vicelike grip. Riley met Hammer's look, and the man again attempted to speak through his damaged mouth. Riley tried to put the bandage on, but Hammer wouldn't let go, and Riley finally desisted. Hammer then picked up the FA-MAS and got to his knees. He pointed to the ramp.

Riley understood what Hammer was doing. He turned to the two women. "Let's go. Down the ramp."

Hammer stood and fired a long sustained burst, first at where Master had been, then around to the left, toward the sniper. When the bolt slammed forward on an empty magazine, he smoothly slipped another one home and continued firing, ignoring the pain and the blood that flowed from his face. Giannini grabbed Lisa by the arm, and Riley pushed them onto the ramp.

As they started down, an explosion behind them threw them all to the ramp. Riley turned and looked. Dewar had finally threaded the needle; the round had passed between the upper cover and the concrete wall, exploding less than four feet from Hammer. Riley caught a glimpse as the blast blew Hammer's shredded body over the wall to the ground forty feet below. Riley shook his head to clear the ringing from the blast's concussion. "Let's keep going," he ordered the two women.

Riley knew that the sniper was directly ahead, but he didn't know if the man had an angle on the walkway. It was a chance he had to take. To stay up on the observation deck was suicide.

Kramer twisted the focus on the PSG1 and scanned down from the deck. Three figures appeared; their lower bodies were below the concrete wall on either side, but their upper bodies were totally exposed to his direct vector. Kramer let the red dot of his laser sight flicker from one to the other to the third, then he settled on his first target.

Ferguson had seen the last explosion on the tower and could only interpret it as some sort of distress signal. He got on his radio and called the Park Service for help as he maneuvered his aircraft in closer.

Master heard the helicopter but it didn't concern him. "Finish them," he ordered Dewar, who obediently blooped another round onto the observation deck.

The round exploded thirty feet behind Riley. "Keep going!" Riley yelled at Lisa. He was surprised when she jerked backward against them, almost knocking Giannini to the ground. The echo of the sniper rifle confirmed his fear as he bent over the woman. A pool of blood was spreading from the wound in her throat.

"Oh fuck," Riley muttered, meeting Giannini's eyes over the body. He reached forward and threw her to the floor, behind Lisa's body.

*   *   *

"Shit," Kramer muttered, as the two dipped below his line of sight. "I got one of them," he reported to Master over the radio. "One of the women. They're about forty feet down the ramp and they're on the floor, out of sight now."

"Got that?" Master asked Dewar, who was lying next to him.
"Yeah." Dewar loaded another HE cartridge, shifted his sights along the walkway, and fired. The round just barely missed, flying over the walkway and exploding in the trees on the far side.

Riley could see the red laser dot flickering against the concrete just above their heads. He estimated they had about a six-inch safety margin that was keeping them from getting their heads blown off. He watched the dot for a few seconds, gauging its movement. Then he heard the chatter of helicopter blades coming closer.
He leaned his head next to Giannini's. "How is she?"
Giannini was searching vainly for a pulse. "She's gone."
"How high do you think we are above the ground?"
"Twenty—thirty feet, maybe."
Riley's hands had begun moving even as he asked her. He unhooked the coiled twelve-foot length of nylon rope that was attached to the right shoulder of his combat harness and swiftly tied a fixed loop on one end. He reached up and flipped it over the metal railing bolted to the inside of the wall. A shot chipped concrete splinters less than four inches from Riley's hand, informing him that the sniper was still on station and alert.
Riley slipped the free end of the rope through the loop and pulled it tight as another HE round flew overhead. Riley grabbed the fixed end of the rope, pressed it into the snap link on the front of his vest, and did two twists. He tapped Giannini. "Here's the plan . . ."

"He's doing something," Dewar reported.
"What is it?" Master asked.
"I don't know."
Master rolled his eyes. "Give me that damn thing," he said to Dewar, grabbing the grenade launcher out of his hands.

Riley jumped up and rolled over the concrete wall, the rope screaming through the snap link, barely slowing him. He slammed the hand holding the rope against his chest, braking barely a foot from the end of the rope.

Kramer snapped off a hurried shot, then tried to settle in on the target hanging on the rope, when the other woman appeared in the corner of the scope, firing on automatic with an FA-MAS. Kramer ducked down as bullets cracked by overhead.

Riley released the brake, the free end of the rope passed through his hand, and he free-fell the remaining fifteen feet to the ground, doing a reasonably good parachute landing fall on the pine needles. He hopped to his feet and immediately ran to the west, 9mm pistol held out front.

The last piece of brass flew out of the ejector port of the FA-MAS, and Giannini turned around and sprinted back toward the observation deck, reloading as she went.

Kramer rolled back to his stomach, put his eye to the scope, and stared in surprise at the empty rope dangling. Then he swung the scope up and spotted Giannini running back up the ramp. He was centering the red dot on the middle of her back when his entire field of vision was blocked out by something close appearing in the scope. Kramer pulled away from the eyepiece and was greeted by the sight of Riley charging toward him, less than thirty feet away. Kramer reflexively snapped off a wild, unaimed shot. Riley halted, swung up the 9mm, and smoothly fired off two shots, the first one hitting Kramer in the shoulder and punching him back, away from the gun, the second hitting him on the point of the nose, killing him instantly.

Riley hurriedly made up the remaining distance and claimed the PSG1 for his own use, grabbing two extra magazines off the dead body.

As Master reloaded the grenade launcher, he had watched Riley execute the short rappel and then disappear beyond the curve of the hill. Master fired at the point where the rope hung over the edge of the wall and was gratified to see that his aim was true as the round landed in the walkway.

Giannini heard the explosion down the walkway and popped up with the FA-MAS to let off a quick burst in the direction of the grenade firing. The sound of the helicopter had gotten louder, and she peeked out. The aircraft was no more than a mile away and heading directly for the observation tower. She sat down, pressed her back against the wall, and waited.

"What are you doing?" the man in the backseat asked Ferguson.

"I think someone might need help," Ferguson answered as he closed on the tower. "It looks like someone is setting off some type of signal up ahead." He slowed down as he approached, trying to figure out what was happening.

Master could see the helicopter closing. About the last thing he needed right now was witnesses. He briefly considered firing on the chopper with the M-203, then just as quickly decided that was a bad idea. He hunkered down and lay low.

Ferguson came to a hover less than twenty feet away from the tower and about ten feet above it. He spotted a body at the base of the tower and also one on the walkway.

"Jesus Christ," he said, taking in the carnage. He added some more choice curses as a woman suddenly appeared on the observation deck with an automatic weapon aimed directly at the cockpit.

"Get us out of here!" the man in the backseat screamed into his headset.

Through the windshield Ferguson locked eyes with the woman. At this range she could put at least one magazine into his bird without much trouble at all. And he knew that a helicopter was an intrinsically delicate piece of machinery—never mind his body also being somewhat vulnerable to bullets. The woman gestured with her free hand, making very clear to Ferguson what she wanted. He wasn't sure he could do it, but looking directly into the muzzle of her gun, he decided he had no choice. He looked again at the sprawled bodies. This woman obviously wasn't afraid to use that gun. He flew closer to the tower.

Through the scope of the PSG1, Riley scanned the trees next to the path below him. He was lying in the prone position about midway between the tower and the spot where the grenades had been launched. He spared a quick glance back at the tower and could see the helicopter pilot maneuvering in close. So far, so good.

Giannini kept the FA-MAS at the ready until the last moment. She felt extremely exposed as she balanced on the rim of the concrete wall, one hand holding onto the overhead, but she had to trust that Riley had her covered. The pilot was slowly edging in the right skid, the blades coming dangerously close to the overhead.

Master stole a peek and suddenly understood what was happening. "Take out the bird!" he ordered Dewar, who was holding the FA-MAS.

Dewar rolled to his knees and sighted in on the aircraft. Riley's first shot was right between Dewar's eyes, blowing him back, the body rolling downhill and over the edge, disappearing into the gorge.

Thought so, Master said to himself, the death of his partner confirming his suspicions about Riley's position. The helicopter would have to be ignored for the time being.

The helicopter skid was only two feet away but it seemed like a hell of a long way to Giannini. She looked at the pilot: his eyes were fixed on the overhang, his hands glued to the controls. She released the FA-MAS, letting it fall to the ground, then stepped out with her right foot, feeling it touch the vibrating skid. She poised for a fraction of a second, then reached with both hands, grabbed the frame around the windshield, and pulled herself across, her left foot letting go of her earthly perch.

She stepped up and into the helicopter and settled into the copilot's seat as Ferguson pushed his cyclic to the side. They separated from the tower. "Get away from here!" she screamed at him. He turned the aircraft and flew rapidly to the south.

With the departure of the helicopter, silence reigned on Clingmans Dome. Master lay motionless, tuning in all his senses, waiting for some sign from Riley. There was nothing. During Master's first combat tour in Vietnam, he had learned that patience was an essential virtue for a warrior; he was prepared to outwait Riley.

Ferguson's first thought was to fly directly to Cherokee and land in the parking lot of the police station. The woman had dropped the rifle before getting on board, so he felt reasonably safe, and he wanted to get rid of his unwelcome passenger as quickly as possible.

Giannini reached up, took the headset off the ceiling, and put it on. "Where are you going?"

Ferguson didn't answer, keeping his eyes focused on the terrain ahead. An ungentle nudge caught his attention. He looked down to see a very large muzzle poking into his side.

"Where are you going?" Giannini repeated.

"Wherever you want to go," Ferguson replied.

"Good answer," Giannini said. She glanced at the couple frozen in the backseat. "Let's drop our guests off first. You got a map?"

*   *   *

Time was not Riley's ally and he knew it. The best tactical course of action was a withdrawal, but he was tired of running. He lifted his cheek off the stock of the sniper rifle. "Hey! You down there. I can't see you and you can't see me, so let's talk."

Master heard Riley, but at the moment he was busy. "I want Surveillance One up here *now!*" he hissed into the portable phone. "I also want you to send a unit to the helipad for that charter company we used. One of our targets is on that bird and I want her policed up. Is that clear?"

"Yes, sir."

"Then do it!" He flipped shut the phone.

"I know you got help on the way," Riley yelled out. "You may even beat that helicopter to the ground, but I doubt it. Because it isn't going back to wherever it took off from. So even if you get me, the chase starts all over again. Let's end it now!"

A half minute of silence dragged by, then Riley was rewarded with a reply. "There's only one way to end this. You know it and I know it."

"That isn't so," Riley called back. "You've got the main person you came for. Lisa Cobb is dead and her body—what's left of it—is up on the tower."

"I can't let you walk. You know too much."

"You don't have a choice," Riley replied. "You might get me, but I'll take a bunch of your people with me. Already have," he added. "My partner's gone and you don't know where she's heading. We know who you are and who you work for; Hammer told us. If you don't let me walk, my partner will tell every damn newspaper and news show in the country. They'll all know what happened here and what's been happening. Knowledge is power and we have it."

A long silence ensued.

"All right," Master said finally. "You can walk."

"Bullshit," Riley said. "I got no reason to trust you and you got no reason to trust me. You know who I am and you'll be after my ass in a heartbeat. Here's the deal. You report back to the people who gave you the contract and say you killed everyone. That's the only way I won't have to look over my shoulder every day."

"What do I get?" Master asked.

"You get to close out your contract right here and now without losing any more people. My partner's free and she won't be easy to find. I'm sure your employer would not be happy with that loose end."

Riley's finger tightened on the trigger of the sniper rifle as Master stood up. Riley forced himself to relax as Master walked onto the tar path. "Let me see you," Master yelled.

Riley stood, keeping the rifle aimed at Master, who held both his empty hands away from his sides.

"I have to give you credit," Master said. "You're the first contract that didn't go down like I planned."

"Murphy's Law," Riley came back, unable to think of a more cogent reply.

"Yeah," Master conceded. "No bad feelings, I hope."

Riley couldn't believe his indifference. There were four dead people up here on the hill—never mind how many had died so far—and it was all in a day's work to this guy. And he didn't want any bad feelings. Riley went along with him: "No, none."

"I'm glad you understand how the game's played," Master added. "Hammer was a loose cannon."

Riley knew Master was stalling for time, but Riley also had to wait. "You think this is a game?" The absolute absurdity of the situation hit him—the two of them standing there making small talk.

Master shrugged. "It's all a game. You just happened to get the upper hand this time."

The sound of the helicopter could be heard again. Riley stood and, keeping an eye on Master, headed for the tower.

Master glanced down the trail, hoping to see his men coming up, but it was empty. He shrugged and sat down on a log.

Riley sprinted up the ramp and untied his sling rope. He looked down at Lisa's body for a few seconds, then continued to the top. He climbed up on the outside wall, then onto the roof.

Giannini spotted Riley standing on the roof and pointed. "In and out fast," she ordered Ferguson. They'd let off the couple in the middle of Andrews Bald. "There may be someone still up there wanting to take a shot at us."

Ferguson didn't need the urging. He raced in expertly, flared to a hover, his skids six inches above the roof. Riley hopped on board and settled into the backseat. Ferguson added power and they popped up into the sky.

CHAPTER 21

GREAT SMOKY MOUNTAINS
1 NOVEMBER, 2:23 P.M.

Two of Master's men came up the path, Simon in the rear, breathing hard from the climb.

"Start securing the bodies," Master ordered. "Dewar is down the ravine here. Kramer is up there somewhere. There's one right there at the base of the tower and one on the walkway."

"We ran into some Park Service people down at the gate," one of the men said. "We gave them the cover story and they bought off on it."

Simon took in the bodies and the blast marks on the concrete of the tower. "What happened?"

Master ignored him and flipped open his portable phone. "Three, have you got the helipad under surveillance?"

"Roger."

"Give me a call when the bird lands."

"Roger."

Simon walked up to the tower and looked at the bodies there. Master followed him slowly. "This is Lisa Cobb," Simon said, "but I don't see Riley or Giannini."

"We got them," Master said coldly.

"Where?" Simon demanded. "I need confirmation."

Master drew his Glock 10mm. "No, you don't."

2:42 P.M.

Ferguson brought the helicopter down low until he was barely skimming the surface of Fontana Lake. To the right the Smoky Mountains were a solid wall; to the left, the Nantahala Mountains loomed. The lake—more than fifteen miles long—was a dammed-up portion of the Little Tennessee River. The helicopter was moving along it from east to west, the dam less than five miles ahead.

Riley was leaning out the backseat, watching the terrain go by on either side, waiting. When they reached an area where there was no sign of habitation on either side, Riley finally spoke into the headset. "All right, this is it. Slow down to ten miles an hour forward speed." He tapped Giannini on the shoulder. "Get on the skid. When you go, interlace your fingers behind your head and keep your feet tight together."

Giannini looked over her shoulder at him. "Would it make any difference if I told you I couldn't swim?"

"What?" Riley exclaimed.

"Just joking," she said, holstering her revolver and taking off the headset. With a firm grip on the doorframe, she stepped cautiously onto the right skid.

"I'd recommend you forget everything that's happened today," Riley told the pilot. "Whatever bullshit story the people who are waiting at your landing pad give you, you probably ought to accept. I'm sure they'll also tell you to forget about today's events."

"Sure," Ferguson said, willing to agree to anything as long as it got these two off his aircraft. "Whatever."

"Keep her low and level until we're gone." Riley took off the headset and joined Giannini on the skid. They were now about ten feet up and moving forward very slowly, at about ten knots. Riley tapped Giannini and she let go, doing as Riley had instructed, fingers interlaced behind her head, body tight. She splashed into the lake. The shock of the cold water took her breath away; then she was on the surface, swimming fiercely.

Riley followed suit, submerging briefly, then kicking to the surface. He pointed at the south shore and they began swimming.

2:53 P.M.

"Master here."

"The helicopter landed but the targets weren't on board."

"All right. Pack it up and get over here. We need help cleaning up this mess."

Master deliberated for a minute, then shrugged and dialed a long-distance number on his portable phone. He reached the voice mail and punched in an extension.

"Yes?"

"All targets are terminated," Master said. "The contract is closed."

"Excellent, but why are you calling? Where's Simon?"

Master glanced down at the body at his feet. "He got caught in the cross fire. I lost two of my men also. It got rather messy."

"Well, clean up the mess. Payment of the remainder of your fee will be made in the usual manner by close of business today." The phone went dead.

3:05 P.M.

"How's it feel to be dead?" Riley asked Giannini as they climbed the steep bank.

"Wet, tired, cold, and hungry," she replied. She grabbed a branch, pulled herself onto relatively level ground, and sat down, water puddling around her soaked body. "We lost, didn't we," she said, looking at Riley as he sat down next to her. "Lisa's dead, and the bad guys are still in business."

"We're alive," Riley noted as he pulled out his pistols and started drying them off.

"But we have to spend the rest of our lives looking over our shoulders."

"Not really," Riley said. He explained his exchange with Master.

When he was done, Giannini shook her head. "We still lost. I can't ever go back to Chicago, and you can't go back to the army. We need new identities—just like the Cobbs." She smiled at the irony.

"I know, but we do have each other," he said, holding out his hand and pulling her close. "It'll be all right."

"It didn't turn out all right for Lisa," Giannini reminded him. She shivered as she leaned against him. "What do we do now? Do you have a plan?"

Riley stood up. "First thing we do is get warm, then I'll have a plan."

Chapter 22

The Ford Explorer came to a halt on the dirt trail, and the front headlights flashed on and off four times. Riley was unable to see the driver because the windshield was heavily tinted, but the signal was correct, the location was correct, and the time was exact.

"Let's go," he said, tapping Giannini on the arm.

They moved out from the concealment of a stand of small pine trees where they had camped for the night. Reaching the Explorer, Riley got into the front passenger seat while Giannini slid into the back. The driver turned to Riley with a wide smile on his lined face. "Long time, no see, my friend."

"Good to see you, sir," Riley replied, noting without surprise that the colonel had not changed a bit in the three years since he'd last seen the man. Six feet tall and still thin as a post, Pike had a rugged, whipcord look about him. The thick hair above his weatherbeaten face was perhaps a bit more silver than Riley remembered.

"And this is . . . ?" Pike asked, twisting in his seat and extending a hand to Giannini.

Riley made the introductions. Calling Pike had been the only thing he could think to do. The colonel had retired four years ago, right after heading the counterdrug operations into Colombia in which Riley had been involved when he was in the 7th Special Forces Group. Since then, Pike had established an international security company, headquartered in Atlanta, which in just three years had turned into a very profitable and respected business. Using his thirty years of experience in military special operations, and the innumerable contacts he'd made in that time, Pike had turned his company into one of the leaders in the field.

It was Pike's contacts and experience that had prompted Riley to call him. If anyone could figure out what to do next, it would be the old colonel. And Pike was a person you could count on. As Riley expected, his friend promised to drop everything and come immediately to pick them up. He'd told Riley to save the details until he got there.

Pike turned the car around and headed out of the national park. "Start at the beginning and tell me all that's happened."

As the Smoky Mountains faded into the background, Riley and Giannini began relating the story.

FALLS CHURCH
2 NOVEMBER, 9:00 A.M.

"The Supreme Court has denied cert on the Cragg case," Jamieson said, looking at the fax message in the file folder in front of her. "No possibility of appeal."

"Then Berson won't ever be called again to testify and is ready to go deep under?" Getty asked.

"Yes. Berson's currently being held in the Third Section. He's a good candidate for sanction," Jamieson offered.

Getty looked out the window of the second-story conference room to the park across the street. "Any word of an outside party that would be interested in paying for sanction?"

"Not yet."

Tucker stirred. "I'm not sure we should start that again quite yet." He looked at Jamieson. "That affair in North Carolina was a fiasco. The director wants to know what happened to Simon, and the whole thing with the Cobbs was a mess. That helicopter pilot made some noise down there and we've had to answer too many questions from the FBI."

Getty returned his attention to the room. "I can handle the director and the FBI. They're not going to lose any sleep over a lowlife who testified against the mob, and they won't get too concerned about someone like Berson. He's a convicted killer, for Christ's sake. And Simon obviously made a mistake and got too close to the action." Getty paused.

"Go ahead and sanction Berson, even if we don't have a supplemental contract. Speaking of which, have we received payment from the Torrentinos?"

"The money was deposited," Jamieson said. "I've already made the breakdown to the individual accounts—after expenses."

"What's that come to?" Tucker asked, the greed evident in his voice.

Jamieson had the number readily available. "Sixty-one thousand four hundred and thirty-four dollars each. The Torrentinos were also quite appreciative of the information Master forwarded us about the contract D'Angelo put out on the Cobbs." She glanced down at a piece of paper. "By the way, the annual income for keeping the Cobb file alive will come to slightly over eleven thousand dollars each."

Jamieson flipped open another file. "What about the Rivers case?"

"Give me a little background on it," Getty said, settling back comfortably in his chair.

CHICAGO
2 NOVEMBER, 10:30 A.M.

Charlie D'Angelo glanced up as Roy Delpino entered his office. D'Angelo knew right away from the look on his right-hand-man's face that there was trouble. A second man was with Delpino—someone D'Angelo had never seen before. The second man went over to the window and stared out, whistling softly to himself.

D'Angelo focused on his old friend. "What's wrong?"

Delpino stood in front of the desk, not quite meeting D'Angelo's eyes. "The Torrentinos know."

"Know what?" D'Angelo snapped, the sinking feeling in his gut belaying the bluster.

"About the contract you ran on the Cobbs. About how you been trying to run things without consulting them."

D'Angelo leaned forward. "Then it's time to make our move openly."

Delpino shook his head. His hand appeared from the folds of his jacket, a pistol in it. "I'm sorry, Charlie."

D'Angelo looked at the pistol, then raised his gaze. "Look at me, Roy. Look me in the fucking eyes and say that."

Delpino met his gaze briefly. "I'm sorry. I got to do it."

"Why? Just tell me why."

Delpino jerked his head toward the door. "Because Mike put it to me real plain. I take you down or we both go down, and both of us going down don't make no sense to me."

The other man, still whistling a tune D'Angelo couldn't recognize, came over and tapped D'Angelo on the shoulder, gesturing at the door. "We're going for a ride. Don't make it any harder than it has to be."

MARIETTA, GEORGIA
2 NOVEMBER, 6:30 P.M.

Pike handed a cup of hot chocolate to Giannini, then one to Riley. He settled down into a leather chair while Giannini and Riley sat down across from him on his couch. Pike's house was near the Civil War battlefield at Kennesaw Mountain on the northwest side of Atlanta.

"You think this Master fellow will keep his word?" Pike asked.

"It isn't a question of him keeping his word," Riley said. "For now, he's got more to gain by following the plan we both agreed on than he does by breaking it. I trust him to look out for his own interests."

"Until a higher bidder comes along," Giannini threw in.

"There is that problem," Riley agreed. "But Master wouldn't be an easy fellow to track down."

"No, he wouldn't," Pike said. "But we need to find him. And we need to uncover the people in the Witness Protection Program who are doing this."

"What do you mean 'we'?" Giannini asked.

Pike graced her with a smile. "That was a rhetorical we, young lady. I think I can find Master with a few well-placed phone calls if what Hammer said about him is true."

Giannini frowned. "Then what?"

"These people in the Program have to be operating on their own." Pike shrugged. "Even if they're not—although I do believe they are— they've gone too far across the line. They are now a liability. There are people in power in our government who don't like that. Liabilities can be embarrassing, and that simply isn't allowed."

Riley remained silent. He knew full well what Pike was talking about. He'd had more than his own share of trying to cover up "embarrassments" for the government.

"I have contacts in Washington and other places," Pike continued, "who will be most interested in hearing about what's going on in the Witness Protection Program."

"I thought you weren't at the top of everyone's invitation list in D.C.," Riley noted.

"That's true," Pike replied with a grin. "But I played the game for more than thirty years, and there are many who still find me useful once in a while. I have contacts the official people can't use," he added somewhat cryptically.

Riley understood just what his former commander meant. Running a private company, Pike was excluded from the scrutiny under which all government agencies found themselves sooner or later. He could do favors for people in those agencies—jobs that couldn't be traced back as officially sanctioned. It was a shadowy world of favors and counterfavors, and Riley had no doubt that Pike was on the positive side of the ledger. It was the only way he could still be in business.

"The first thing we need, though, is some names. I should be able to find out who's behind this, but I'd like to be one hundred percent sure before I give them up. And I have to know more about what really happened before I can decide who to tell. This needs to be cleaned up as neatly as possible for your sake."

Riley drained the last of his hot chocolate. "You find me Master, I'll confirm the names."

Pike stood. "Good. That's taken care of. I'll do some checking with my sources also. The other question I have is whether you two want to surface after the smoke clears."

Giannini looked at Riley, and he met her gaze full on. He thought for a few seconds, then shrugged. "I think we need to stay under for a little while. Then let's keep our options open."

CHAPTER 23

Master locked the doors to the gym and walked out into the brisk fall air. He felt good, his body refreshed by two hours of weight lifting. He enjoyed working out alone after the regular patrons of the club left, and he paid the owner well for the privilege. The sound of his footsteps echoed off the dark buildings on either side of the parking lot as he walked toward his armored Mercedes.

Another set of footsteps, louder than the echo, caused Master to halt and turn. A slight, dark figure stood at the corner of the gym. Master reached into his windbreaker, his fingers curling around the butt of the Glock 10mm, when a woman's voice called out from his left.

"You can take it out, then you can put it down on the ground and kick it away from yourself."

Master froze, only his eyeballs swiveling to try and find the owner of the voice. He estimated the woman was above him, probably on the roof of the warehouse next door. He turned slightly and was rewarded with the red dot of a laser sight flickering across his eyeballs, then settling on his left cheek.

"She means it," the man to his front called out.

Master recognized the voice and relaxed slightly. "Riley, I did what I said—"

"The gun," Riley interrupted.

Master took out the Glock and carefully placed it on the ground in front of his feet.

"Kick it away," the woman called out.

"That'll ruin the finish," Master complained.

"I'll ruin your life." The dot moved off his face, and he could feel a subsonic round flicker past, kicking up sparks as it ricocheted off the tar. The dot returned to roost on his skin.

Master kicked the gun reluctantly, putting about six feet of distance between him and the weapon.

Riley walked forward out of the shadows into the illumination cast by the streetlights fifty yards away. He bent down, picked up the gun, and tucked it into the back of his waistband. He was dressed in dark green jungle fatigue pants, a T-shirt, and a brown leather jacket. A pair of old, scuffed boots were on his feet.

"As I was saying," Master continued calmly, "I did what I said I would. You and your friend Giannini—who I assume is up on the roof there—are officially dead. I kept my end of the deal."

"We kept our end," Riley said, circling to his right, putting the streetlights behind him. "We didn't go to the press or the authorities."

Master pivoted to maintain face-to-face contact. "Well? Why are you here then?"

"I just want to confirm some information."

"What?"

"The people who made the contracts for the Witness Protection Program. We've done a little research—actually the information isn't hard to find, since it is a federal agency—and the control staff for WPP is headed by a fellow named Getty. Official title, Section Head, Witness Protection Program, U.S. Marshal's office. Civil service, GS-16 grade level. Although he does live well even for a GS-16. Rather nice house in Alexandria, wouldn't you say? Six bedrooms, four baths, with an indoor pool. In that neighborhood such a house goes for what? Two million? Then you have a Mr. Tucker, GS-13, official title, Deputy Assistant for Operations, Witness Protection Program. Drives a red Jaguar. Has a rather nice boat docked in the marina."

"A boy with his toys," Giannini called out.

"Wait a second—" Master started.

"Then a Ms. Jamieson, GS-13, official title, Deputy Assistant for Security, Witness Protection Program."

"Let's hear it for equal opportunity," Giannini's voice floated out of the void. "She may even be a little smarter than the others—she doesn't flaunt her wealth. It took us a couple of days, but we did find she was worth more than a million and a quarter in various mutual funds and stock options. She just had to keep that money growing. Should have buried it in the backyard if she wasn't going to spend it."

Master remained silent.

"There was a fourth member," Riley continued. "A Mr. Simon Jenkins, official title, Deputy Assistant for Intelligence, GS-13, Witness Protection Program. Seems Mr. Jenkins—or shall we simply call him Simon?—had a little accident while out boating on the Chesapeake with Mr. Tucker, who was kind enough to fill out the accident report. It says poor Simon fell overboard—quite clumsy of him—and his body was badly chewed up by the propeller. His funeral service was a week ago and rather poorly attended, I must say. Nice coffin."

A long silence descended over the parking lot. The red dot was still on Master's face, and Riley stood silent, unmoving, ten feet away. Master finally spoke. "So what? Are you trying to impress me?"

"I just want to know if the first three I mentioned are the ones who let the contracts on the Witness Protection Program. I want to know if it stops with them or if it goes up through the U.S. Marshal's program."

Master laughed. "Shit, it might go all the way to the attorney general. Maybe the president."

"But Getty, Jamieson, and Tucker for sure?" Riley asked, not letting Master distract him.

Master shrugged. "Yeah, those three for sure."

"How'd you get your contracts? Who contacted you?" Riley asked.

"Usually Simon on the actual contract. Sometimes I talked to Getty. I only dealt with Jamieson once. Tucker was the money man." Master tried to discern Riley's face. "But what good does that information do you?"

"It keeps us from making a mistake," Riley said quietly.

"I told you before and you didn't listen, but you'd better listen now. Drop it." Master pointed at Riley. "You still don't understand, do you? After all the shit you've been through, you just don't get it. This is our government you're up against. There's nothing you can do."

Riley ignored him. "So what's your excuse? Money?"

"I don't need an excuse," Master snapped. "Yeah, I don't say it isn't part of the reason, but those people *are* criminals. Seemed like I was doing society a favor."

"What about all the innocents who got in the way?"

"Innocents didn't get in the way, until we ran into the Cobbs."

"How many were there before the Cobbs?" Riley asked.

Master didn't answer.

"This fellow Getty has been in charge of the Witness Protection Program for six years. We haven't been able to find out much else, but you have to figure that at least several hundred people a year go under in the Program. What percentage of those do Getty and his partners figure deserve to die? And does it just happen to be a happy by-product that they can keep the money allocated to support those people in their new lives? The federal budget for the Program was forty-three million last year alone. How much of that do they keep? How many people with a green status in the computer never got picked up by another section?"

"Listen," Master said, "I just did a job, all right? You've done the same thing. You've been on missions where the objective was a pile of shit some politician pulled out of the air after twenty seconds of deep thought. Or your mission was denied after the fact because some bureaucrat wanted to cover his ass. That's just the way it goes."

"So that's how you justify it?" Riley asked.

"It's not justification," Master said. "It's reality."

Riley nodded slowly. "Uh-huh. Well, guess what? You fucked up."

"What do you mean?"

"Did it ever occur to you that this whole operation with Getty and his people wasn't sanctioned?"

For the first time Master was slightly disconcerted. "I work for the government on a contract basis. They contacted me—"

"I know you work by contract," Riley cut in. "That's how we found you. That's also how you were able to use government facilities like the hospital at Bragg to get rid of bodies. *You're* official," Riley said, "but Getty isn't. He's acting on his own."

"Bullshit," Master spat.

"Tell me why it's bullshit," Riley said. "How do you *know* your Witness Protection Program assignments are sanctioned? What proof do you have? Hell, what proof do you have that any of your assignments are sanctioned?"

Riley didn't wait for an answer. "There's no paper trail because the people who give you your jobs can't have one. And I can't deny that you probably think you're doing the right thing. The right people contact you—they work for a government agency. They have the money. And they have a job they can justify and you can believe might be sanctioned by the government. The only problem you have is that it isn't."

Riley watched Master's face in the dim light. "Kind of changes everything, doesn't it? In fact, Getty was receiving payment from the Torrentinos on top of the money he had for the upkeep of the Cobbs. Double-dipping. So, ultimately, you were working for the Torrentinos too. You really fucked up when you wasted Jill Fastone and then dumped her body in Chicago. You thought you were sending a message to the mob, but you were actually sending the wrong message to the person footing your bill."

"I did what I was told," Master protested. "If Getty was rogue, that wasn't my fault."

"Just following orders, eh?" Riley said sarcastically. "That's a rather weak justification."

"What are you going to do about it?" Master asked, the tone of his voice indicating to Riley that he was accepting the information. "I still work for other agencies that—"

"No, you don't," Riley cut in again. "A little bird is whispering information to all those people in the government you used to work for, and the bird is telling them about all of this. I think you're out of a job." Riley turned to walk away.

"You expect me to just let it go like that?" Master demanded. "I gave my life to this. My people died doing those bastards' dirty work."

"You have no choice but to let it go," Riley said.

Master laughed, and the sound had a manic edge that caused Riley to turn back. "Now who's the one who isn't in reality?" Another odd laugh. "I know you exist and you know I exist. Sooner or later that's going to cause one of us trouble. I don't feel like waiting for that time."

Master didn't wait. He stepped forward with his left foot, then across with his right behind, and snapped a side kick with his left foot, aimed for Riley's midsection, except Riley wasn't there. He was moving back with the attack. Master expected that and continued with the forward flow by planting his left foot down and spinning, striking out with a back kick with his right foot.

Riley hopped to his left, let the kick fly by, then snapped his own turn kick directly into the left center of Master's exposed chest. Master's breath exploded out of his lungs and his ribs splintered under the impact of the toe of Riley's left boot.

Riley lightly moved away on the balls of his feet as Master labored to regain his breath and overcome the blinding pain. Squinting in the dim light, he could see the dull gleam of the metal tips on Riley's boots. "Not fucking fair," he gasped.

"To quote someone," Riley said, "ain't it a bitch."

Master bent down, hand snaking for his ankle, and Riley burst forward. As Master's hand reached the ankle holster, Riley's front kick caught him square in the jaw, breaking the bone and lifting the larger man off his feet, throwing him back onto the ground. Riley kicked down on the right hand, cracking the bone, and the small .22-caliber gun fell to the ground.

Riley instinctively stomped down on Master's already wounded chest. He twitched, then died.

Riley took Master's small pistol and his watch and wallet, then turned and swiftly walked away, linking up with Giannini as she came down the fire escape from the building where she'd provided cover. The telescoping stock on the long-barreled MP-5 was collapsed, and she hung it on a Velcro hook on the inside of her coat.

"Why did he do that? He should have just walked."

"He knew he fucked up. If we could find him, others could. Besides, he didn't trust us. He gave it his best shot."

"Jesus," Giannini said. "This is too damn crazy."

Riley couldn't have agreed more. That had been his reaction when Colonel Pike told him the rumors he'd uncovered, through some of his underworld contacts, about Getty and the Witness Protection Program people. "Let's call the colonel and tell him his information is correct."

CHAPTER 24

MARIETTA
11 NOVEMBER, 9:00 P.M.

"It's a mess, but a solvable one," Pike said. He was standing at a large bay window, looking out at the looming bulk of Kennesaw Mountain. "Like I told you yesterday, the best information I could uncover is that Getty and his folks were working for the Torrentinos and whoever else could foot the bill to kill someone entering the Program. That's besides pocketing the expense money for those witnesses they were supposed to be supporting."

"What are we going to do about it?" Riley asked. Giannini was drinking a cup of coffee on the other side of the room, having listened as Riley filled in Pike on what Master had said and the fatal results of the meeting the previous evening. Pike had been at his office the entire day, contacting people all over the country.

"*We're* not going to do anything about it," Pike said. "At least not directly. Let me explain the big picture here. Master worked for Getty, thinking Getty was authorized to order these missions. But Getty was actually working for himself and—in the case of the Cobbs—the Torrentinos.

"Charlie D'Angelo—the man you," he nodded at Giannini, "said was in charge of the Torrentino gang on the outside—was working for himself. That explains two different sets of people after you. D'Angelo's people are the ones who killed Tom Volpe and attacked you in the alley in Chicago. They're also the ones," he turned to Riley, "who got killed by Master's men outside your apartment in Fayetteville.

D'Angelo was after the two million and didn't know about the Torrentinos' contract with Getty.

"My source in Chicago tells me that D'Angelo has disappeared, so that's one loose end tied up. Although we didn't plan it, Master took himself out of it last night. We still have the problem of Getty, who thinks you two are dead and would not be happy to see you surface. So here's what I'm going to do: I'm going to whisper in somebody's ear and see what happens."

"Whose ear?" Giannini asked.

Pike turned, placing his back to the window. "There's one other loose end—the two million that Philip Cobb stole. No one seems to know where that is, and as far as I can find out, the location died with Philip Cobb. However, we can use that information to our advantage. How do you think the Torrentinos would react if they found out that Getty double-crossed them for the two million and that Getty had Master kill Jill Fastone?"

Riley smiled for the first time in a while. "I think the Torrentinos wouldn't like that very much at all."

"I believe," Pike continued, "that we should let the Torrentinos clean up the last loose ends."

"What about us?" Giannini asked.

"Once this is closed out," Pike said, "you both can go back to your old lives."

"I left two bodies lying in an alley in Chicago," Giannini noted. "I don't think my former employer is going to be too thrilled about that."

"They're not thrilled," Pike said, "but they are pragmatic. I talked to someone in the Chicago PD I trust—and who owes me a big favor—and laid out the situation. He said my information solves two homicides for them, which they always appreciate, and that no one is going to miss those two scumbags you killed anyway."

"If I go along with that, it doesn't make me much different from Master," Giannini said.

"You didn't kill those two men for money," Riley said. "You did it to save your life, and you were involved in the whole thing in the first place because you were trying to help someone."

"Correct," Pike said. "And Dave, you're on extended temporary duty until it's safe for you to go back to Bragg. In the meantime, why don't you two enjoy a little vacation here? I've got business to attend to." Pike left the room.

Riley turned to Giannini and held out his hand. Giannini took it and joined him on the couch. He lay back, holding her in his arms.

"What do you think the people in D.C.—" she began.

"Hush," Riley said, gently placing a finger over her lips. "It's out of our hands now. The colonel has always given me very good advice and this time I'm going to follow it. So no more talk about what happened or what's going to happen. I thought I lost you back in Chicago and it made me do some thinking. Now you're here and that's all I care about. Here and now." He leaned forward, his lips meeting hers.

EPILOGUE

The man waited in the crawl space of the house with his eyes closed, his head leaned back against his small bag of tools. He had unscrewed the drainpipe two hours ago and made all the necessary connections. He cocked his head as he heard the dull echo of footsteps above. He checked the time on the slight fluorescent glow of his watch—just about right.

He heard the sound of the toilet flushing and then the rush of water to his immediate left through the PVC piping. With a slight screech, the shower was turned on, and water immediately began pouring out the open end of the pipe to his right, flowing onto the concrete. He moved quickly, taking a metal plumber's snake and slipping the free end into the flow of water. He slid the snake up into the pipe, his fingers feeling the metal as it went. He'd left a piece of tape at the desired length; when he felt the tape, he stopped. The end of the snake was just below the metal drain cover of the tub above.

He grabbed a heavy rubber-coated wire that he had prepared earlier and connected the metal alligator teeth at the end onto the snake. Taking care to move away from both the water and the snake, he then picked up a small metal box that he had wired into the house circuit. He flipped a switch on the side of the box and began whistling.

Four feet over his head, Jamieson was frozen in the river of electricity that coursed through her body from the water below up to the showerhead. Her body shook in a spastic dance as synapses fired uncontrollably, her body's normal neural functioning overwhelmed by the voltage.

235

The man had started counting slowly when he'd thrown the switch; when he reached thirty, he turned it off. He heard a deep thud as Jamieson's body fell to the bottom of the porcelain tub. He withdrew the snake and coiled it; quickly reconnected the drainpipe; and disconnected his box from the house current, restoring the circuit breakers.

He exited from the crawl space into the backyard and picked the lock on the back door. Once inside, he made his way directly to the bathroom. He checked Jamieson to make sure she was dead, then took her hair dryer in gloved fingers and plugged it into the socket next to the sink. He turned it on and, holding it by the cord, dipped it into the toilet. A hiss told him that the water had completed the circuit and the plastic was melting. He kept the dryer there for five seconds, until the circuit breaker kicked in. He removed the dryer and placed the device into the tub with Jamieson. It looked like a stupid accident, but people died of stupidity every day. His job done, he left the way he had come in, making sure the door was secure behind him. He checked his watch as he strolled down the street.

6:15 A.M.

The heated water slid smoothly over Getty's skin as he dove gracefully into the pool. The sky outside was still dark and the lights around the wall of the pool reflected off the surface. Getty swam one lap, flipped expertly, and turned and was heading back, his body slowly warming to the exercise. His wife was still asleep and would be for another two hours. This was his time to work out and relax before driving to work.

On his eighth lap he caught a glimpse of a dark shadow as he made the turn. Slowing, Getty raised his head out of the water and pulled up his swimming goggles. A man dressed in dark slacks and a sweater was standing at the near edge, whistling a tune Getty found vaguely familiar.

"Who the hell are you?" Getty growled, treading water.

The man lifted his right hand. Getty started, then relaxed, seeing that the man held only a small plastic spray bottle.

"What do you think you're doing?" Getty demanded, slowly backing away.

With three smooth pulls on the plastic trigger, the man released a fine mist that drifted in the air over the pool. He turned and was gone out the back door, quietly closing and locking it behind him. Getty started to swim across the pool, going for the phone near the house door to call the police, when he felt a tingling sensation in his right arm. As he grabbed the edge of the pool, his left arm was affected and he lost his grip, splashing awkwardly back into the water. In ten seconds he could no longer kick and keep his head above water.

By the time his wife found the body two hours later and the police arrived, the muscle inhibitor had dissipated. Cause of death was listed officially as accidental drowning.

ANNANDALE, VIRGINIA
21 NOVEMBER, 6:45 A.M.

The traffic along Route 650, known locally as Gallows Road, was light this time of morning, and Tucker enjoyed gunning the engine on his Jaguar and weaving in and out of traffic, playing beat the light and beat your neighbors. He pressed down on the gas, gave the steering wheel a slight tug to the left, and ignored the bleat from a blue BMW as he cut in front and roared toward the next traffic light.

The light turned yellow, which he took as an indication to speed up. Too late, he saw the tow truck coming from the left, its driver not slowing one bit for the upcoming intersection. Tucker slammed on the brakes and threw the wheel to the right. The laws of physics overruled the quick prayer Tucker screamed out. The high steel bumper on the tow truck smashed into the left side of his car at twenty miles an hour.

Tucker ducked. That move saved his life as the left roof post was sheared off and glass exploded inward. He felt a searing pain as the left front wheel was punched back through the wheel well, compressing the entire control console against his legs, breaking both of them and pinning him in the seat. The steering wheel had also been knocked back and pressed against his chest, causing his breath to come in slow, labored gasps.

In the sudden silence after both vehicles came to rest, Tucker heard a door slam. A face peered around the edge of the bumper into the wreckage of his car. Tucker twisted his head, trying to ascertain how badly he was hurt.

"I can't get out," he gasped. "Help me."

The tow truck driver leaned forward, having difficulty reaching through the torn metal. He awkwardly got one hand on Tucker's neck.

At first Tucker thought the man was checking his pulse, but the fingers curled around and gripped his jaw.

"What are you—" Tucker started to say when the man jerked his arm back, pulling Tucker's head around with it and snapping his neck.

"I need some help here!" the tow truck driver yelled, stepping back from the two cars into the gathering crowd. "Somebody call an ambulance!" As he moved away, he began to whistle, his hands laced behind his back. He waited until the crowd had grown large enough, then he slipped away from the stolen truck and the scene of the fatal accident.

The Author

Bob Mayer, a West Point graduate, spent several tours of duty with both the Infantry and the Special Forces. He served two years as the commander of a Special Forces A team and two years as the operations officer for an SF Group overseeing military deployments across Europe. After leaving the Army, he moved to the Orient to write and study the martial arts. His first novel, *EYES OF THE HAMMER,* takes a Special Forces team into Colombia to battle drug lords; his second, *DRAGON SIM-13,* follows Green Beret Dave Riley and his team to China; in *SYNBAT,* third novel in the Special Forces series, Riley faces a shockingly inhuman threat. Mayer is currently in the Reserves as an instructor at the Special Forces Qualification Course at the John F. Kennedy Special Warfare Center and School at Fort Bragg. Mayer, originally from New York City, now lives in Clarksville, Tennessee.